A GRUESOME DISCOVERY

Cora Harrison

This first world edition published 2017
in Great Britain and the USA by
SEVERN HOUSE PUBLISHERS LTD of
Eardley House, 4 Uxbridge Street, London W8 7SY.
Trade paperback edition first published
in Great Britain and the USA 2019 by
SEVERN HOUSE PUBLISHERS LTD.

British Library Cataloguing in Publication Data
A CIP catalogue record for this title is available from the British Library.

ISBN-13: 978-0-7278-8758-0 (cased)
ISBN-13: 978-1-84751-874-3 (trade paper)
ISBN-13: 978-1-78010-936-7 (e-book)

Typeset by Palimpsest Book Production Ltd.,
Falkirk, Stirlingshire, Scotland.

ONE

St Thomas Aquinas
'. . . potest, igitur, lex naturalis deleri de cordibus
hominum, vel propter malas persuasiones, . . . vel etiam
propter pravas consuetudines et habitus corruptos.'
(. . . natural law, therefore, can be blotted out from the
human heart . . . either by evil persuasions, or by
vicious customs and corrupt habit.)

There was a dreadful stench from the trunk. Damp, perhaps. Stronger than that, surely. Decay of some sort, thought the Reverend Mother, bending over it. Fifty years of working in the slums of Cork, a city where periodically high tides and south-easterly winds drove the river to flush out the sewers and empty them onto the streets and into houses, had inured her to smells of all kinds: excrement; rotting carcases of rats, dead cats and dogs; bodies unwashed for years, an everyday experience for her; and occasionally an overlooked corpse of a beggar who had died behind the convent chapel.

And yet this seemed to be a worse stench than most she had encountered. She was not surprised, now, that the men who had delivered it to her had hesitated to follow her orders about depositing it in a classroom and had suggested placing it in this century-old, unused outhouse at a distance from the school and the convent. She had acquiesced. There would be no point in disappointing the children next morning if the trunk only contained rubbish and now that she looked at it more carefully, she was afraid that would prove to be the case.

An old trunk with broken corners, disfigured by greyish patches of mould. A printed label in the precise centre with the name and address of an auctioneer on Princes Street, and beneath it, on another label, written in indelible purple pencil, in large, even, block capital letters: 'THE REVEREND

MOTHER, ST MARY'S ISLE'. The Reverend Mother stretched forward a hand, withdrew it and looked at the trunk dubiously. Like all who seek charitable contributions, she was gifted frequently with items that, on examination, she would designate as rubbish. There was another, smaller label in a different hand, a brown luggage label, attached to the handle of the trunk. '*Old School Books*' it said in fancy, ornate handwriting, finishing by a neat and perfectly rounded full stop, with a hollow centre. Useless, probably, she thought, imagining torn copies of *The Christian Brothers Latin Grammar*. But perhaps not. Heavy, anyway. The auctioneer's men had staggered under their load. They could well be hardback books, even perhaps expensively bound. The poor of the city did not send their unwanted goods to auctioneers. The rag-and-bone man would be the destination of their leavings. These might be good books, despite the appearance of the trunk.

The Reverend Mother stretched out a hand to open the lid and then stiffened as a voice from behind her said softly, 'I think that might be my property, Reverend Mother.'

The Reverend Mother did not reply. She did not turn around or draw attention to her name on the label. From the corner of her eye she could see the belted raincoat, the slouched hat, pulled well down. Almost a uniform for the proscribed Republican movement. Bother, she thought. Usually the convent was not troubled by their nefarious doings. There was something about the assumption of authority in that soft voice which annoyed her. Without answering, she leaned forward and flipped open the lid of the trunk. It moved more readily than she had expected, flopped over quite suddenly, striking the side of the table with a slight thud. And then there was a terrible stench of putrefaction, a sour, sickening smell.

She had not thought to bring a candle; the small, old roadside building was well lit by a gas lamp on the pavement outside the window. There were shadows everywhere, but there was enough light to see the contents of the trunk.

Not school books, but a man, a body, a corpse surely by that smell. The Reverend Mother forced herself not to recoil, and bent a little more forward so as to examine it. The body was wedged into the trunk. A small body, but it barely fitted, the legs doubled up, with the knees pressed up against the chest. A man, a very short, stout man, dressed in a respectable frockcoat, black broadcloth, starched white shirt, top hat rammed down upon his head, the eyes, just visible below the rim, stared up at her.

But that was not all. As her own eyes became accustomed to the dark, the Reverend Mother saw that there was something else. Packed all around the body were the rotting skins of dead animals, green, white, glistening silver with decomposition, gobbets of blood, lumps of fat, some crawling maggots.

There was a sudden gasp from the man at her shoulder and the Reverend Mother turned back to her companion. Bigger than his father, was her first thought, but not as tall as his younger brothers. She knew them better, but Fred was instantly recognizable. He had been the only red-headed child in the large family. She hadn't seen him for a few years, but the face, oddly, had changed very little since childhood, the eyes wide with apprehension, the vulnerable mouth, bottom lip trembling, the aspect of a child who dreads a blow, she had often thought.

'It's Fred Mulcahy, isn't it?' she enquired. And then when he made no reply, she added calmly, 'Surely that is your father. What has happened?'

He backed away from her hastily. 'I know nothing about this, nothing whatsoever.' He cast a sick look of loathing at the body and then averted his eyes. In the light from the street gas lamp his face was almost as white as that of the corpse before them.

'But you were expecting something?' She looked at him closely. His outstretched hand was shaking. His breath came quick and fast.

'Not that, not that at all. I was expecting something. It was to be handed over at the Douglas Street Sawmills, just outside the Sawmills, that was what they said, these were my orders. I was to go to the Sawmills and receive a trunk, supposed to be landed at Douglas Passageway. Come by sea. Not that at all.' His voice was high and breathless. Awkwardly, he removed his soft, slouch-rimmed grey hat and stood clutching it to his breast. 'When I saw this trunk on the back of a van I followed it. I thought that they had taken the wrong turning but I was

slower – got stuck behind an old donkey. They had carried it
into the convent before I could stop them. I thought the men
had made a mistake.'

The Reverend Mother surveyed him dispassionately for a
moment. Cork was a small city and she knew most of the
inhabitants and she certainly knew all about the Mulcahy
family.

The dead man, Henry Mulcahy, had been a country boy
who came to the city well over fifty years ago. He had worked
as a barrow boy for his uncle for a few years and quite soon
had seen a way to profit from the busy meat market at Shandon,
buying hides of cows and skins of sheep at very low prices,
and transforming them into marketable leather and sacks of
wool. He had married well; she had heard that his wife had
been the daughter of a prosperous farmer; had sired ten sons
but neither of the older boys, she had been told, was keen to
follow their father in his trade. Fred, she knew, had rebelled
and left home. Rumour said that he had joined the Republicans
and rumour, she thought, surveying his slouch hat and belted
raincoat, had not lied.

'You were expecting a trunk, but not this trunk?' she queried
and then as he turned away, she called after him. 'I shall have
to say that I saw you, Fred, so it may be as well for you to tell
me what you were expecting to see when the lid of the trunk
was raised,' she warned as he went towards the door.

He stopped abruptly, started violently and then turned
towards her. She could see how his face grew even paler. He
produced a revolver from his raincoat and pointed it directly
at the starched bib that lay over her chest. Her heart skipped a
beat, but she stood very still, not looking at him, but eyeing
a small maggot that crawled across the dead man's trouser
knee. The boy's face was chalk white and his hand shook.
There was a possibility, remote, but nevertheless present, that
he might fire. Guns were an evil invention, she had often
thought. They allowed killing to be at a distance, they deper-
sonalized it. Much harder to stick a knife or a sword into
living flesh than to pull a small trigger from a remote point.
She said a quick prayer; should be an act of contrition, she
thought, but incongruously only the words of St Thomas

Aquinas: '*Grant me, O Lord, a penetrating mind to understand*' came to her thoughts.

'I think, Reverend Mother, you would be best to forget that you have seen me.' His voice was high, shaking and his face grew even whiter. She wondered when he had last eaten. 'Give me your word that you will say nothing of seeing me,' he screamed at her impatiently.

She made no reply to this, but studied him speculatively. He would be one of the republicans, one of the Irish Republican Army, as they named themselves, one of those who had rebelled against the treaty that left the six most northerly counties still as possessions of Britain. It was, of course, a lost cause by now. Michael Collins was dead; but the government he had set up was firmly established as a *Dáil*, a parliament. The ceasefire with the rebels had been agreed, de Valera was out of the country. Only the very dedicated, the very fanatical and the very desperate still kept the rebellion going. Which of these was the young man in front of her? The last, she thought. He must be about twenty now, she thought. It was a stubborn age. Only complete desperation would now drive him to return to Shandon as a prodigal son. While there was a cause to be fought for, then he kept away from his father.

And the man lying dead in front of her would have been unlikely to kill the fatted calf in celebration at the return of his son – more likely, she thought, to send him out to the yard to work on flaying the calf's skin.

'When did you last eat?' she asked and then when he did not reply, she added, 'I was thinking that if I showed you the telephone, you might ring Inspector Cashman and tell him the story. No need for you to await his arrival. I will deal with that. But at least you would not render yourself the first suspect in the killing of your father if you were the one that reported the finding of the body. But before you go, you must have a cup of tea and a slice of Sister Bernadette's fruit cake. You remember Sister Bernadette, don't you? She always had some little treat for you when you were a boy and when Bridie used to bring you here.' The reference to the past might calm him, make him feel less threatened. Did Bridie still work for the

Mulcahy family, she wondered. Recently the woman had ceased her visits to the convent that had once sheltered her.

'I don't want anything to eat and I don't want anything to do with police or with . . . that carrion.' He spat out the words, but his voice trembled and the hand that held the gun trembled even more.

'Your mother must be told,' said the Reverend Mother in a practical tone of voice. 'Death brings its duties,' she added, keeping her voice calm and resisting the temptation to ask him to put that pistol back into his pocket.

'A happy release for her, poor woman, after all those years of slavery.'

'Nevertheless,' she said persuasively, 'over twenty years of marriage brings its own affections, its own bonds.'

He didn't reply to her comment, didn't even turn his head, but he had heard her, she was sure. A clever boy, she had learned this from Bridie, who had worked in the Mulcahy household since his birth; young Fred had done well at Farranferris Seminary but had declined an offer from the priests to become a clerical student and progress to the priesthood. He wanted to go to university to study mathematics while his father had wanted him to become a feather merchant. No doubt the poor boy was now hiding out somewhere in a derelict cottage in west Cork. Let him go now, she prayed, let him lose himself in the back streets, or make for the Western Road and be outside the city before a hunt was organized. And once he had left the premises, then she could go indoors to the convent, lift the phone to telephone Inspector Patrick Cashman and leave the matter to him. Dead bodies were his affair; live, young, undernourished bodies and minds were hers.

But he did not go. He lifted the pistol with great deliberation, taking care to steady it by placing his left hand beneath his right wrist, aimed it carefully, not at her, but at the man in the trunk. There was a small explosion, a strong clean smell and then the rancid odour intensified. Light from the roadside gas lamp flooded in as the door was opened and receded as he closed it behind him. He had left and now she was alone with the body; the body which had just received the outpouring of a pistol.

The Reverend Mother took several seconds to recover. Her legs were trembling. Old age is no excuse for cowardice, she said to herself severely as she forced her unwilling limbs to move forward and to stand beside the trunk. No blood, she thought, nothing really to be seen without bending over the body. And even then it was impossible to see anything. The well-tailored black broadcloth would conceal any stain of blood.

But she had a strong impression that Fred Mulcahy had shot his father through the heart. For a moment she stood very still, visualizing the scene and picturing the angle of the pistol; picturing the young man steadying his shaking hand; trying to remember the sound. She looked back again. She had been very sure that the man was dead when she had opened the lid, but the smell of decay had been so strong that it was an obvious conclusion. It had been a little later when she had noticed the rotting hides and skins. She forced herself to look again. Yes, he was undoubtedly dead. The maggots continued on their grisly work, undisturbed, and one even crawled across the dead man's rigid eyeball.

Abruptly the Reverend Mother closed down the lid of the trunk. There was no key. She remembered now how quickly and easily she had opened it. The small latches had been well oiled, she thought, as they clicked into position with the slightest of pressures. She had opened it just by sliding the round metal lock. There had definitely been no key protruding from the lock and nor were they tied to the handle of the trunk. She slid her hand along it to be sure and then went resolutely to the door of the old building, taking out the large bunch of keys from her capacious pocket and turning back to lock it after her.

There was no one around in the hallway, or in the corridor beyond when she had gone back into the convent. A rattle of tea cups and a sound of voices came from the convent refectory. The nuns were at tea. The Reverend Mother continued down towards the back door, and unhooked the telephone receiver from the side of the instrument.

'Get me Inspector Cashman, will you, Miss Clayton,' she said wearily. She should, of course, give the number of the police barracks, but she was too tired to look it up.

'Yes, of course, Reverend Mother. He should be still in his office. I'll have him on the line in a moment.' Miss Clayton sounded alert and interested. The Reverend Mother reminded herself that she would need to be careful or else sensational stories would be flying around Cork within minutes. As she waited, she could hear a muffled sound. Miss Clayton had her hand well over the receiver, but her telephone speaking voice was penetrating and shrill and she could distinguish the words: 'she wants the guards'.

'Good evening, Reverend Mother.' Patrick sounded fairly breathless. 'Not in his office,' she could imagine Miss Clayton telling her fellow workers.

'Good evening, Inspector,' she said formally. Face to face, she called him Patrick and still saw him fondly as an earnest, hardworking, determined six- or seven-year-old boy in her school, but in public she always addressed him as 'Inspector' and the telephone exchange, she often reminded herself, was a public place. 'I was wondering whether you could spare the time to come here to the convent, if you are in the neighbour-hood,' she continued feeling unable to invent an innocuous reason as to why he should come swiftly and perhaps bring the police doctor with him.

'I'm on my way down there just now and will drop in, Reverend Mother,' he said obligingly and his speed of response made her realize that there had been a slight shake in her voice. She carefully hung up the receiver, touching it to make sure that it was in position. Her cloak was a light one. No doubt that was why she was shivering and so she went swiftly to her room and donned a heavier cloak over the top of it. It and the heat from the fire gradually warmed her. Sister Bernadette, she was touched to see, had not only brought in her tea, but had placed the teapot, with a fancily knitted woollen cosy protecting its swelling sides, on the hearth just in front of the glowing fire. She poured a cup from it, not bothering to add milk, but conscientiously taking some sugar, although she loathed the taste. Sugar is good for shock, her old friend, Dr Scher, had told her that. It would keep her going until Patrick took the responsibility from her hands.

And then she thought of something else, something puzzling.

She braved the icy corridor again and went purposefully down towards the back door. Once again she unhooked the receiver from its hook beside the telephone and spoke into it after the immediate greeting.

'Oh, Miss Clayton, I wonder would you be kind enough to get me the telephone number of Mr Hayes, the auctioneer.'

'Yes, of course, Reverend Mother.' Miss Clayton sounded unsurprised. Probably knew all about the trunk-load of books already, thought the Reverend Mother, too shaken to smile to herself. She took in a deep breath and set herself, while she waited, the task of counting backwards in sevens, starting at one hundred. This, she knew, required concentration and kept other images from her mind, as it traversed the lines of numbers from 100 right back to 2. She had just reached 23 when a series of clicks brought the auctioneer onto the line.

'Reverend Mother! I was just about to phone you to make sure that the books arrived safely.' Probably Mr Hayes was going to do nothing of the sort, but he was an excessively polite man and would not like even to hint a surprise at hearing from her. Still he had confirmed that the trunk had been meant for her and that was something that she had wanted to know.

'Yes, indeed, and thank you very much for sending them over,' she said. Were they a 'left over' when the sale had finished, or did someone deliberately send that trunk to her? She had only to wait expectantly and Mr Hayes, as usual, would fill the silence with his fluent, rapid delivery.

'Not at all. It's a pleasure, Reverend Mother. I hope you find them useful.' He gave a little chuckle. 'Grist to the mill, eh! They were left to the end of the sale of Mr Mulcahy's goods, the stuff that he wasn't taking with him to the new house. You know Mr Mulcahy, "Mulcahy the Skins", Reverend Mother? Well, he's moved to a fine new house in Montenotte and he had a lot of stuff in those houses of his in Shandon Street that he wanted cleared out – good stuff, you know, but a bit battered. Twelve children grew up in those two houses, ten of them boys and you know what boys are like, Reverend Mother! They will tilt their chairs, and kick the legs of the tables and slam the doors of the cupboards. Not that it wasn't good, serviceable stuff. Quite a few bargains, there, for those who had an eye for a well-made piece of furniture. Yes, we had a nice dining-room set, some wardrobes, be as good as new if a carpenter did a few repairs, one of those big, old tables, sand it down and you'd have it looking good, quite a few oak presses, a couple of trunk-loads of curtains and cushions, an old clothes horse, that sort of thing. Good stuff, but not what the man wanted in his new house in Montenotte and not what the new owners wanted either. You know the way it goes, Reverend Mother. New house, new furniture! That's what—'

'And the trunk that you sent to me.' Mr Hayes, as a true auctioneer, was able to cram ten words into each second, and would, like a wound-up clockwork toy, go on with great fluency until interrupted.

'Well, your cousin, Mrs Murphy, was still there from the sale before, bought herself a lovely old croquet set, the young ladies will enjoy that if we ever get a summer; that's what I said to her. So I tipped her a nod when it came to the trunk of school books – I knew that you would like them, Reverend Mother, so as soon as Mrs Murphy said, "half-a-crown", well, I brought my hammer down and said "sold!".'

So it was her cousin, Lucy, who had purchased the books. For a moment, the Reverend Mother wondered what to say. Mr Hayes, when he heard the truth of the contents of the trunk, sold for half-a-crown to Lucy, would be disconcerted and angry, perhaps, that she had said nothing. However, Patrick had to be the first to know about the grisly contents of the battered old trunk.

'Well, Mr Hayes,' she said eventually, 'you've solved one puzzle for me, and now here comes Inspector Cashman to solve another. Goodbye, Mr Hayes, and thank you, again, for thinking of us.'

And then decisively she hung up the receiver. Despite the events of the past hour, she felt a smile begin to warm her lips as she pictured Mr Hayes's machine-like brain rapidly shuttling reasons for any connection between a trunk-load of old books and the arrival of a senior member of the local Guards. 'Tommy,' he would say to his assistant, 'did you take a look inside that trunk, at all? It was never a load of dirty books that we sent over to the Reverend Mother in St Mary's Isle. Would you tell me, Tommy, was there any chance of that, at all?'

The Reverend Mother went straight towards the front hallway once she had replaced the telephone receiver. Patrick had said that he was on the way down – those had been his words – and so he would not be long arriving. He was probably on his way to pay a visit to his elderly mother, she thought with some compunction. Now his evening would be filled with activity, people to see, orders to be given, reports to write. She waited by the front door until she saw the lights of a car illuminate the garishly coloured glass of the convent front door. She checked, as was automatic with her, that her bunch of keys were still in her pocket, and then stepped over the threshold, pulling the door shut with the softest of clicks in order not to disturb Sister Bernadette at her evening meal.

But it was not the brand-new, shining black Model T Ford, the property of the Cork Police Barracks, which drew up at the edge of the pavement, but a battered, old, grey Humber with a large dent on the mudguard of its front wheel. And the man that climbed out from the driver's door was not a slim, young police officer, but a rotund and elderly figure. The Reverend Mother went to the gate.

'Dr Scher, how nice to see you. In fact, I am expecting Patrick. Did he telephone you?'

Dr Scher took a little time to slam a recalcitrant front door into submission and then shook his head.

'No, I was with him when you telephoned. He said that your voice was shaking. I came along as support.'

'I'm perfectly well,' said the Reverend Mother sharply and then she relented. 'Well, I have had a rather unpleasant experience. Something most unexpected has happened. But where is Patrick?'

'Well, we were on our way when Patrick must have spotted a man that the police were looking for, young fellow, standing outside the door of a van, leaning on the bonnet, smoking a cigarette, young fool. Patrick stopped his car, just in front of me, miracle that I didn't go smack into him. He jumped out to arrest this young fellow. Young fool pulled a gun on him, but it didn't do any harm, no bullet in it, hadn't been reloaded after the last shot, according to Patrick who took it off him. And then along comes another lad on a motorbike, drives straight at them, shouting "Jump, Fred!" Patrick stood back to save himself and the young fellow jumps on the back of the motorbike and off the pair of them went. Patrick went after them, though I don't think he has much chance of catching up with them. Those motorbikes weave in and out of the donkeys and carts, the cars, and the pedestrians. I'd say that he wouldn't be here for an hour or so, but in the meantime, you've got me. Cold out here! Shall we go inside?'

'I want to show you something first,' said the Reverend Mother, 'but tell me who was arrested? What was his name? The young man with the unloaded pistol. Who was he?'

'I heard Patrick say his name. I bet that he was mixed up in that raid up Douglas Passageway. They seized a barracks just beside the harbour. Something in the *Cork Examiner* about it this morning. There was a lot of shooting went on. A couple of soldiers killed, so I heard. I think that the young fellow's name was Mulcahy, that's it. I remember Patrick saying that name. He said, "I arrest you, Fred Mulcahy, under the suspicion that you were involved in the raid on the barracks in Douglas and in the death of two members of the Free State Army".'

TWO

W. B. Yeats
'The best lack all conviction, while the worst are full
of passionate intensity'

E ileen had spotted Fred Mulcahy immediately. She had been happily riding down the quay on her brand-new motorbike – at least it was brand-new to Eileen. It had been sold, second-hand to her, by her friend Eamonn, when his wealthy parents had bought a new model for their only son. Eileen adored it, had cleaned every inch of it, repainted it a shiningly austere black and rode it all over the city, wearing a leather helmet, a tweed jacket, a pair of breeches, and her beloved knee-high leather boots.

And now there was Fred, just about to be arrested. He had his hands up in a helpless fashion and a proud, suffering look on his face. Only one policeman, there, thought Eileen scornfully, as she accelerated noisily. Why doesn't he make a run for it? Everyone knows that the guards were unarmed, except for a truncheon. Why is he so stupid, always posing? He seemed to be forever trying out the role of martyr, another Patrick Pearse who would be shot by the British.

Still, when it came down to it, Fred had been one of the six young men and two girls that had shared a house, shared danger and daring exploits, when she had lived in a Republican hideout in Ballinhassig, south of the city of Cork. He was a show-off and a nuisance, but she could not let him down now. Rapidly she illicitly overtook a lorry on the left-hand side, skidded to a halt in front of them and shouted in her gruffest voice, 'Jump! Fred, jump!' and then to cause more confusion she palpitated the horn rapidly with her thumb, filling the quayside with the alarming sounds.

It galvanized him into action, anyway. He flung himself onto the back of her bike, riding pillion and she kicked the accelerator quickly. There was a satisfying roar from the engine and then she was off. She overtook the lorry again, again sliding past on its left side and pulling out ahead of him. The lorry driver blew his horn and she blew hers back with a jolly little beep-beep. She could hear, from behind them, the civic guard, poor eejit, blow his whistle but that wouldn't help him much. The *Garda Siochána,* the guardians of the peace, were thin on the ground and by the time that he got to a telephone box to summon the army from Victoria Barracks, then she and Fred Mulcahy would be well out of the way.

'Where do you want to go, Fred?' she yelled back at him.

'Douglas,' he said into her ear and she gave a nod. Douglas was a good choice. They would be in Douglas village in under ten minutes and she would not have to go through the town and risk meeting a lorry-load of soldiers coming down from the Victoria Barracks, summoned by a policeman who had lost a suspect. She was a little surprised that Fred had not wanted to get back to the safe house in Ballinhassig, but she was also relieved. If she drove fast, she could drop him off at Douglas and be back at the printers, where she worked, before they shut for the evening. She had been sent out to a shop to get details of some posters that they wanted printed and had promised to return with the instructions before the end of the day. Her job was important. She wanted to do well, to be regarded as reliable. She liked the money that she earned and liked that she was involved in printing propaganda leaflets and Republican arguments.

'What did the guard want you for?' she shouted over her shoulder to Fred when they had climbed to the top of Douglas hill and were well on their way to the village.

'The raid on Douglas Barracks, this morning,' he shouted back and she nodded. Pretty stupid to be hanging around after that. But then Fred was a bit like that. Always wanted to be the centre of attention. She slowed down to a stop in order to wait for the Cork to Douglas tram to get out of her way.

'That fellow took my gun,' he said petulantly into her ear.

'Jesus, you didn't shoot one of the Civic Guards, did you, Fred? All hell will break loose if you did that.' She looked around at him in alarm and saw that there were tears in his eyes. Embarrassed, she looked away.

'The gun was empty. There were no bullets in it.' His voice was choked with emotion. She guessed that he was crying and so was careful not to turn around again.

Stupid, though, thought Eileen. If you are going to shoot, well, shoot. Don't go around trying to fire from an unloaded revolver.

'Don't worry about it, Fred,' she said. 'It's just as well that you didn't shoot one of the guards. That causes no end of trouble. They'd go through the city with a fine comb looking for you.' And then her curiosity got the better of her. 'Why was it empty? Did you fire at someone else? What did you have a gun for, in the first place?'

'There was supposed to be a trunk-load of guns, unloaded from a Kerry trawler. They came from America and were picked up near Cape Clear Island by some of our men. They were supposed to commandeer a trawler. I was supposed to be the armed escort.'

'Go on,' she said impatiently. He had only answered one of her questions.

'Well, I met a Kerryman, couldn't understand him very well, speaking in Irish, he said something about Douglas Sawmill and then I got hold of a donkey and cart, took them from an old fellow, told him I was requisitioning them. I thought it would look . . . I thought . . .'

'Tell me afterwards.' Douglas Sawmill? She had often wondered why Douglas Street and Douglas Sawmills was in the city, not in Douglas village, itself. Rich people lived in Douglas and they had managed to get this nuisance of a tramway set up between the city and their rural village.

'Watch out for tramlines,' Eamonn had warned her when he was teaching her to ride the motorbike. 'You can easily come a cropper if you get a tyre stuck in one of them,' he had said and so she went carefully, determined not to injure her beautiful bike. The tram had trundled on, so she accelerated again, adroitly weaving her way in and out of the traffic. For a few minutes she concentrated on her driving, taking great pleasure in her skill and she put thoughts about Fred to the back of her mind. Time enough for that when they reached the village of Douglas.

Douglas seemed quiet when she arrived. There was a civic guard on duty outside the Douglas Barracks, but he was chatting to a woman and so she sped past, hoping that Fred had the sense to turn his face away. By now there were pictures of most of the active Republicans stuck on the walls of the barracks throughout the city and its suburbs.

'Down here, down this street, stop by the post office,' he said in her ear, and obligingly she turned off and drew up to a halt.

'You're not going in there, are you?' she asked in alarm. Post offices, also, had pictures of wanted men stuck up in them. She turned back to look at him. He had that expression again, that noble hero look which had often annoyed her. He took no notice of her words, now, just slipped off the back of her bike and strode into the post office, looking, she thought, with his belted raincoat and his slouched hat, every inch a wanted IRA man. She kept the engine running, glancing apprehensively around, but all remained quiet until he came out again. Looked terribly white. Should she make an effort to get him back to Ballinhassig where he would be safe?

'Down that road, there. That leads to the shoreline,' he ordered, climbing back on to the bike. He had been a long time in there. What on earth was he up to?

Eileen kicked the bike to a start but restrained her impulse to roar down the street. It would relieve her annoyance, but it was dangerous to draw attention to oneself in a small place like Douglas.

'Next left.' Fred seemed to gulp out the words, and she had an uneasy feeling that he might be crying again. She followed his muttered directions again and to her surprise came to what was obviously a harbour. Not the river, but the real sea. Waves crashed on the shore and she thought she could smell salt on the damp air. She had not known that Cork harbour came right in as far as Douglas. Shows you how much I know of my own city, she reflected and planned, now she had a job and a motorbike, she would go on trips all around the city and even down to the sea.

'Stop here,' Fred said in her ear and she pulled up just beside a pier and got off the bike. He didn't move, though, just sat there, staring out at the water with a frozen expression on his face.

'What's wrong, Fred?' Eileen suppressed the word 'now' and listened with annoyance to the church bell sounding the half hour. Half past five. Would she be able to get back to the printing works in time? The compositor worked late on a Friday and liked to get the week's jobs finished if possible before he went home.

'It's gone,' he said. 'That trawler from Kerry is gone. I'd know it. It had a repaired mast, a piece of wood of another colour nailed to it.' He scanned the boats bobbing on the water, moving in and out of the harbour. 'Curses! I wanted to get out to that American ship. It's probably still moored out there near Cape Clear Island. I have to see those men from the trawler. I was going to ask them to take me with them, to bring me to the American ship. I wanted to go to America.'

'You and another couple of million Irish people,' said Eileen. He sounded a bit like a spoiled child, but that was Fred. Always going on about his father and his hard childhood.

'They'd allow me. I'd ask for sanctuary,' he said. 'I shot a man.' He pulled his hat down over his eyes and turned away from her.

'What, a civic guard?'

'No, not a civic guard. Someone else.'

'Who then?' She was getting tired of Fred. The last time she'd met him, he managed to get himself shot by showing off and since then he clearly hadn't improved. He was standing there, gazing out to sea, the hat pulled down to hide his eyes, but from his voice she guessed that he was weeping. Eileen felt a little ashamed of herself.

'What's the matter, Fred? What's wrong?' He was shivering now. Older than herself by at least a couple of years, but he seemed very young to her. A sob broke from him and she wondered whether he was having some sort of a breakdown.

'Have you really killed someone, is that it?'

'I don't know. I don't think so. I fired my gun at him, but

I think that he was dead already. He looked dead.' And then, almost absent-mindedly, he said, 'There were maggots crawling around on top of him.'

'Maggots!' Eileen swallowed hard. 'Sounds dead,' she said in as judicial a manner as she could muster. 'Someone killed him earlier, perhaps.' Days ago, she thought. She wasn't too sure about maggots, but didn't think that they would appear on a newly-dead corpse.

'Let's get you back to Ballinhassig,' she said. She had to give up the prospect of getting back into Cork before the printing works closed. On Monday she would explain her failure to return. They were all patriots in the Lee Printing Works. They would understand that she had no choice in the matter. She had to rescue a fellow Republican in dire straits.

'No, I can't do that. I can't bring trouble on them. I'm a wanted man.' He gazed out to sea showing his profile in a heroic fashion.

'That doesn't matter. The soldiers will be after anyone who took part in that raid. That's why there are safe houses. Tom Hurley will hide you, get you out to west Cork or something.'

'Not if I'm wanted for the death of my own father.'

'What! Was that who you shot? The dead man.' She had heard Fred's tirades, often enough, against his father when she had been living out in Ballinhassig and now she felt a little sick. 'But he was dead, already. You said that there were maggots crawling over the body.'

'Well, I've confessed to the murder. That's why I wanted to stop at the post office. I sent a confession to the Civic Guards. I signed it too.'

'What! A confession! Where is it now?'

'I posted it. I wrote out a confession. I told them how it was. I wrote a full account. I told how I went up to Shandon Street, how I pleaded with him, telling him that I wanted to go to university to study mathematics. If he had enough money to build a big house in Montenotte, then he had enough money to educate his eldest son. He refused and I shot him. I wrote it all down. I signed my confession. I put it in the post box. I just made the post. The woman in the post office told me that. She said a minute later and I would have missed it. I saw the bag of letters going off in the post van down to Cork.'

Eileen looked at him, speechless for the moment. And then something about his pose annoyed her.

'You want to be hanged, is that it?' she snapped. 'It wouldn't be a very noble death, though, would it? Shooting an unarmed man. And your own father, too! Not exactly dying for Ireland, was it? So what's so terrible about him that he deserved to be killed? At least your father didn't skip off to England as soon as your mother was pregnant, just like my father and the father of loads of others did. No, he stayed and worked hard and sent every single one of you, all twelve of you, girls as well as boys, to school and even to secondary school. What good did it do for Ireland shooting him?' And then she melted slightly. 'But you didn't, did you? Tell me that you didn't.'

'Yes, I did,' he said stubbornly. 'And I'm not going to Ballinhassig. You'd better leave me now. I have only one chance and that is to get out to that American boat. That fishing boat over there might take me. Have you any money?'

Reluctantly, she took her leather wallet from the inner pocket of her jacket. It held three brand-new one-pound notes issued by the Bank of Ireland. Her whole week's salary. He snatched it from her before she could say anything and then he was off, striding down the pier looking out to sea. There were numerous small fishing boats heading in towards Douglas Harbour and behind her, men with donkeys and carts were arriving to purchase the day's catch to deliver to the shops and the markets in the city. Perhaps one of these fishing boats would take him to Cape Clear. Eileen doubted that, though. The sea was very rough around west Cork and these fishermen would trawl the easier waters on the east side of the city. Most of them probably did not venture more than half a mile outside the harbour.

I can do no more for him, she told herself, as she turned her motorbike to head back to the city. If he has really killed his own father, and been stupid enough to write a confession to the Civic Guards, then Tom Hurley would not welcome his presence in Ballinhassig and would do nothing to help

him. It was annoying to lose her wallet, though it was a
second-hand one. But losing her salary was terrible. It meant
that she had nothing to give her mother for food this week.

Nevertheless, she felt almost glad that he had done that,
had stolen from her. It did, she thought, absolve her from
taking any more risks on his behalf. In the meantime, she had
better get quickly out of Douglas before she was identified as
the friend of a murderer. She would ride at a reasonable speed,
she thought. Give no one the notion that she was escaping,
but she wouldn't stop until she reached the printing works off
South Terrace.

And then, quite suddenly, her motorbike spluttered and
stopped. She clung to the handlebars, jolted by the sudden
jerk. No petrol? Surely not. She was meticulous about filling
it up, had felt glad that she had done it this afternoon, or else
Fred might have taken even more of her money. Nevertheless
she got off the bike, carefully parked it by the pavement and
then examined the petrol tank. No, that wasn't the problem.
It was almost full. She did a few tests that Eamonn had showed
her, but could find nothing wrong.

'In trouble, sonny?' The post-office van slowed to a halt
across the road from her. She wished that she could grab his
bag of letters, but that was stupid, so she just nodded.

'Garage just down the road, you'll have to push the old
bike,' he called out of the window. He jerked his thumb towards
a side road, just a few yards ahead of her. 'Down there; they'll
sort it out for you.'

And then he was gone, bringing the fatal letter to the Cork
sorting office. It would probably be on the superintendent's
desk in Barrack Street in the morning post. Eileen got off her
bike and began to push it. Perhaps that hill up towards Douglas
had been too much for it. She hoped, desperately, that she
could afford the repair. She had about ten shillings in her
purse. Would that be enough? And would the garage be still
open? It was getting quite late in the evening. She turned down
the narrow side road and was cheered to see lights and a petrol
pump only a few yards down the road. Puffing heavily she
rolled the bike inside.

'Broken down, are you?' The man inside seemed sympathetic.

'That's right.' She took off her cap and ran a hand through her damp hair. His grin widened.

'Don't get many young ladies pushing motorbikes in here, do we, Tommy? Take a seat over there, girlie, and we'll have a look. Run out of petrol, I'll be bet.'

'Run out of petrol, that'll be it,' echoed Tommy.

'I checked that,' said Eileen and watched indignantly as Tommy lowered the dipstick into the petrol tank.

Half an hour later, though, she wished that it had been that, even if it had made the two men laugh. Running out of petrol would have been an easy thing to cure. The longer the two men worked over her beloved bike, the more that they pursed their lips and shook their heads.

'Carburettor,' said Tommy and the tone of finality in his voice made her heart sink.

'Carburettor,' agreed the first man.

'Can't do it tonight, missie,' he said to her. 'I'm afraid that's a long job. We'll have to strip the whole thing down. You'll have to leave it with us. Come around tomorrow at about five and we should have it done for you.'

'Oh.' Eileen gulped a little.

'Where do you live?'

'In the city?'

'That's all right, don't you worry. The trolley buses keep going until late. Go back into the village. You'll get back to the city in no time.'

Eileen nodded. At least her mother would not be worried if she got the trolley bus back. She could get off at the quay and walk home.

'How much will the repair cost?' she asked.

'Could be anything up to about £3, I'm afraid.' He must have seen the shock in her face because he said, 'Sorry, love, but carburettors going wrong make for a big job. And there could be parts needed, a needle valve or something else. You never know until you get the thing stripped down. Still, keep your fingers crossed, love, might be able to do it for a bit less.'

'Thank you,' said Eileen. She felt slightly dazed when she walked out. Where could she get the money to pay for that?

And then a wave of anger came over her. How dare Fred help himself to all of the money in her wallet? She started to run back up the road and then turned down towards the harbour. She would get that money back from him.

THREE

St Thomas Aquinas
'CONCEDE mihi, misericors Deus, quae tibi sunt
placita, ardenter concupiscere, prudenter investigare,
veraciter agnoscere, et perfecte adimplere ad laudem
et gloriam Nominis Tui.'
(GRANT me, O merciful God, to desire eagerly, to
investigate prudently, to acknowledge sincerely, and to
fulfil perfectly those things that are pleasing to Thee,
for the praise and glory of Thy Holy Name.)

The Reverend Mother thought about Fred Mulcahy for a moment or two after Dr Scher's words. There had been something very odd, almost theatrical in the way that he had fired at the body of his father. And then he had an unloaded gun when he encountered Patrick and his men. Lucky for some civic guard, for Patrick perhaps, that he was unable to fire. Perhaps even lucky for the boy himself. This business of the assault on Douglas Barracks was probably not anything that Patrick would be too involved in. Douglas was a small village, certainly a few miles at least outside the city boundary. The army would take over there. It was probably quite difficult to get evidence that any particular young Republican had been involved in an attack, but a shot policeman would have meant certain death by hanging. Then she switched her mind from the problem of the son to that of the father.

'Have you a torch in your car, Dr Scher?' No doubt, she could find one in the convent, but for the moment, she did not want any interference in the community's hour of rest and relaxation.

He gave her an appraising look, but then went towards his car without question, returning with an impressively large torch, clicking on the beam and testing it against the convent wall. She thought of saying 'Prepare for a shock', but then decided that dead bodies were the norm for a man who was professor of anatomy at the university and who regularly conducted autopsies for the police.

And so, walking steadily, and saying no more, she led the way to the old disused coach house, inserted her key into the lock of the door and pushed it open. The smell now filled the chilly building and she saw him stop and sniff the air, before he switched on a powerful beam which illuminated the whole building. Once again, but this time with apprehension, she clicked open the latches, and cautiously lifted the lid of the trunk. The stench seemed even worse now and in the light from the torch the maggot activity increased rapidly.

'Well, well, well,' said Dr Scher. 'What a woman for surprises you are, Reverend Mother! Where did this come from?'

'From Mr Hayes, the auctioneer, number 23 Princes Street,' said the Reverend Mother precisely. 'Purchased for me by my cousin, Mrs Murphy,' she added.

'A friend of yours?' he queried, with a nod towards the macabre contents of the trunk.

'Known to me,' amended the Reverend Mother. 'That is Mr Mulcahy from Shandon Street, a hide and skin merchant.'

'I see. Well, that accounts for the sere cloths,' he said flippantly.

She should reprove him for this frivolity, but his calmness in the face of death somehow comforted her. A certain measure of steadiness flowed back into her legs. She straightened her shoulders and found the courage to ask the question which had been troubling her.

'How long has he been dead?'

'Couldn't tell you that until after I get him on the table,' he said. 'And that will be Monday, I'd say. I have a poor girl who was dragged from the river to see to first, not that anyone seems too interested in her, poor thing. Pregnant, I suppose, pregnant and hungry, condemned by church and state. Nothing to live for.'

The Reverend Mother bowed her head. There were too many bodies taken from the river these days. Whether it was a case of suicide, murder or a political street battle, the two channels of the River Lee were dumping places for the unwanted dead of the city.

'Perhaps you could give me some idea, very roughly, of when death could have occurred, and . . .' She hesitated. 'How did he die?'

He gave her a quick glance, turning the beam of the torch in her direction. He said nothing, though, and bent over the body, touching the skin without hesitation and flexing the joints of the dead hand.

'Depends on where he has been kept,' he said, 'but in an unheated room in this dank fog, I suppose that he could have been dead a few days. Would have been popped into the trunk when he was fresh, though, I'd guess. Why do you ask about how he died?'

'His son shot him through the heart about an hour ago. In my presence,' she added.

'Well, well, well.' Once again he bent over the body and shone the powerful beam of the torch onto the black coat, delicately lifting the lapel of the broadcloth with finger and thumb and peering down at the starched shirt front. He made no comment, but now she could see for herself that there was a small, shiny, dark patch of stiffened blood on the white linen. And once she had identified that, she could see that the black cloth of the man's jacket and waistcoat also had been stained with blood.

'Was he shot?' She asked the question, but knew that he probably could not tell her the answer to it. The blood on the shirt, the blood on the black coat; that blood was old blood, hours, perhaps days, old.

'That or knifed,' he said. 'Killed anyway.'

'But not by his son, not ten minutes ago.'

'Who's his son?'

'Fred Mulcahy, the man that you were talking about a little while ago.'

'The young fellow wanted by the police. So he had paid you a visit previously.' Dr Scher looked startled. 'You were here with him, alone? You should be more careful. There are a lot of dangerous men around, Reverend Mother. I would be wary of inviting strangers in off the street. You have a good lock on your gate so keep it locked.'

'I didn't invite him. I think that he must have followed the auctioneer's men in. He just appeared at my shoulder after they had left. He thought this trunk was for him. He expected a delivery. It was to be handed over to him outside the Douglas Street Sawmills. I think that he was as shocked as I was when the lid was opened.' She would have to tell her story again to Patrick, but in the meantime Dr Scher's matter-of-fact reactions were a comfort to her. Death was death, she told herself. Whether it happened in a hospital bed or violently, like this one, the result was the same. An abrupt cessation of living functions, decay, dissolution and eventually reintegration with the earth. When the police were finished with the body, then a decent burial would have to be organized.

'And he was surprised to see his father, this young friend of yours?'

'I think so.' She hesitated over that for a moment but she did not add anything. Time enough later for a more precise recall of that moment when she had thrown back the lid of the trunk.

'Here's Patrick.' Dr Scher had begun to move towards the door before she had fully registered the sound of a car outside the convent fence. He handed her the torch and then went outside, closing the door behind him. Left alone, she went on thinking. Why had Fred Mulcahy shot his father in that ostentatious gesture? What was the point of it? Surely a gunman would know that the man was already dead? Even to her, the man had looked like a corpse. And what about that stiffened plaque of blood on the man's clothing? Someone had killed him. But why should Fred kill his father. He had escaped from the family home and the work that he disliked so much. She turned away from the body and went towards the door to meet the two men. Patrick was looking grim-faced and worried. Dr Scher gave a half-shake of his head when she looked at him and so she decided to ask no questions.

'Any more bodies for us, Reverend Mother?' queried Dr Scher and she gave a half-smile in appreciation of his efforts to normalize the situation. Patrick did not smile. He had a tired look and the Reverend Mother was not surprised that he was worried about the situation. Douglas was less than two miles away from where they stood, but Cork Harbour was an enormous one; the second largest in the world, she understood. It was nine miles long from end to end if you measured a straight line from its entrance at Roches Point, but its sides snaked in and out of villages and small seaside towns. By the terms of the treaty, Britain still owned Cork Harbour and British troops were on Spike Island – still some Americans around, also, she seemed to remember hearing. Nevertheless, given the huge volume of ships coming in and out of the harbour with passengers and goods on them, and the amount of yachts, pleasure boats, rowing boats and dredgers, it was probably an easy way to smuggle in weapons. The superintendent of the police barracks would be annoyed when he heard that young Fred Mulcahy had managed to give the slip to the inspector.

'Well, that's in the hands of the army, now, they're out looking for them, but this looks like my affair.' Patrick gave a nod towards the trunk. 'It turned up, sent to you by an auctioneer, Dr Scher told me.'

'It says "school books" on the lid and that, I suppose, is why my cousin purchased them for me. She paid a half-crown for the trunk, according to Mr Hayes, the auctioneer, when I phoned him. He said that she bid half a crown and that he immediately knocked it down to her, the trunk and its contents, and that must have seemed to be quite a bargain. I said nothing to him, of course. He took it as a natural curiosity about the donor. I haven't, as yet, spoken to my cousin, but I presume she could tell no more.'

The Reverend Mother was pleased to hear how steady her voice sounded. She did not avert her gaze from the gruesome sight in the trunk but forced herself to utter a short prayer for the man's immortal soul.

'I'm frozen,' said Dr Scher. 'Reverend Mother, would you take me indoors and offer me a cup of tea. We'll leave you and the sergeant to make arrangements, Patrick.'

'You know where the telephone is, Patrick,' said the Reverend Mother, but was not surprised to find that the sergeant followed them out and before they had re-entered the convent, the police car was speeding its way along the wet road. Joe had been sent to fetch a van and the man's body would be conveyed to the police mortuary ready for Dr Scher's autopsy. There was no point in them waiting. She knew how methodical Patrick was. The first task would be to have the body taken care of and after that he would take her statement. He would wait for the result of the autopsy before speculating too much on who may have killed the man. In that, she thought, he was quite unlike Dr Scher who would be full of questions, surmises and sudden brainwaves. Patrick was reticent and discreet. Dr Scher was impatient, indiscreet; prone to sudden leaps of the imagination and wild theories. An excellent doctor, though, and a good friend to the community of nuns, all of whom liked and trusted him.

She left him to exchange greetings with Sister Bernadette and some of the other nuns and made her way to her own room. She had plenty of time to hang up her cloak and to take her customary seat in front of the desk before he came bustling in, rubbing his hands. He closed the door carefully behind him, heaped an extra shovelful of coal upon the dull fire, riddled it energetically and then turned to her.

'Now, Reverend Mother, you can tell me all about that unfortunate man. And, of course, I suppose that you know by now who murdered him.'

She thought about the question seriously. It would be important to get this matter cleared up as quickly as possible. There would be a lot of whispering and of speculation once it became known that the dead body of the hide and skin merchant had ended up in the convent on St Mary's of the Isle. But who had killed him, and why?

'He must be quite a rich man by now,' she said aloud. 'I remember, quite some time ago, someone telling me that he made a lot of money during the Boer War – selling leather for boots and belts. And he would have done equally well out of the Great War as by that stage he had developed the wool side of the business; a huge amount would have been needed for all of those uniforms. War, I read once, is good for business. There is little haggling, little beating down of the prices.

An enterprising man who can produce the required goods reliably and punctually, and in sufficient quantity, can charge what that service is worth to the army.'

Dr Scher listened with attention. He was a man with a deep interest in his fellow townsmen. She had often noticed that about him, and had thought that if he were not a doctor, he would have made a good novelist. 'So a rich man. And now where would his money go, Reverend Mother? I'm sure that you know that.'

She thought back to Bridie's words about the family row when young Fred left his father's house. 'If he made a will, and not everyone does that, well then I doubt whether he has left any money to his eldest son. He had ten sons and two daughters, all younger than Fred who must . . .' Once again her mind went back to the time that Bridie had left the convent and had gone to work for the Mulcahy family. Fred had been a baby then and had helped Bridie to come to terms with her sorrow and her loss. 'Fred must be about twenty now,' she said aloud. 'I think it is about a year since he left home and joined the Republican Party. I understand that the break with his father was because Mr Mulcahy wanted the boy to go into business, as a feather merchant, apparently, and Fred wanted to go to university and study mathematics. A singularly useless choice, in his father's eyes, I understand.' The Reverend Mother pondered on that self-made man, on the story of rags to riches. 'I would think that it is very possible that he did not make a will at all,' she said after a minute. 'He would not have been an old man and he would not have felt himself to be old. His business was prospering, he had just had built a fine new house in Montenotte which he had filled with brand-new furniture. 'No, he would have felt that he was embarking on a new and successful part of his life, not ending it. It will be interesting to see, but I will be surprised if he did make a will.'

'So,' said Dr Scher thoughtfully, 'how did that boy, Fred, get on with his mother? You know the family, do you, Reverend Mother?'

'Only at second-hand,' she replied. 'A former lay sister in this convent went to work for the family when she left us and she kept in touch. Fred was often here when he was a young boy. I suppose I have retained an interest in him and the older children of the family. As time went on, of course, we saw less and less of Bridie. But, to answer your question, yes, I do believe that he was his mother's favourite. Bridie used to say that often. Of course, Fred was a great favourite with her when he was a small boy and she may have exaggerated his mother's fondness for the child. And I'm not sure about the mother's relationship with him now that he has left home.'

'But this Bridie still works for the Mulcahy family, does she?' Dr Scher turned around as Patrick, after a discreet knock, pushed open the door and entered the room. He shook his head to the offer of cake and tea but held out his hands to the blaze from Dr Scher's fire.

'The body has been removed now, Reverend Mother. A certain amount of excitement in the street, I'm afraid, but these things always do get out, sooner or later.' He glanced at the clock on the mantelpiece. 'I'd just like to take a brief statement from you, if you don't mind, and then I'll be on my way.' As he spoke, he produced his notebook, licked the tip of his indelible pencil and began to write rapid shorthand, as she spoke.

'At about five o'clock of the evening, a trunk was delivered to the convent at St Mary's Isle. It was sent by Mr Hayes, Auctioneer, Princes Street and was labelled "school books", and with the name and direction of "The Reverend Mother, St Mary's Isle". When they left, I decided to check the contents. On opening the lid, it was found to contain the body of a middle-aged man. The man was dead.' She finished there, thinking about the dramatic event that followed. He looked up from his notebook and across the room at her and she responded immediately.

'The trunk was placed by the auctioneer's men in an old outhouse because the trunk looked so dilapidated and smelled bad. The men suggested putting it into an old outhouse, which was once the convent coach house a hundred years ago and I agreed to that. When I went in to check on the books to make sure that the children were not disappointed, I was followed by a young man. I was only aware of his presence when he spoke to me. He claimed that the trunk was for him, but once I had opened the lid, he said that he had not expected that. I believe,' said the Reverend Mother carefully, 'that his words were: "I know nothing about this, nothing whatsoever." He went on to say that he expected a trunk to be delivered to him outside the Douglas Street Sawmills, but with a different contents.'

'Guns, I suppose,' said Dr Scher as Patrick continued to write rapidly.

'He was about to go when I rather unwisely suggested that he should be the one to call the guards and that alarmed him. He pointed his pistol at me, not, I think, with any real intention of using it and I mention this only to show that when I spoke of his mother and his duty to tell her, then he fired his pistol at his father's heart. The man, of course, had been dead for some time; even I, without any medical knowledge, could have told that.'

'What made him fire at his father?' asked Dr Scher as Patrick's busy pencil scribbled across the page of his notebook.

The Reverend Mother thought back to that scene in the shadowy coach house. 'I believe it may have been the mention of his mother that provoked the shot.'

'The lad must have known that the man was dead,' said Dr Scher, more to himself than to anyone else. 'It was impossible that he thought he was alive.'

'Certainly I believed that I was looking at a corpse, not at a living man.' The Reverend Mother looked at Patrick when she said that and saw him nod and make another note. He waited for a moment, and then snapped a rubber band around his notebook, replaced it and the pencil into his jacket pocket, glanced again at the clock on the mantelpiece and then got to his feet.

'Thank you, Reverend Mother. Now I'd better be off to see the auctioneer and hear what he has to say. I've sent Joe up to Shandon to tell the wife. Apparently they have sold one of the houses that they lived in, two houses joined together, but they are keeping one on as an office and she's still there, seeing to the disposal of the furniture and the cleaning out of the place. Joe is good at that sort of thing, breaking bad news. I'll have to see her myself when she has got over the first shock, but in the meantime, I'd like to see what the auctioneer has to say.'

And then he went swiftly through the door and they heard the determined tramp of his boots on the wooden corridor outside. No sound of voices. By now Sister Bernadette and the other nuns in the kitchen probably knew all about the macabre discovery in the old coach house and were busily discussing it in the kitchen.

It would be a good way for an auctioneer to get rid of his enemies, wouldn't it? Shoot them, pop the bodies in some trunks and then sell them for a few pounds,' remarked Dr Scher as he helped himself to another cup of the dark orange tea which Sister Bernadette made specially to suit his taste.

'I believe that it only fetched half a crown,' said the Reverend Mother absent-mindedly. 'I must speak about it to my cousin, Mrs Murphy.' It was, she remembered, the auctioneer's own idea that Lucy should bid for this trunk, but that was understandable. 'Presumably no one had bothered to look inside the trunk, although it was not locked when it came here.'

'And no keys?' asked Dr Scher.

'No, no keys, but it did look very old, didn't it? It may have been fifty to sixty years old. None of the boys went away to school, they were all educated at Farranferris Seminary in Shandon itself, and I suspect that they were not a family for holidays, so it may be that the trunk came with Mr Mulcahy himself when he journeyed from Tipperary as a boy to work with his uncle in Shandon.'

'And I suppose he took another journey, his last journey before his funeral, with it from Shandon to the auctioneer's premises. Very, very strange. I wonder how Patrick is getting on with the auctioneer.'

FOUR

Eoin O'Duffy, Police Commissioner
'I say that a brave guard is braver than a brave soldier.
A soldier goes into the fight under the command of his
officers. It is altogether different with the policeman.
He is at once the commanding officer and private. He
fights his fight alone. His enemy, the criminal, ever
exists. For the guard it is a fight to the finish. It is a
question of either his life or that of his antagonists.'

P atrick was familiar with the auctioneer's rooms on
Princes Street. When he had first obtained a coveted
place on the newly-formed Civic Guards' cohort in Cork
city, he had grimly saved almost all of his weekly wage. His
boarding, in the barracks, was free and he had few other
expenses. After a couple of months he had saved enough to
buy a small house for his mother in a laneway on St Mary's
of the Isle. He had said nothing to her, just gone on saving
while she went on living in one room in a tenement. And it
was then that he had fun for the first time in a rather bleak,
and very hard-working, life. Week after week, he had haunted
the auctioneer's premises, watching, listening, gauging the
mood of the buyers and, one by one, he had bought a bed, a
kitchen table, an easy chair, and then had added a few
cupboards, another chair for a visitor, a wooden press for her
clothes and even, a great extravagance, a wooden dresser with
a few colourful plates and cups. The little house had been kept
warm with rick of turf, stored outside the back door. Every
few days he had lit a fire and gloated over the growing contents.
It still affected him, whenever he remembered his mother's
reaction to the paradise that her only child had purchased for
her and there were tears in his eyes when he turned into the
auctioneer's premises on Princes Street.

A sale had just finished and people streamed out, chattering amongst themselves. An evening at the auctions was an evening out for a lot of people and those Friday night auctions were very popular.

Mr Hayes, he was glad to see, showed no memory of him. The auctioneer was perturbed and uneasy.

'Is it about that trunk; that's it, isn't it?' he asked immediately, once Patrick had introduced himself and meticulously shown his identity. 'I thought that there must be something wrong when the Reverend Mother telephoned me and I've been making a few enquiries. I didn't look at the thing, myself, you know, inspector. I just sell the stuff as it comes in; that's the way that things go in our line of business. We'd never be able to get through everything if we had to weigh up each item. Half-a-crown, that's what it was sold for, well, I ask you, inspector, what's half-a-crown these days. I couldn't go inspecting everything that goes for half-a-crown. Now, you're a fair man, inspector, you wouldn't ask that of me, would you, now?'

'I understand that Mrs Murphy, the solicitor's wife, placed the bid for it,' said Patrick stolidly. *Get as much out of him before you tell him why you are here*; that was the advice that he would have given to his sergeant and now he heeded his own instincts. The man was a talker and a talker usually told what you wanted with just the minimum of questioning. Mr Hayes had the reputation of knowing everything worth knowing about the citizens of Cork. Keep him talking and soon Patrick would know what could be known about the Mulcahy family and about the dead man himself. Already a cascade of words were pouring from the lips of the auctioneer.

'Well, that was the way of it,' he said waving a hand expansively, 'and it was myself tipped Mrs Murphy a wink. That's what happened, without a word of a lie, inspector. You see, I know that Mrs Murphy is the cousin to the Reverend Mother. She bought a Victrola for her once; I remember that. She had it delivered to the convent so that the girls could learn songs from it. And so this trunk-load of old school books – well, that's what I thought it was, that was what the label said. Well, I saw that Mrs Murphy was still there, chatting to a friend. I said to myself the Reverend Mother would like this and so I gave the nod to her and as soon as she made a bid, well, I counted it out pretty smart, and then I brought my hammer down on it. I thought,' he said, beginning a winding-down process, 'that I was doing a favour.'

'And you had no idea about its contents?'

'Not an idea, in the world,' said Mr Hayes with emphasis. 'But I've heard that the trunk was taken off to the barracks, and now here you are . . .' He made a sweeping gesture with his right hand and then collapsed onto the edge of the seat of a tall stool. The show was over as far as he was concerned. Now it was for the inspector to uncover the goods.

'There was a body of man in the trunk,' said Patrick, endeavouring to make the words sound normal and every day.

'Really!' Mr Hayes did a good imitation of a man who is stricken by total astonishment, but Patrick had a feeling that the man knew of that all the time. Cork was a small city, filled with excitable, gossip-loving people and it was hard to keep anything a secret within its bounds. The van driver, the man at the mortuary, someone at the telephone exchange, the word would have gone out. It was a pity; he would have liked a true reaction to his startling news, but there was nothing that he could do about that just now.

'I suppose that you've heard who it was,' he said grimly.

Mr Hayes did not acknowledge or deny, just looked expectantly at Patrick. There was a noise of heavy footsteps on the stairs outside, a knock against the banisters that made Mr Hayes wince and then a crash from overhead.

'We're getting ready for the sale tomorrow,' he explained. 'Death of Major Heffernan, you'll have seen it in the paper a while back. Only relative is out in India, we've had an auction at the place itself, out in Fota, and these are just the remnants. They'll go in with another lot.'

'So when did you collect the stuff from Shandon?' asked Patrick.

'A couple of days ago, on Tuesday, we made two journeys. Very steep hill that. I didn't want the lorry to be overloaded coming back down it.'

'So nothing was sold at the house, was it? You didn't have an auction, there, did you?'

Mr Hayes shook his head. 'No, no, it doesn't work like that, inspector. "Fota" now, a big house, nice area, people go for the day out and then they get tempted to buy, but Shandon, wouldn't say a word against it, decent, hardworking people live up there on Shandon, but you wouldn't have people going all the way up there for an outing, now would you, inspector?'

'But you went up yourself, didn't you? When was that?'

'Must have been a couple of days ago,' said the auctioneer cautiously.

'You keep a notebook, a diary, something like that, do you?'

'*Book of Sale*,' said Mr Hayes. 'I'm never a one to scatter information into different nooks and crannies. Everything goes into the one book in date order. Now let me see, where did I put it.'

The book of sale was lying conspicuously on the top of the bureau in Mr Hayes's office, but Patrick allowed him to go through a little fiction of looking for it. The man was an actor and he had to be given his moment on stage. Prosperous business, he thought. From memory, there was a sale on there almost every day of the week, many of them going on into the evening when the cheaper goods were sold off.

'What sort of commission do you take, Mr Hayes?' he asked as with a cry of triumph, the auctioneer removed his hammer from on top of the book and brought it across the room.

'Usually fifteen per cent. Don't get much on the sale of a trunk for half-a-crown,' responded Mr Hayes.

Patrick said nothing, though it did cross his mind that, once the news got around, these rooms would be full of curious people wanting to see the exact spot where the body of one of their prosperous citizens reposed until it was despatched to the Reverend Mother at St Mary's Isle. Fifteen per cent on the contents of Major Heffernan's splendid house out in 'Fota' would amount to quite a sum. And he had a feeling that Mr Hayes had charge of the sale of the houses in Shandon as well.

'Ah, here you are.' The book opened neatly at the right page and a small scrap of torn paper fluttered to the ground, its function as a marker over and done with. 'That's right. Three days ago. I went up to the house on Tuesday evening. You see my system, inspector. All the information is kept on that one page. I put the total at the bottom once everything is wound up, once the houses are paid for and the furniture and fittings disposed of and then I take my cut and transfer the profit to my accounting book. Not much money in it, but we struggle on, inspector, we struggle on. If my poor father could see what the takings are, these days, well, he'd turn in his grave, poor old man. In his day there was big money coming in, but now all the wealthy people are leaving the country. Not that I'd take any side on politics, you know.'

'And did you see Mr Mulcahy when you went up to the house on Tuesday evening?' Patrick gave a cursory glance at the neat page but declined to be sidetracked into speculating on the profitability of an auctioneer's business in these troubled days.

'Yes, I did, but just for a couple of minutes. He had to go off. He wanted to get off to his new tanning yards. You know there's been a bit of trouble about that land that he bought near the old *dún*. People don't like it. They say that the *dún* is sacred, and of course, there is the *cillín*. Supposed to be bad luck to interfere with one of them. Superstition, of course, but when all is said and done, I suppose you have to say that there were a lot of poor little unbaptized babies buried there and it doesn't seem right to some people that concrete had been spread on the little graves, and there are tons of hides and skins heaped up on top of it and the stink, of course. Have you ever smelled that stuff they use to soak the skins? He'd be used to it, of course, but when I saw him a couple of months ago, well, I told him straight. "Move the tanning yard, Mr Mulcahy, move it away from those houses if you want to sell them". That's what I said to him. I told him straight. "Jesus Christ himself," I said to him, if you'll pardon the expression, inspector, "well the good lord, himself, couldn't sell those houses for a good price if that tanning yard at the back is still there. You'd hardly notice the smell now, I suppose; you're that used to it. Well, that's as maybe," that's what I said to him, "but someone coming new to the area wouldn't like it.

Wouldn't like it at all." Well, I told him straight, inspector
and he took my advice. Got the piece of land beside the *dún*
dead cheap. Belonged to the bishop. I arranged the sale with
his lordship myself . . .'

'So you didn't speak to him, to Mr Mulcahy, for long.
What did he say in that time?' Patrick thought he should keep
to the point with the auctioneer, but he was interested in the
story of the local reaction to Mr Mulcahy's new tanning yard.
The man had stirred up enmity in Shandon.

'Just the usual. Get it from all the clients. Telling me to get
as good a price as possible for the furniture. As if I would
throw it away! Well, I wished him a good evening and took
myself off. I'd seen all that I needed. See, look here, I made
a note. Look at it. A cross beside the word 'stairs' and a tick
beside 'windows'. That means that we'd be better taking the
heavy furniture through the windows and lowering the pieces
down onto the top of the lorry than trying to bring down that
big heavy stuff around the bends of the stairs. Carpenter
built, on the spot, the most of it, anyway.' Mr Hayes ran down
like a clockwork toy and collapsed onto one of his own chairs
and looked interrogatively up at Patrick.

'Who left the house first, you or Mr Mulcahy?' Patrick
made a note and then looked back at the man.

'I knew you'd ask that,' said Mr Hayes triumphantly, 'but
you know I can't be sure and that's the truth. I heard him
shouting at his wife, or perhaps it was his daughter Susan.
They were out cleaning up the yard behind. Have it smelling
of Jeyes Fluid, and have the rat catcher in again; that was my
advice to him. One of the houses had been sold; all the
carpentry work done, but there was one still to go. We'd lost
a sale on that because the wife didn't like the smell in the
outbuildings. He had some sort of idea of keeping this one as
an office, but I knew he'd change his mind on that. Build
himself an office up next to the tanning works – that was the
thing to do. He saw sense in that.'

'So you left the premises and came back down into the city
and possibly Mr Mulcahy was still there when you left.'

'That's right,' said Mr Hayes obligingly, 'but I think, now
that I get to remembering, I think that he was already gone

up to his new tanning yard. I'll tell you what you should do, inspector, you should go up to the cathedral and have a word with the verger, he'll show you that tanning yard that the poor man bought, though I have to say that he hadn't paid for it yet. I'm going to be in trouble with the bishop over that, I can tell you, but you go up there, inspector and then you can see for yourself, and who knows but the verger, Mr Sweetman, will be able to give you chapter and verse about seeing Mr Mulcahy on that evening. And you'll probably find the poor wife and daughter up there, and some of the young lads, too. Ten of them, he had, and all of them fatherless now, and the two girls, the twins, of course.'

Mr Hayes cast an agonized glance at the ceiling where some more bumps were to be heard and Patrick took pity on him. The man had probably told all that he knew. Patrick got to his feet.

'Just one more question, Mr Hayes, do you think that the body was in the trunk when it arrived here, or was placed there some time yesterday, or even this morning.'

Mr Hayes hesitated. He had been placed in a dilemma, of course. The notoriety would be enormous as rumours flew around the city of Cork. Patrick could see him falter. What if the man were actually killed on his premises? Would that bring the crowds? But the hesitation did not last for long. When it came to murder on the premises or off the premises, Mr Hayes' instinct was to opt for the latter.

'Not a chance of it happening here, inspector. I wouldn't say it to anyone, but yourself, inspector, but the people of Cork are a light-fingered lot. I've always got one of my lads in these rooms, keeping an eye open. No, not a chance. That man arrived in a trunk and left in a trunk and I'm only very sorry that I didn't check the contents myself and that it gave such a shock to the Reverend Mother. I must go and apologize to her as soon as I get a minute to myself.' Mr Hayes gave an agonized glance at the antique grandfather clock that stood in stately splendour in the corner of the room. It chimed just as he finished speaking and Patrick took the hint, rising to his feet and thanking the man for his time. Once outside, though, he did not hail a cab to take him up to

the heights of Shandon, but walked rapidly across the South
Mall and made his way back to the barracks. With a bit of
luck, Joe, a conscientious and hard-working sergeant, might
still be on duty.

'You've seen Mrs Mulcahy, Joe. What did she say?' He put
the question as soon as Joe was seated in front of him and
had to repress a moment's impatience as the young man
fumbled in his pocket for his notebook. He himself had trained
Joe never to rely on memory, always to refer to his notes, so
it was illogical to wish that he'd hurry up a bit.

Joe looked at his notebook, frowned and then put it down.
'Not a lot, to be honest. I asked her when she had last seen
her husband and she told me that it was last Tuesday. Came
out with that very quickly, as though she had the answer ready.'

'Odd, that,' said Patrick. 'Didn't she think to make any enquiry
about him?'

'Yes, I asked her about that,' said Joe. 'I just said, quietly,
"And this is Friday, Mrs Mulcahy."'

'What did she say to that?' asked Patrick.

'She just looked stunned. But then I pressed the question
and she told me that Mr Mulcahy, she kept calling him that,
was living in the new house, keeping an eye on the builders,
was how she put it and that she didn't expect to see him
because the tanning yard had been moved. Sounded an odd
story to me, but I didn't push it. She looked so distressed. She
had her daughter with her, Susan, her daughter Susan, she's—'
once again Joe looked back at his notebook – 'she said that
she was nineteen, but I'd have taken her for fifteen, tall, but
very skinny and pale, rather spotty, usually girls are over that
by nineteen, but she didn't look too healthy. She just sat there,
beside her mother and when I told them eventually that Mr
Mulcahy was dead, they both just stared at me in a frightened
way. And then Mrs Mulcahy said, "God rest his soul" just as
though she had heard of the death of a neighbour or something,
and then one of the boys, John, was his name, came in. Before
I could say a word, she told him and he just looked at her and
then looked at me and said nothing. And then, after a while,
quite a while it seemed, she said to him that they would

have to arrange the funeral and she asked him to go and see the priest and he said "Right-ho" and just went, just like that, without another word.'

'Interesting family,' said Patrick. Joe, he thought, should have questioned the boy before allowing him to follow his mother's instructions, but he decided to say nothing. The mistake was his. He should have sent Joe to the auctioneer and tackled the grieving family himself. 'Were they in shock, do you think, Joe?' he asked.

'Could be.' Joe thought about that for a moment. 'No, I thought they all seemed scared, that was my feeling. I didn't think that they were shocked. It was more . . .' Joe hesitated for a moment and then finished by saying, 'more fear than shock, that's what I thought, anyway.'

Patrick consulted his watch. It was late, but not too late for a visit.

'You go off duty now, Joe,' he said. 'Thanks for staying late. Any word from Dr Scher?'

'He's doing the autopsy first thing in the morning,' said Joe promptly. 'He came back to do that poor girl tonight.'

'It will be interesting to see whether Mr Mulcahy was shot or stabbed. It would be one or the other as there was blood on the chest. That was a strange business about the son firing at the dead man. Well, off you go now, Joe. I'll lock up here.'

The superintendent had locked his own room and the keys of the police car were presumably inside it. Patrick gave a dubious glance out of the window. The fog and mist of the afternoon had now settled down into that soft rain, so familiar to the people of Cork, a rain that is as wetting as a downpour. It couldn't be helped though. An umbrella would be nothing but a nuisance on the very narrow and busy pavements of Shandon Street. He locked the doors of his office, turned up the collar of his coat, settled the brim of his cap over his eyebrows and set off walking rapidly.

The cathedral, first, he thought, as he climbed the steep hill. He passed the two houses owned by the dead man. There were lights in one of them. He would call in there on his way back, but he would see the verger first.

He was barely in time. Benediction was over, the church

was empty and an elderly man was quenching candles at
the back of the church. Patrick watched quietly for a while.
Very old, almost doddery, he thought with a feeling of disap-
pointment. Probably doesn't know the time of the day – a
favourite saying of his mother's and one that had great
relevance for a policeman looking for evidence that would
stand up in court.

'Good evening, Mr Sweetman, I wonder whether I might
have a word with you,' he said stepping forward from the
shadows. The hand that held the candle snuffer did not
tremble at his sudden appearance and the old man went on
methodically quenching until nothing but a few trails of
smoke were to be seen, eddying sleepily around the statue
of Saint Anne.

'I hear that we've had a murder here in Shandon; that's
what brings you, I've no doubt.' The voice also was quite
steady. He glanced keenly around the church, his gaze sweeping
up and down the side aisle, checking that all was well and
then rubbed the candle grease from the snuffer until it was
burnished to a high shine. Meticulously he replaced it in the
exact centre of a high shelf in the cupboard at the back and
then reappeared at Patrick's side.

'Come and have a cup of tea with me in my house; I don't
like talking about things like murder inside the cathedral.'

Patrick suppressed a sigh. He was not over-fond of tea and
these ceremonies did take up so much of his time. Still he
couldn't persist in asking questions if the verger did not feel
they were appropriate to a sacred setting. He followed the man
across the graveyard, but then stopped him.

'Where is the land that Mr Mulcahy purchased from the
bishop for use as a tanning yard?'

The man gave him another keen glance and then pointed.
'Over there, inspector, over by those trees, the only trees left
in Shandon. No one dared to cut them down, you know. No
one dared to interfere with a sacred place. Not until . . .'
Patrick looked back at him and saw the man shake his head.
There was a look of fury in the old eyes and then he set his
lips firmly and lowered his eyes to the ground.

'I don't know much of the history of Shandon,' said Patrick

apologetically. 'I'm from the southside, myself. Could you tell me a little about that place over there?'

'You young men have learned Irish, haven't you? *Sean Dún*, you know what that means, the old doon, the ancient enclosure.'

It was, when Patrick looked more closely, circular in shape. Even from a distance large rocks of dark red sandstone were visible, strewn around as from a collapsed wall. Here and there among the trees, he could see small hillocks, which probably contained more rocks, or perhaps parts of ancient buildings, monks' places, perhaps. Patrick wondered about it and its origins. It was a small oasis in the busy built-up world of Shandon, part of the ancient history of the city of Cork. He had a sudden impulse to explore it before the light faded. Resolutely, he turned to the old man.

'I won't disturb your evening cup of tea, Mr Sweetman. I just wanted to know whether you saw Mr Mulcahy here on Tuesday evening. Did he come up here at all on that afternoon, or early evening? Did he have a word with you about that land over there?'

He waited anxiously. The most likely answer was that the man could not remember and that would mean that he'd had a wasted journey. He hadn't realized that the verger would be so old. However, the elderly man was shaking his head very firmly.

'Not on Tuesday, inspector. No one came to talk to me on Tuesday. The bishop himself blessed the graves on that evening and I was leading the procession with the holy cross in my hands. When it was all over, I went inside and served tea and biscuits to the clergy and the choir and after that I went back to my own place. Didn't see anybody until the next morning.'

This was indisputable. This man certainly did not appear to be doddery, or in his second childhood. He was alert and quick-witted. There was almost no point in questioning him further. Still, Patrick never left a matter until every single stone had been unturned and so he persisted.

'Perhaps when he saw you busy, he just slipped across to his new property. Would that be possible, do you think, Mr Sweetman?'

The old man shook his head decisively. 'Anything is possible,' he said, his voice giving a lie to his statement, 'but, you know, inspector, I keep a sharp eye out during these ceremonies. I'd be on the alert for anything.'

'I'm sure that you would, Mr Sweetman. Thank you very much for your help. Now I'll leave you to have a cup of tea and a rest.'

It should be possible to find a few people in Shandon who were in attendance during the blessing of the graves and ask for their corroboration – I'll get Joe onto that, thought Patrick as he walked away as rapidly as possible. As for himself, he was fairly satisfied that Mr Henry Mulcahy had probably met his death somewhere within his house. Why kill a man out here in a graveyard and then drag his body all the way down the hill, and into a house, just in order to place it in a trunk? Nevertheless, he was curious about the new site for the tanning yard and he made his way across to the ancient site.

A slice of the history of old Cork, he thought, as he gazed around. There had been a fort there; that was still obvious. A few portions of the original rounded wall of the enclosure still remained, but that was not all. There had been a monastery, also. He was almost sure of that. In one corner of the circular site stood the remains of an arch, low and empty of its door, but the marks of the hinge were still there engraved into the stone.

And everywhere he looked there were small mounds of earth, a few grieving parents had attempted to carve a name onto one of the stones lying around, some mounds had a wooden plank on them, the letters softened by the Cork rain and now indescribable. One or two had the remains of a few roadside flowers, a bunch of dandelions, now nothing but empty seed heads. One stone with the word, '*Rosie*', scratched into it. Most were unreadable, thick with moss and crumbled with age, only a small number had a legible name, and one, heartbreakingly, he thought, just said, '*my baby girl*'.

He knew what it was, of course. No unbaptized infant could be buried in the licenced graveyard. The church did not admit the possibility of their future admission into heaven, but condemned them to an everlasting limbo. But the mothers, most of them, wanted some sacred site for their dead baby's resting place and this ancient place, hallowed in the past, provided this.

But not all was ancient here. As he pondered on the sadness of those grieving parents, Patrick raised his eyes and saw, beyond the trees, a new building. He went closer and examined it. Made in the cheapest and ugliest fashion from shuttered concrete, flimsy and garish, it clashed with the quiet dignity of the ancient stones. There was more concrete on the ground, probably encroaching over and across the ancient graveyard, and a large tank filled with a foul-smelling mixture, a terrible smell of dung and urine and the sharp, acrid stink of dog droppings. In smaller tanks, raw hides, with skin and blood still adhering were piled in heaps, interlayered with the peaty dust from turf sods. The stench was worse from these and no doubt infested with vermin; Patrick saw a rat slip past stealthily.

He walked away briskly. The cathedral bell was sounding the hour of eight o'clock. Not too late to see the grieving wife and family.

But as he walked down the steep pavement, his mind was busy with the mothers of the infants buried in this ancient and holy place. What did they think of the man who had brought his noisome trade to such a sacred spot?

FIVE

Everything looked different when Eileen came panting back down towards the shore. Even from a distance she could see how all the donkeys and carts of the fishmongers from the surrounding villages were moving sharply away, the owners standing up, sometimes in empty carts, and urging on the unfortunate animals with voice and whip. Although it was now getting late, the small fishing boats seemed to be moving away from the harbour and pier, turning to cross over to the other side towards Cobh or to take refuge in Mahon. Something was happening.

There was no sign of Fred, at first, but then she saw him on a rowing boat, tied to a mooring post by the pier. There were three people in the boat. Two men, and Fred himself. Not one of the three took any notice of her, after a quick glance. All of them were looking in the opposite direction, focussing on the water, hands shielding eyes. The fog had died down and there was a low sun in the west that dazzled the eyes. And then a cloud came over the sun and Eileen saw what they were looking at. In the distance, was a large fishing boat: a trawler. Its deck was covered with a seine net. Her long-sighted eyes could make out a glint of silver from it, mackerel, she thought. By the morning they would be piled up on the market stalls. But there was another boat going behind it. In pursuit, she thought. Flying a flag. More of a ship than a boat. Loaded with men. The tricolour of the Free State flew from it. She gazed at it fearfully. The gleams of sunlight picked out glints of metal; these men were holding guns in their hands. Not aiming at Fred and his two friends, but pointing towards the fishing boat.

There was going to be trouble in a few minutes. Eileen had been in enough skirmishes to know that. She cast another swift glance at it. No time to be lost.

Without hesitation, she thundered up the pier, grabbed the rope post and leaned down into the boat. 'Fred, give me back that three pounds,' she said. 'I need it badly. My bike. It broke down. It's the carburettor. I need that three pounds. Give it back to me, it is mine, you know.'

He looked at her then, looked at her furtively and gave a nervous laugh, glancing at the other men for approbation. It infuriated her.

'Give me back my money, Fred,' she hissed and put a hand on the gunwale of the small boat. Her eyes were on his breast pocket. He had shoved her wallet in there when he had demanded it from her. With determination, she reached into the boat, letting go of the rope in order to grab his coat. He shrunk back, but she got her free hand into his pocket, felt the wallet and shouted, 'Thief! You're just a bloody thief! Give me back my money!'

And then with a scared look, he stopped resisting. 'Always a bit of a mammy's boy, our Fred.' Eamonn used to say that when she and her friend Áine shared a Republican safe house with six young men. 'First to talk and last into action.' Danny used to say that. Now he tried to shrink back when he felt her fingers on the wallet in his pocket.

But then everything began to go wrong. The boat rocked violently, almost leaped in the water. One of the men had started up the outboard engine. In a second's time, Eileen had lost her balance. For a moment she wavered over the water between pier and boat. The man holding the tiller looked back and swore. Then his friend grabbed her firmly by the wrist and pulled her. She staggered, almost lost her balance, but after a minute, she found herself seated on one of the cross planks. There was barely room for her, and she swore aloud, as much from fury as from fright. He put one of his hands over her mouth and the other clamped her wrist.

'Looks like you are coming with us,' he said in a whisper. 'Now keep your head down like a good girl and don't say a word, will you? There's a bit of trouble going on, but we'll try to put you on shore before things get serious.'

'Oh, shut up,' said Eileen, wriggling free from his hand. She still had hold of Fred's pocket and she was going to keep it that way.

There wasn't any need for silence, in any case. The outboard engine had exploded into a series of ear splitting bangs and thumps. The small boat leaped in the water. Eileen's fingers felt something in Fred's pocket. He was looking over his shoulder. In a moment, she retrieved the wallet and thrust it deep into her own pocket.

'It's mine,' she said, more as an explanation to the other men than addressing Fred. 'He took it from me,' she added and then looked all around her, wondering how to get back to shore.

Fred did not protest. It seemed as though he hardly noticed her action. His eyes were fixed on the two boats further along the Douglas Passageway. Someone was shouting into a loud hailer from the ship filled with Free State Army soldiers. The new government in Dublin had plenty of soldiers, many of them inherited from the English army, but so far they had no navy. That ship was no warship, it looked quite like a passenger ferry. But it was every bit as deadly. Every man on it was armed with a gun and there was a small cannon on the deck. The fishing trawler abandoned all pretences of fishing and leaped into action, speeding through the water. The path to the outer harbour was blocked by the Free State ship and so the fishing trawler had turned back towards the land. Eileen looked at Lough Mahon. The trawler was making for there. She could see guns now in the hands of the men and the net with its glistening mackerel was thrown overboard.

But then a shot rang out. The Free State Army boat aimed directly at the fishing boat. Another shot. A return shot. Several shots. The mackerel trawler lurched. It had been hit. It was easy to see the ragged hole in its side.

'Stay right where you are; don't move. We're coming on board,' came the voice. A Dublin accent, thought Eileen. Another few shots were fired from the trawler. On its far side a dingy was lowered. She could see that men were streaming

off the trawler, diving from the prow. It wasn't going to work
though. The Free State ship was full of men. Coming from
the large island of Haulbowline, in the outer harbour, she
guessed. Ireland had no navy, yet, but they had a troop of
soldiers on Haulbowline and soldiers, on a ship handled by
professional sailors, was just as effective as any navy, or so
she had been told.

In any case, the Republicans seemed to be getting the worse
of the encounter with the Free Staters. An effort to unload
another dinghy from the trawler had failed. The boat was
already riddled with holes and now it was bombarded. It
lurched dangerously and the bows began to sink. The few
men left on it were galvanized into action. A small lifeboat
was launched over the side. It hit the water with a tremendous
splash and then righted itself. The men already in the water
swam towards it and a box was lowered down to them, and
then another box.

'The weapons!' said Fred and instantly the man at the
propeller started up the little outboard engine. Shots rang out
and Eileen crouched at the bottom of the boat, pulling a
tarpaulin over her head. Let me not be shot, she prayed
earnestly. It was cowardly, but life was good at the moment.
She was having fun. She didn't want to be killed.

There was a scream and the boat rocked. The man at the
engine slumped into a heap.

'He's got a bullet in the stomach,' said Fred, his voice
shaking and then there was a splash. The man had been
thrown overboard. Eileen gulped. Cautiously she unfolded a
corner of the tarpaulin. Had he been still alive? No word had
been spoken and the action had been almost immediate. Had
it been Fred who had done that? She thought it had been
Fred. The outboard engine was still running and the boat
was being steered in a zig-zag way in order to avoid shots.
The man at the tiller was still at his post. No, it had been
Fred who had thrown the wounded man overboard.

And then a savage whisper from the man at the tiller. 'Dive,
it's our only chance! They're getting too near us.'

Two splashes.

The engine spluttered and then died.

Eileen was left alone on the little boat.

She glanced around. Boats were a new thing for her. She had never, during her eighteen years in a coastal city, even seen the sea. Could she manage this boat on her own? They could not be too much different from motorbikes, though, and she had mastered her motorbike with a couple of half hours of tuition. She edged up towards the prow of the boat, pulled the cord of the outboard motor, holding it in one hand and the tiller of the boat in the other. Cautiously and keeping the engine speed to a low level she began to move away from the boats on Lough Mahon and down the narrow channel past Passage West.

She would, she thought, avoid the place of action. She knew what was going to happen. The Free State soldiers were going to be victorious in this action. Fred and his two companions would not do much, she thought dispassionately, about delaying the inevitable outcome for the men in the fishing trawler and for the goods that they carried in those heavy wooden boxes. Guns, she thought, thinking of Fred's feverish gabbling. She knew where she would go and how she could wait out the conclusion of the battle.

There was a voice in her ears. A voice from the dim and distant past when she was only about eight years old. The voice of the Reverend Mother telling the children the story of the famous Englishman, Sir Francis Drake, who was desperate to escape from the Spaniards. He had sailed into Cork Harbour, *knew it well,* said the Reverend Mother; sailed up through the outer harbour, the Spaniards close behind. He had reached the spot where the Owenbue River discharged its waters into the harbour. 'Cleverly knowing,' had said the Reverend Mother to her eagerly listening class, 'the exact spot where there was a deep pool.' He had cast his anchor there, and waited, knowing full well that the tide was ebbing and that his enemies' large ships would be stranded useless and sunken into muddy sand.

And now more than three hundred years later, that same place might save her life. The tide had turned. She could see how the water ebbed out towards the outer harbour, towards

the sea. It was going to be difficult for that warship to get
back out, unless they came quickly, but Eileen was well ahead
of them in her rapid little boat and she would get to safety
before they spotted her.

Eileen knew the Owenbue, well. The river flowed through
the valley at Ballinhassig, below where the Republic safe
house was located that she and Fred had shared not so long
ago. Looking across, she could now see where it reached its
destination, the place where fresh water met salt water, the
small channel that led up to the small seaside town. She tried
to picture the atlas, tried to remember her Geography lessons.
She had got a first-class honours in Geography. Yes, she
remembered now. It was Carrigaline. She would take advantage of her education and of her teacher's gift for telling
interesting stories and she would follow the example of the
sixteenth-century hero/pirate from Elizabethan England and
make for Drake's Pool. She would spend the night there,
and then when dawn rose, she would cautiously negotiate her
way back, hopefully to Douglas and pick up her motorbike.
At least now, she had her money back. She imagined herself,
nonchalantly telling the story to Jack at the printing works
and imagining his horror that she had got herself involved in
such a dangerous operation.

And then a shot hit the water in front of her. She had been
too confident. She should have stayed where she was until
darkness fell. Even then, she should not have switched on
that noisy and intrusive outboard engine, but should have
endeavoured to move the boat, slowly and cautiously, with
the aid of those oars that she could dimly see, lying in the
bottom of the boat.

Still, there was no good wishing the past undone. Now was
a moment for boldness. Eileen opened up the throttle to full
speed and made the little boat leap through the water.

Another shot was fired. It split the water next to the boat
and a fountain sprang up, and almost swamped her. She
could not change action now. She was right in their sights.
There was only one thing that she could do and although
she slightly despised herself for thinking of it, she snatched
off the leather helmet that she wore on her motorbike and

allowed her very long, black hair to blow, like a sail, behind her.

The shots stopped. That was a surprise. It had been an act of desperation, but it had worked. As she sped through the water of the channel, the little boat cleaving a passageway almost like a knife through butter, Eileen prayed that it might last. She had her eyes on the Owenbue River and her faith was firmly in that story, told so very long ago in that classroom.

And then there was another shot. Not at her, this time, but at the men with the boxes of rifles. Another and another. She saw the man who had pulled her aboard the boat when she had been rifling in Fred's pocket, trying to get back her wallet. The man who had told her to keep her head down and to be a good girl. He would never say that again. She saw the shot that hit him, saw his hands go up into the air, saw him topple over and fall from the boat and into the harbour water. The top of his head had been blown off.

Don't look, her mind whispered that to her. There was no point. No point in trying to be heroic, trying to help, trying to rescue. There must be about ten men there, all in great danger. The chances were that few of them would be alive in the morning. She fixed her eyes on the group of trees near to the shoreline and drove her boat at full speed towards them. Drake's Pool, her mind said as she steered adroitly away from the scene of action.

There was a small island in her sights, not a real island, more like a piece of higher ground in the harbour, perhaps a cluster of rocks that had accumulated sand and debris. There were some tall reeds growing there, no longer flourishing and green, pale straw in colour, but standing up tall and straight, about six foot high, she reckoned. She drove her boat to behind them and then slowed almost to a stop, the tick of the engine seeming almost quieter than the thud of her heart.

The battle, skirmish or whatever one could call such a one-sided affair, seemed to be almost over. The man with the Dublin accent was bawling down the microphone, and there were no more shots. How many were now left alive, she wondered, but dared not move in order to look. Had Fred been taken, or was he still at liberty? Perhaps she should try to search for him, but somehow she did not want to. She did not want to have anything more to do with Fred Mulcahy. She shuddered a little when she thought of his strange confession. If he had really killed his father then he would be hanged, if found.

And she? She had taken no part in the battle, but even so. She had been in the company of Republicans. Once arrested, she would be recognized, identified, tied in with that daring prison break. She would be lucky to escape with a short prison spell, but she did not want that, not for Fred Mulcahy, who had robbed her and involved her without scruple when she had saved him from arrest. She moved the boat carefully, reaching out and clutching bunches of reeds, one after the other and moving the boat by that means. Without the noisy outboard engine or the splash of oars, the boat glided along almost soundlessly. Any sound from the reeds could be from some of those long-legged birds. She moved on until she was just at the end of the shelter and peeped around cautiously.

The fishing trawler was now on its side. Some ill-advised men, who had lent their boat to the Republicans, were now going to be without means of making a livelihood. It still held some guns, though, in their long boxes and these were being handed up into the Free State ship. Eileen could hear the shouts of the sailors beckoning the soldiers to get back on board. And then she noticed something. The Reverend Mother's story was right. The tide was ebbing fast. She could see how it was dragging some clumps of dead reeds and even an empty bird's nest, in a fast swirling track of water out towards the sea. And, yes, she thought, the level was definitely sinking. She would be safe. They wouldn't be able to approach her now. There was not enough depth of water left for a ship of that size.

The ship was moving out trying to catch the tide. It blew its horn and under the cover of the noise, she risked starting up her engine again. She needed to get down that estuary. She could see lots of boats moored there, yachts with white and coloured sails. Rich men's toys. Eamonn had said something like that once. But if she could get amongst them she would not be conspicuous, and, even if the soldiers spotted her, they would not risk injuring a rich man's toy.

And so she took a gamble, opened the throttle, went recklessly at full speed in that direction. The water was ebbing fast out of the estuary. The anchored boats and yachts swung on their ropes. Most were heavily tilted to one side. It would be hours before they could take to the sea again. Still her boat was very small and shallow. She would perhaps be able to make her way to the village beyond.

But not immediately. There would be troops all around. An unknown face coming ashore from the battle. She would be questioned. Where was Drake's Pool?

And then she saw it. It was obvious. A large yacht was anchored there and it stood proud, not leaning, plenty of water there. Drake's Pool. Not muddy, not ebbing, deep water, she could be sure. She saw a sea creature, smooth-headed, perhaps a whale, rise up and then dive deep into the smooth, reflective water. Carefully she steered her little boat across, the engine chugging away happily.

SIX

St Thomas Aquinas
*'Et secundum eandem rationem sequitur quod tristitia
causet odium.'*
(And in the same way it follows that hatred arises
from sorrow.)

Saturday was a good day for the Reverend Mother to meet her cousin Lucy. School finished at half-past eleven in the morning and the nuns then had Saturday afternoon to themselves, a free afternoon to do some shopping, to take a walk, to prepare lessons or to pray, according to their individual tastes. From time to time, once breakfast was over, she glanced at the clock, but her cousin was not an early riser and so she hesitated to contact her and instead tried to concentrate on a submission to the newly formed *Dáil* on the importance of funding secondary education for all children and not just subsidising it for the children of the well-off.

'Mr Hayes, the auctioneer to see you, Reverend Mother,' said Sister Bernadette, putting her head around the door after a polite knock. 'He doesn't want to disturb you, but he'd be grateful for a quick word, if you can spare the time.'

'Yes, of course,' said the Reverend Mother cordially. 'Will you come and remind me that I have a class at nine o'clock, sister?'

'By all means, Reverend Mother.' Sister Bernadette respectfully withdrew, without even a single glance at the clock standing conspicuously on Reverend Mother's mantelpiece showing the time to be now five minutes to nine.

Mr Hayes was already in full flow when ushered in by Sister Bernadette. *The terrible times* was his theme. 'Dreadful the things that happen in these distressful days,' he was saying as he paused for breath and allowed the sister to tap on the

Reverend Mother's door. It was a good phrase, was her thought
as she called out 'Come in, sister.'

'Dreadful' and 'distressful' had the advantage of sympa-
thizing with the community about the mischance of a dead
man being delivered to their convent, if they knew all about
it, and, if they didn't, of being interpreted as a general verdict
on the prevailing malaise in the city.

When left alone with the Reverend Mother, though, Mr
Hayes fell silent, thrust out his open palms in a gesture of
despair, before saying, 'Reverend Mother, what must you think
of me?'

This was an unexpected opening and the Reverend Mother
took immediate advantage of the dramatic moment of silence that
followed it. 'How nice of you to come, Mr Hayes, do sit down.
I was thinking only this morning about you and the auctioneer
business and I wondered whether that trunk was in your main
saleroom, the place where you conduct the auctions.'

Mr Hayes looked taken aback at this abrupt approach.
'No, it wasn't, Reverend Mother. We only put the better stuff
in the main showrooms. That would have been upstairs, or
perhaps in the hallway. I'd say it would have been upstairs,
though. But, to be honest, I couldn't tell you for sure.'

'So how did my cousin, Mrs Murphy, come to bid for it?'

'Well, you see, Reverend Mother, we work like this. Small,
valuable objects are brought up to me into the main showroom
by one of the boys. I hold it up and then start with a low
figure and raise the bidding step by step. But the furniture and
the heavy stuff doesn't get moved at all. We'd be all day over
one sale if we did a thing like that, so for each sale we get a
load of leaflets printed out. I go out to the house and scribble
down a list of everything to be sold, you see, Reverend Mother,
and I get them printed up by a little printing works just off
South Terrace – nice little girl, Eileen MacSweeney from
Barrack Street, came to school here, didn't she – well, she
types it up, lovely and neat; sweet little girl, well, they run
off a hundred copies on their printing works, we put them in
the windows of shops, leaving them outside our own premises
so that anyone can take a leaflet and on the day of the sale
one of my boys hands them out to the people there. I always

tell them to give one to everyone in the building whether they are interested in the lot or not. People put a bid in, you see, Reverend Mother, when the bidding is low and then they get interested. It catches them, like; they get carried away. And I use the same leaflet to get through the sale, go through them quick as I can. Keep everything lively and moving fast, make people think they'll lose a bargain if they hesitate. That's how it works. There was another trunk, too, among the goods, nothing worth much in it either, old curtains, cushions, table-cloths. Someone had stuck labels on the trunk giving what they held, you see. One of the family, I suppose.'

'And the trunk marked "Old School Books"?'

'Number 159,' said Mr Hayes. 'I think that number will be on my tombstone. I'll never forget it. I came to it, called it out, said it was a trunk full of old school books, twelve children, the man had, you know, Reverend Mother, and I'd say they'd passed the books down from one to another of them. Well, I gave the details and then I looked straight across at Mrs Murphy, God help me! And I said, "Now who will start me off at half-a-crown?" And she raises one finger and I look all around the room, give it a few seconds, and then I say, "Sold to Mrs Murphy for half-a-crown." And then I just went onto the next item. I never waste time with the small stuff. Clear it out and make room for the next sale. That's always my motto. Can't even remember what that next item was now. I've been in such a state about the whole thing. I've been in the business for fifty years, man and boy, and never a thing like that has happened to me before. I came over to apologize to you, but God knows, I don't know what to say to you, Reverend Mother.' Like a gramophone whose turntable had slowed to a stop, Mr Hayes fell silent and mopped his face with a large handkerchief.

'My dear Mr Hayes, you must not feel so badly. The whole thing has been much more of a shock to you than it was to me. I do hope that the unpleasant affair has not affected your business?' The Reverend Mother had her eye on the clock. There was a sound of a door closing in the distance and then the click of Sister Bernadette's metal-tipped shoes going to the convent door. This would be the postman, a very punctual man who always delivered his letters before nine o'clock in the morning.

'Well, now, I wouldn't say that. You know Cork people. Very curious, they are,' admitted Mr Hayes. 'It's made for a lot of interest in the city.' He began to look more cheerful as he thought of that. 'In fact, when I came out here this morning, there was already a queue of people waiting for the doors to open and then popping in to get a leaflet for today.'

'Splendid,' said the Reverend Mother. The click of heels now came from the corridor and she rose from her seat. He stood up, also, though he looked as though he had more to say, but Sister Bernadette's knock sounded on the door.

'Ah, sister, you are summoning me to class. Are the children in? Goodness, is it that time?' She held out her hand. 'It was unnecessary, but very, very kind of you to come to see me, Mr Hayes, and please do be assured that I value your kind intention very well. We are grateful for all contributions to our work here.'

'If anything else comes up, then you can be sure that I'll think of you, Reverend Mother,' said Mr Hayes, his cheerfulness quite restored. 'No, no, don't worry, sister, I'll find my own way out.'

'Mrs Murphy telephoned when you were with Mr Hayes,' said Sister Bernadette as the door closed with a reverentially careful snap behind the auctioneer. 'She just wanted to leave a message that she was going to drop in this afternoon. She'll be here at three o'clock unless she hears from you. I told her that I thought you were free and that you would be pleased to see her.' Sister Bernadette beamed her pleasure. Touchingly the whole convent were solicitous for their Reverend Mother's health after her gruesome discovery.

'Thank you, sister,' said the Reverend Mother as she went rapidly down the corridor and into the classroom where the senior girls, under the stern eye of Sister Mary Immaculate were studying a poem about daffodils which the good nun had decreed they were to commit to memory. Their bright, pleased faces when she came in cheered her somewhat. She had, she remembered, promised a debate on whether girls should be allowed to wear trousers by parents and schoolteachers, something that had seemed to be of great interest to these young ladies who were certain that the 1920s had changed all and that they could look forward to a brighter future than their mothers.

'Well, let's start by summarizing the advantages,' she said cheerfully as soon as Sister Mary Immaculate had closed the door behind her. 'How do you think that wearing trousers would make life easier for girls?' Little by little was always her motto. First the easy stuff, then the more difficult work of getting them to look on the other side of matters, to see things from the point of view of the older generation, to appreciate the point of view of those who had, as she had thought earlier when meditating on Mr Mulcahy, come up the hard way. By the time that the lesson was over she was happy with her hour's work. These girls were not natural readers or writers, but they were great talkers, all of them, and talking was the way whereby they could be led to formulate thoughts. A few groaned when she asked them to write down the arguments, but most seized pens eagerly while the ideas were still fresh in their heads. When all was peaceful and the only sound was the monotonous dipping of steel nibs into inkwells, her mind wandered back again to the Mulcahy murder. Could the hard life imposed by the man onto his family, his wife and children, even if it had been done with the best of intentions, with a fanatical impulse to raise his family into the upper echelons of the city of Cork, could this have resulted in one amongst them being driven to murder?

But of course, actions, rather than intentions, are what are remembered. Would it be probable that at least some of Mr Mulcahy's twelve children hated rather than revered their father? She endeavoured to recall the expression on Fred Mulcahy's face when she had thrown back the lid of the trunk, but all that she could remember was the impassionate denial that he had anything to do with it. No sorrow; none that she had seen. And, of course, his words about his mother.

And then as she sat in the silent classroom her ear caught the sound of the convent doorbell and the cheerful voice of Dr Scher joking with Sister Bernadette. Now there would be some answers. She gave him a few minutes to be settled in her room, fed with tea and cake by the kitchen and then organized the collection of the scripts, promised a small prize for the best argued of the submissions and dismissed the girls for a five-minute run around the playground before their next class. It would, she thought, not be in the best of taste to discuss the autopsy with Dr Scher as he gulped down the strong tea and relished the sweet cake.

Dr Scher, however, did not seem to have much diffidence about approaching the subject. 'You'll never guess what I found when I opened the man up, Reverend Mother,' he said with his mouth full of cake as soon as she came into the room.

'Gunshot, or knife wound?' she asked, after thoughtfully waiting until he had stopped chewing and had swallowed another slurp of tea.

'Neither,' he said, his chubby face alight with amusement.

She frowned in puzzlement.

'What then? What killed him?'

'He was hit on the back of the head with, I would guess, an iron bar. Killed him instantly. What do you make of that? Bled profusely, of course.'

'What about the shot fired by Fred Mulcahy?'

'Didn't kill him, of course, bullet went right through the body and out the other side. Embedded in the skins. I've ruined those skins, I'm afraid, doused them in formaldehyde; mind you they were soaked in the man's blood. I'd say that he might even have obligingly fallen into the open trunk after the blow that killed him.' He was speaking lightly, but she could see that he was scanning her face for evidence that the matter might be upsetting to her.

'That, I should imagine, is of small consideration,' she said impatiently. 'But that was unexpected, was it not? So where did the blood come from, the blood that we both saw on the man's coat?'

'We're not too far advanced in those things,' he said with an apologetic air. 'I wouldn't be too sure, but I think that it is fairly likely that it came from the dead man. There's a massive wound on the back of the head. Of course, that doesn't rule out the possibility that the man who dealt the fatal blow might have been punched on the nose by Mr Mulcahy. It wouldn't be the first time in my experience that a punch on the nose might have led to a murder. I suppose that it's possible that it came from someone else.'

'I see,' said the Reverend Mother. 'You are hinting that perhaps Mr Mulcahy had an argument, an argument or a fight with someone. That someone could have resented the blow, resented the shedding of blood . . .' Deliberately she refrained from using a pronoun. Was the argument, the fight, the blow received and then returned, perhaps, was that with his wife, one of his sons, or perhaps even his grown-up daughter. Susan; that was the name. She remembered her well. A clever girl. Bridie had been proud of her, though Fred, the eldest of that large family, was her great love.

'That's a possibility,' he admitted. 'There could have been an altercation. All that I can, in my poor scientific way, tell you is that someone, with a reasonably strong arm, picked up an iron bar and hit the man on the back of the neck. He would, I think, have been killed instantly, would have dropped to the floor and never moved again. The injury to the brain was massive.'

'And school books,' asked the Reverend Mother. 'Were there school books there? Were there books beneath the body, beneath the hides and skins?'

Dr Scher shook his head. 'No, there were no books in it.'

'I'm not surprised, really, when I think about it. After all, why try to sell off old school books when the youngest Mulcahy boy is only six years old. Mr Mulcahy may have made enough money to build himself a house in Montenotte, but he wouldn't be the type to waste money. No, I'd say that the school books would all have been carefully kept. Was there anything else in the trunk?'

'No, nothing was in that trunk except the body of the man and the hides and skins that were packed around him.' He hesitated for a moment, almost looking inwardly into his memory of the morning. 'I would be pretty sure that the skins were in the trunk first,' he said slowly. 'They were packed down, weighed down by the body, blood-soaked. Perhaps the skins were in the trunk, perhaps for carrying purposes. Make what you like of that.'

'I see,' she thought about it for a moment. 'When I first thought about those skins, untreated, crawling with maggots, I felt that it was an action of hate that had packed them around the body of the dead man,' she said slowly. 'But now that you tell me they may have been there before the body, then there may be a different interpretation. In that household, skins of dead animals were a normal fact of life. If it happened as you suggest, then it looks as though the murderer had no normal distaste for handling these objects. Whatever way it was, this is a strange and unsettling crime and I feel very worried about it.'

'Worried.' He had picked up that word and there was an interrogative note in his voice. 'Why worried?' he asked.

'Murder is always worrying,' she replied. 'There is always a great measure of fear attached to the deed. I remember a child, you remember him, too, Dr Scher, little Jimmy, clever little fellow, and he used to say to me, very earnestly, the way that those young boys impart information to elderly nuns, he used to say, "Be very careful of a cornered rat, Reverend Mother. No matter how big you are, they will bite you if they can't escape you". There may now be other people in danger because of that initial murder.'

'You suspect that the wife or one of the children, one of the boys, have had something to do with it. Is that right? Or could he have been involved in some criminal activity?'

The Reverend Mother thought about it. It was, she supposed, a possibility, that this man, this self-made man, this man, who according to his own account of himself, arrived as a barefoot man in the city of Cork; yes, it was a possibility that he was engaged in some nefarious dealings. On the other hand, he could just have been a hardworking merchant, a dealer in hides and skins, who had a knack of exploiting the market, a knack of marketing his goods to the highest bidder.

'Who else could have killed him?' she said the words aloud and looked interrogatively at the doctor.

'An iron bar striking a man across the back of the neck looks like anger to me, Reverend Mother. This murder doesn't bear the mark of a business rival deciding to get rid of a man more successful than he. You imagine someone picking up an iron bar and hitting a man across the back of the head. That, to me, spells raw and uncontrollable anger. A business man or some political rival would be much more likely to put a bullet into him on some dark night, perhaps when he was up there at his new tanning yard, or anywhere, in fact. There are parts of Shandon where the sound of a shot would have the residents locking doors and drawing curtains across windows. No, I have a feeling that this is a domestic murder. Strength would have been needed, but then, I've heard that the wife and family worked long hours in the tanning yard.'

'And the blood on the front of the coat, we have to go back to that. Was it the result of a fight? Was there any mark on the dead man, other than the final fatal blow?'

'No, no mark that I could see. He was a man who had worked with his hands all of his life and the hands were calloused and scarred, but no, there were no fresh marks on him. So if there was violence, he was the person who inflicted wounds, not received them.'

'How much strength would have been required to hit a man on the back of the head with an iron bar, hard enough to kill him? Would it have required great strength?'

'I'd have to see the iron bar, first. I suppose the shorter the bar, the less force that would have been required. Patrick is up there now, up in Shandon, looking around the house – the most likely place, I suppose, but he's also looking in the new tanning yard.'

'The new tanning yard?' she queried.

'Yes, apparently he wanted to sell the other house, but there was a problem with the tanning yard located just behind it, so he bought some land from the bishop – a piece of land just behind the cathedral. There's been trouble about that, so Patrick tells me. It's been used through the centuries as a *cillín*. You've heard that word, have you?'

'A *cillín* . . .' The Reverend Mother breathed the word and then was silent. The connection was strong between a *cillín* and a member of the merchant's household. She sat very still while a feeling of sorrow came over her. She had been harsh and judgemental in those days over twenty years ago. Afraid of the consequences to the convent that she ruled over.

Afraid of an English newspaper getting hold of the story. Or perhaps just afraid of the bishop. Would she have made a different decision about poor Bridie if Dr Scher had been physician to the convent at that time? She looked across at him with affection. Pragmatic, kind, never judgemental, truly Christian, she thought wryly; he had become a friend and a confidant and sometimes she wondered whether she could have gone on so long without his cheerful and reliable presence, gone on bearing the heavy burden of ever-increasing poverty and despair among those whom she tried to care for. Over the years she had learned to trust him more and more and to come to have complete reliance in his discretion. If only he had been around then . . . Nevertheless, she did not finish her sentence, but left the two words to hang in the air.

'Yes, a *cillín*, a place where poor mothers, poor families, who had lost an unbaptized baby, placed the little bodies. Supposed to be a sacred place. Poor things,' said Dr Scher compassionately. 'Well, Patrick went up there yesterday evening. Went to talk to the verger of the cathedral, to check whether Mr Mulcahy had gone up there on Tuesday. He told the auctioneer that he had to see the verger. The verger says no, says that he was leading a procession that afternoon, a blessing of the graves' ceremony and then was giving tea to the choir and to the clergy afterwards. He definitely did not see the merchant.'

'So it looks as though . . .'

'Yes, doesn't it? Looks as though the man was killed in his own house and his body shut away into the trunk. Tuesday would fit well for the day of death. I couldn't be sure, but I'd say he was about three days' dead when I looked at him this morning.'

'Would the body have been put in the trunk immediately?'

'Probably. Much easier to cram the body into the trunk before he began to stiffen. And the hides and skins were soaked in blood. Animal blood or human blood? I am inclined to think the latter. Yes, I think that after the fatal blow, he either fell or was heaved into the trunk. Probably fell. That was what I said to Patrick. He was a small man, this Mr Mulcahy, but he was a heavy man. I weighed him. Fifteen stone. A lot

of muscle as well as that layer of fat which came with afflu-
ence, I suppose. But he would have worked very hard as a
young man and built up a solid frame. You're looking very
worried.'

'It's not a pleasant thought to think that one of a man's
household may have murdered him.' The Reverend Mother
had been about to use the word family, but then rejected it
for the more appropriate word, household. Her mind was on
one person ever since the mention of the *cillín*.

'It may not have been anything to do with the wife or
those boys, if that's what is upsetting you,' said Dr Scher
consolingly. 'Give Patrick a chance to unearth more evidence.
The man could have gone down to the city, called into his
bank, had a word with a business rival, gone down to the
quays to make sure that his leather was safely packed for its
voyage across the channel. He sells a lot of it to England,
you know, so someone at the university told me.'

'I'd find it hard to imagine that he was killed down in the
flat of the city and his body taken back up to Shandon and
placed in a trunk there in one of the empty rooms. And don't
tell me that the body in the trunk originated at the auctioneer's
rooms. The old trunk was one of the items that Mr Hayes
noted down on his visit to the house on that Tuesday afternoon.
He read out from his book to me. There were several containers,
each filled with various goods from the house, curtains, cushions, various soft furnishings, and, of course, the trunk load
of books. Or so the label said,' she added.

'There are all sorts of reasons why a man like that could
have been killed. He could have been followed home by
someone who had made up his mind to kill him. Very easy
for someone to knock on the door with a tale of problems at
the docks. And the yard is open all of the time, of course.
Someone could easily have been invited into the house.
Those women, well, they might not have felt that the visitor
was any business of theirs. I would say that the man had them
well trained to appear when he wanted them, and to keep to
themselves when he didn't.'

The Reverend Mother thought about that. It made sense
according to all of the hints dropped by Bridie over the years.

Fred's words about his mother had shocked her, but she had
to admit, reluctantly, that these words, harsh as they were,
had not surprised her.

There was, undoubtedly, a possibility that the suspect list
for the murder of Henry Mulcahy, Hide and Skin Merchant,
may well have been quite large.

SEVEN

St Thomas Aquinas
'Fac me, Domine Deus meus, patientem sine
murmuratione, humilem sine fictione, hilarem sine
dissolutione, maturum sine gravedine, agilem sine levitate . . .'
(O Lord, my God, make me patient without
grumbling, humble without pretence, cheerful without
dissipation, mature without undue heaviness,
quick-minded without levity . . .)

Lucy arrived at the convent punctually at three o'clock in the afternoon, followed by her chauffeur carrying an enormous bouquet of flowers, as though to an invalid.

'I'm not dead yet, you know,' said the Reverend Mother mildly, while Sister Bernadette hurried off to the kitchen in search of a pair of vases that would do justice to such expensive-looking blooms. She looked across at her cousin with an amused expression. Lucy always liked to do the right thing; to make the right gesture.

'I wish you wouldn't keep getting yourself mixed up in these sordid affairs,' complained Lucy, but her small, neat-featured face was full of interest as she sank into an easy chair and stretched her hands towards the fire.

'Who was it that actually sent me a present of a corpse in a trunk, then, Lucy?' said the Reverend Mother getting this in quickly just before Sister Bernadette and a young novice appeared, carefully carrying two well-filled vases. The novice proved to be neat-fingered with flowers, plucking blossoms from Sister Bernadette's hasty efforts and rearranging them to display their best features. Lucy was loud in her praise and the Reverend Mother prayed a silent prayer for patience.

'Rupert said that I must be sure to ask you whether there were books in the trunk after all,' said Lucy, once the door had closed. 'He has a bet on with one of the solicitors on the

Mall that you took them out, wiped them down and placed
them on the shelf of your classroom before you sent for the
police.'

'I'm sorry to disappoint you, but I have no idea what was
at the bottom of the trunk. I know that there were untreated
animal skins, hides, packed around the corpse.'

'To stop it moving around, I suppose,' said Lucy with a
dramatic shudder. 'We're under suspicion, of course, you do
realize that, don't you?'

'You? Why, on earth?'

'Well, Rupert had no end of trouble with that man. I told
you, didn't I? He's plonked that awful new house just in the
way of our view of the river. Rupert tried to oppose the sale
of the meadow to him. That didn't work. And then Rupert
tried another tack. He appealed to get the house moved to
one side of the field, but he got nowhere. They say that
Mulcahy bribed someone on the city council. One shouldn't
speak ill of the dead, I know that, but he really was a most
unpleasant man, Dottie. So unreasonable. He could have easily
moved that house fifty feet to one side and then we wouldn't
be bothered with them, but he seemed to take a delight in
being a nuisance to us. And then he even had the cheek to
ask Rupert to act for him at the sale. Rupe was incoherent
with rage. It was the Cork Law Society dinner that night and
he could talk of nothing else. I was wearing the most fasci-
nating dress, but the whole evening was a complete flop.
Rupert was just totally obsessive. Quite put everyone off their
beef, going on about the man setting up his tanning yard
under our very noses and describing the whole process just
as if he were born to the trade.'

'But Mr Mulcahy didn't actually do that, build a tanning
yard next to his new house, did he?' pointed out the Reverend
Mother. 'He bought land from the bishop, up there in Shandon,
so Dr Scher told me. He built a shed there and concreted part
of the land so it must have been some little while ago, mustn't
it? That's what I have heard, anyway.' Mr Mulcahy, she
thought, was unlikely to have really wanted to set up a tanning
yard under the noses of Rupert and Lucy. The move to
Montenotte represented a move in status. By that, he would

have joined the gentry. The fact that he had retained, for the moment, as an office, the ground floor of one of the two houses that he owned in Shandon, until he could build an office by his tanning yard, showed that he had no intention of moving his business to the salubrious slopes of Montenotte where Cork's merchant princes dwelt. It had probably been a fuss about nothing. Rupert, she knew, though a kind-hearted person, was a highly-strung man, an extremely fastidious person who got easily worked up about things.

'A most unpleasant fellow who caused trouble where ever he went,' said Lucy roundly.

'He came up the hard way, I suppose. Do you remember that my father used to say that? It was a great expression of his, though I suppose it was true of most of the citizens of Cork. Gentility depended, then, as now, I suppose, on how far back "the hard way" was. Two generations makes everything respectable, isn't that right, Lucy? Our own ancestors proved that.'

'But you must admit that to make your money by buying and selling tea as our great-grandparents did, was a lot more respectable than by flaying the skins and hides of dead animals,' said Lucy with a shudder.

'And that's a very nice leather handbag, that you have, Lucy,' remarked the Reverend Mother.

'Oh, don't be so pious, all of a sudden,' said Lucy. 'One can have a leather handbag without probing too much into how it was made. Mr Mulcahy, the late Mr Mulcahy, was an unpleasant man with an unpleasant way of making money. But, now, the big question is who actually did kill him in the end. And I forbid you to say Rupert.'

'I was thinking of you, actually. You are the one who sent me the body. Did you see this trunk at all, Lucy, before you so kindly purchased it for me?'

'Well, of course, I didn't. Perhaps if I had noticed that a trunkful of school books was going for half-a-crown I might have decided to buy it for you, but I would have opened it up and looked at the books first of all, to make sure that they weren't Latin and Greek or that sort of thing. Funny that no one did, isn't it? Was it locked?'

'No, no keys,' said the Reverend Mother. That, she thought, was strange. 'And I'd say that the lock had been recently oiled, or just well-used,' she said. 'I remember how easily the latches clicked open.'

'Very strange.' Lucy brooded on this for a moment. 'What did the trunk look like?'

The Reverend Mother thought about it as dispassionately as she could. 'Dilapidated, dirty, disreputable.'

'Stop showing off that you know all about alliteration,' ordered Lucy.

'And it smelled bad, but I couldn't think of a word beginning with the letter "d" and describing accurately the way it smelled,' admitted the Reverend Mother. She felt slightly ashamed of the way that she and her cousin often reverted to their youth in the way that they swopped wisecracks when they came together.

A man has died and his son is in danger of being hanged for the murder, she reminded herself.

'Smelled bad, looked bad,' mused Lucy. 'I'd say that the auctioneer's men would have put that somewhere out of the way. He has them all very well trained; I'll say that for him. The foreman, Mr Gregory, must have been with him for a good forty years or so.'

'Lucy, have you met Mrs Mulcahy? I'm not sure that I've ever even seen her.'

'Nor have I, now that I come to think of it. It's odd, isn't it? A man builds a big new house just in full sight of our place. He's there every few days. I've heard him. He had a voice like a foghorn. In fact, you could hear him half a mile away bellowing at the builders. But do you know I don't think that I ever saw her there. Imagine a woman not wanting to be around while a new house was being built for her. You'd think that she would want to have some sort of say in it? I used to see him coming down the road. And I used to shut my window if it were open. He didn't drive, you know. He always walked or if it was raining very hard he might come by cab.'

'But never brought his wife, so you think?'

'I'd say that we'd have heard if she made an appearance,' said Lucy. 'Rupert was so bad tempered every time he saw or heard that man that the servants got all worked up about it. I'd say that the gardener or the housekeeper or one of the parlour maids was bound to tell him that they had seen Mrs Mulcahy that day. You know how servants are. They love to make a sensation. If Mrs Mulcahy had been seen, then they would definitely have announced it. Rupert says that he heard she was very badly treated and that he had her out there working in his tanning yard when the woman was pregnant. She had twelve children, you know, so the unfortunate woman was probably pregnant for most of the years of her marriage, poor thing. The eldest ran away to join the Republicans but the rest are all still at home. Twelve children in twenty years of marriage. Just imagine!'

The Reverend Mother nodded silently. What was it that young Fred Mulcahy had said? *A happy release for her, poor woman, after all those years of slavery.*

'And they say that the children were badly treated too,' went on Lucy. 'My housekeeper told me that by the time the boys were six or seven years old, as soon as they came back from school, they would be sent out with buckets to gather up dog mess from the streets. He used that for the tanning of the hides, you know. And if they didn't come back with a bucketful there would be no supper for them.'

Frantically building up a business, thought the Reverend Mother. Any of the Mulcahy children that she had seen looked well-nourished and Fred had certainly grown into a fine looking young man. The threat of no supper had probably not been carried out. Neighbours would have been quick to judge. But when she compared them with the many families that she had dealt with, there had been no neglect. All of the Mulcahy children had been educated, sent to secondary school, also, which showed that Mr Mulcahy had been ambitious for them. He had baulked at university for Fred, but that, given the man's own background, had not been surprising. He probably thought that university was a waste of time and that the boy would be better off setting up in some business.

Judge not, she thought and changed the conversation back to the trunk.

'It seems amazing to think that the trunk lay for a couple

of days in the auctioneer's rooms and no one attempted to open it or to check on its contents. Why do you think that happened, Lucy?'

'It's a big building, full of stuff, really jam-packed with goods. Unless someone was interested in school books, I can't see anyone poking around in an old trunk. No, I wouldn't be surprised that no one looked at it.' Lucy was an auction addict as were several of her friends. A cosy hour could be spent looking for bargains or the perfect object to fit an unfurnished corner. And then followed by lunch in the Imperial Hotel where the sale would be discussed, and perhaps, afterwards, a return visit to the auction rooms. Lucy would know the ins-and-outs of the practice at Hayes' Auctioneers very well, indeed. How long had the trunk rested in those rooms?

'I'm sure that I wouldn't bother looking at an old trunk full of school books,' finished Lucy. 'And I'd say that would be true of most people. You know what old school books would be like. Probably scribbled on. Rude words and silly drawings all over the back pages.'

'And, of course, its appearance and the smell coming from the trunk would probably have put people off touching it,' said the Reverend Mother. 'What do you think, Lucy?'

'That's very likely,' said Lucy. 'And, what's more, the majority of people there were left over from the previous sale. You remember Ashgrove, on the old Youghal Road, well, the contents of house and garden were being auctioned off. I was there for that sale and so were lots of others that I saw. It's always tempting to hang around for the next sale and see what comes up – Mr Hayes knows that and he always runs one into the other.'

The Reverend Mother nodded. It did seem feasible. A battered, smelly old trunk with mould on it. Why should anyone bother much with it while the expensive contents of Ashgrove House were laid out for them to admire and covet?

EIGHT

St Thomas Aquinas
Ex quo patet quod misericordia non tollit iustitiam,
sed est quaedam iustitiae plenitudo.
(Hence it is clear that mercy does not destroy justice,
but in a sense is the fullness of justice.)

The Reverend Mother tapped her foot impatiently on the well-polished hall floor as she waited for her taxi to arrive. Already she was quite late. Why did the bishop always choose a Monday morning to call together all of the headmasters and headmistresses of the religious schools in the city? Surely any man of intelligence could guess that Monday morning was almost always crisis time in schools. Things happened in families during the weekend and the trouble was brought into school on Monday morning. Already she had phoned the guards on behalf of a woman with a very black eye and a broken arm who wanted to find some safe haven for herself and her child, away from her drunken husband who had threatened to set fire to the tenement in which they lived; had rummaged in a cupboard to find a gymslip, blouse and cardigan for a girl whose clothes had been pawned by her mother in order to fund a Saturday night drinking session in her local public house and who, poor child, had arrived in school wearing nothing but a torn petticoat and a huge and filthy shawl; had phoned up the city council on behalf of a family who had received a notice from their landlord to quit their one-roomed home within three days; had doled out some rat poison, safely stored in a sealed tin box with a hole large enough for a rat, but too small to allow little fingers to poke at the deadly contents. She had listened with sympathy to the sad news of the death of a baby, promising earnestly to pray for the little soul; had amalgamated two of the infant classes to cope with the absence of one teacher and sent for a plumber to fix an ominous drip from the kitchen ceiling. By the time that the taxi arrived, she was tired, irritable and her head ached badly. She was on the verge of getting Sister Bernadette to tell a polite lie about a sudden illness to the bishop's secretary, but when she saw the taxi draw up at the gate she forced herself on. It would never be worth absenting herself. The bishop would only feel bound to call to see her and that would be a worse waste of her time as he would insist on inspecting the whole school, addressing the children, boring them, she told herself and firmly refused to feel guilty. And, of course, his visit would result in bringing down all sorts of unwelcome suggestions on her head. He might even bring up the matter of the money that she spent so recklessly in order to run the school. No, it would be better to go and get it over with and so she was pleased that the arrival of the taxi had taken the decision out of her hands. Rapidly she left the shelter of the porch and advanced towards the gate. Luckily it was a motorized taxi, not a horse-drawn one. She hated to see an animal struggle up the almost perpendicular heights of Shandon Street.

And, of course, she admitted to herself, Shandon Street was of interest to her at the moment. She had done as much as she could do for now, she told herself with a backward look at her school. All was quiet and orderly within its walls. Hungry children had been fed, warmed, and the naked clothed and that was all that she could do for the moment. She made a firm resolution to be very polite to the bishop and to listen with interest to his various suggestions for the efficient running of a school. She might even find some way of avoiding the ceremonial and lengthy lunch provided for all.

Interesting place, Shandon, she thought, as she escaped from the bishop's palace a few hours later. The lunch, on this occasion, had been a new-fashioned buffet which made things so much easier, and quicker. She had swallowed a cup of tea, nibbled a ham sandwich, tastefully shorn of its crusts – where did the crusts go, she had wondered – and then she had tasted a biscuit, adroitly swiped a plateful of silver-paper-wrapped chocolates into her purse from under the nose of a hungry Christian Brother – the needs of her children were greater than his; she had mentally wafted the message to the man, eyeing his large, well-fed stomach and then she had slipped out of a door. Hopefully, she would not be missed at the bishop's closing address and the prayer for guidance.

The day had turned fine after the morning's rain. The Shandon bells on St Anne's Church played merrily and the clock showed that it was barely two in the afternoon. Or at least one face of the clock showed two o'clock and the others showed, 2:03, 2:04 and 2:07. 'The four-faced liar', the clock was nicknamed in Cork, but whichever face was right, she had plenty of time. The school day did not end until four and so there was no rush about getting back to the convent ready to meet and greet those mothers who turned up to collect their children and, usually, to get some advice and help from the Reverend Mother.

She would walk, she decided. The sun had come out and the pavements, although frighteningly steep when one looked down, were steaming and almost dry in places. She would go slowly, keeping close to the wall, and she would look around her. She greeted the verger who was sharing a few sweets with some of the children on their way home for the midday break. A nice man, she thought. The name, Mr Sweetman, suited him. What a shame that he and his wife had no living children. He would have made a very good father. She smiled and raised a hand, but did not interrupt his chat with the children. One of his great pleasures in a dull and dreary life.

She saw the sign for the Mulcahy business almost immediately, only about a hundred yards down from the cathedral. The two handsome gabled houses belonging to the dead man, built in the era of George IV, she guessed, fronted onto the street. And the workplace, the hide and skin business, its large yard and outbuildings had been behind the houses. She hesitated for a moment and then crossed over the road. The yard was only a few paces down a side lane and the sign was clearly visible from the street. 'Henry Mulcahy & Sons'. Rather touching, she thought. Like Mr Dombey, the man had wanted to found a dynasty. She walked down the lane and stood for a moment at the gate looking around the yard. It was scrubbed clean, and a strong smell of Jeyes Fluid met her nostrils. And then a familiar figure came out from one of the outhouses, carrying a pail.

'Good afternoon, Bridie,' said the Reverend Mother. She was faintly embarrassed to be caught peeping in through the gate, but Bridie gave a cry of delight and came forward instantly, dropping her pail in the middle of the yard.

'Reverend Mother,' she said enthusiastically. 'You've come for the condolences. The Missus will be ever so pleased.'

And it was, of course, a reasonable excuse. Ever since the announcement of the death in this morning's *Cork Examiner*, troops of people, led by compassion, neighbourliness, or sheer curiosity would have been streaming into the place to give their condolences to the sorrowing widow and children. The Reverend Mother allowed herself to be led around to the front of the houses. The front door of one of them had its knocker decorated with a large mourning wreath. Bridie led her towards this one, turned the knob and ushered her in through an empty hallway and into the front room of the house.

The small bare room here had been used as an office when the Mulcahys and their twelve children had occupied the two joined Georgian houses. That was plain. There was a desk, a few wooden chairs, a telephone and behind it, covering the whole back wall of the room, was an elaborate, though roughly made, oak cabinet, containing innumerable small drawers. The widow sat on the chair behind the desk, a girl beside her and two tall boys, younger brothers of Fred, she reckoned, were standing awkwardly behind their mother's chair. There was no sign of the rest of the family, probably the younger boys were at school, or being looked after by the other sister, but perched on the corner of the desk was a small man, thickset, his face elongated by a spade-shaped beard, several shades lighter than his bushy eyebrows. When the door opened, he looked up alertly and then leaned across the desk to say something to Mrs Mulcahy.

The woman looked dead tired. The Reverend Mother eyed the queue ahead of her, all waiting to shake the hand of the grieving widow and felt contrite that she was going to add to the poor woman's troubles. She could see the strain on the drawn face as Mrs Mulcahy tried to reply to the conventional expressions of sympathy. Bridie had slipped away once she had escorted the Reverend Mother inside the door. There had been an immediate movement, to her embarrassment, as the polite people of Shandon Street moved aside and encouraged the holy nun to go to the top of the queue.

'This is the Reverend Mother from St Mary's of the Isle, Mam.' It was one of the daughters. Susan, she guessed. Susan's voice was very composed, her manner respectful, but assured. Reputedly a very clever girl, she had attended St Vincent's Convent in Shandon and had won prizes when she sat the Intermediate Certificate. According to Bridie, this girl Susan had wanted to go on with her education but her father wouldn't hear of her becoming a bluestocking and told her that there was enough to do in the house and she could help her mother with the younger children. Had that rankled? The girl looked composed, but who knew what she felt like underneath. Did she mourn her father's death? Or was there always a measure of relief when the hand of a tyrant, even a benevolent tyrant, is removed?

The Reverend Mother delivered her condolences. The unfortunate wife was at the end of her tether, eyes circled with black, hands tightly clenched, to restrain the tremor. It was merciful to be short and conventional.

'You're very good. Thank you for coming.' The phrases came mechanically to the woman's lips. Then she turned with an effort to the man who had got off the desk and was now standing beside her chair, waiting expectantly.

'This is Mr McCarthy, my husband's friend, Reverend Mother.'

'The family appreciate your presence, Reverend Mother.' His tone was hushed and his voice slightly husky. He spoke as though he were an important member of the family. Perhaps he was a cousin, or a nephew. Odd that Bridie had never mentioned his name amongst the tons of information that she poured out about the Mulcahy family. A person one would find difficult to ignore, she thought, with a quick look at the heavy jaw and the determined china blue eyes. 'We're all very grateful to you for coming,' he finished with a quick glance around the room, his beard jutting out aggressively. And obediently a small murmur rose up in response.

'You must come and have a cup of tea, Reverend Mother.' Susan rose to her feet almost before her mother had finished speaking. The Reverend Mother made her farewell as quickly as possible and followed the girl out to the hallway.

'Your poor mother,' she said, once the door of the office closed behind them. 'Thank God that she has such good children to give her support. I suppose that Sally is looking after the younger boys.'

The girl looked slightly startled at the Reverend Mother's knowledge of her family and so she added quickly, 'I remember you in your pram, the two of you. Bridie used to take you visiting the convent.' Did the girl know about Bridie, she wondered. She had a keen intelligent face. Even as toddlers, it was easy to pick out Susan from Sally. Susan was the one that was always grimly investigating everything within reach while the prettier twin, Sally, was content to be handed from one nun to another, beaming placidly.

'That's right, Sally is looking after them. They're over in the new house. There's no room here for them, no furniture much even in this place, now,' said the girl. There was a defensive note in her voice. 'We'll be having the burial tomorrow morning. The police said that we could. They'll all come over for that. And then they'll have to get back to school, all of them.'

A good half an hour's walk from Montenotte to Faranferris School in Shandon, she reckoned, and some of the boys must still be quite young – probably about six or seven, the youngest ones, thought the Reverend Mother. It would be hard for the boys to do that walk twice in every day, but then the Mulcahy children would not have been brought up to expect an easy life. She just nodded her head in agreement, though. Susan wanted no more conversation; that was easy to be seen. She opened the door to the back room where Bridie stood awkwardly, waiting for guests with a teapot in her hand, and Susan ushered the Reverend Mother in and then closed the door firmly on her.

The house was almost devoid of furniture. There was nothing

here but a small, rather rickety, table with a huge metal teapot and a large plateful of sandwiches. Some coarse earthenware cups, many of them without saucers, were set out on the table, but it didn't look as though anyone had availed of the hospitality that had been got ready for the sympathizers.

'Sit down, Reverend Mother,' said Bridie. Nervously she dusted off the scratched paint on the window sill and then stood awkwardly, poised with teapot in hand. 'Sorry not to have somewhere nice for you to sit, Reverend Mother. We're in a state here. Nearly all of the furniture has been taken off to the auctioneer's place, just left us a couple of beds and this old table. It's just been the Missus, and Susan and myself left here. The other house has been sold. They used to join, you know. They joined in the attics. The children used to run between them. The fun that they used to have, chasing each other from house to house!' Bridie's nervous, white face softened into a smile at the memory. 'It's all boarded up now that the one of them has been sold,' she said regretfully. 'You'll have a cup of tea, Reverend Mother, and a sandwich, won't you?'

'Nothing for me, thank you, Bridie,' said the Reverend Mother decisively. 'I've just been having lunch with the bishop.'

'You'd have the best of everything, there,' said Bridie respectfully. And, then, almost as though she could not resist it, she said anxiously, 'I suppose there was a lot of talk about our trouble up there at the palace.'

'Yes,' admitted the Reverend Mother. 'I did hear it mentioned. Everyone was very sorry for the children and for Mrs Mulcahy, of course.' And there had been lively debate on who among his business rivals might, to quote one of the Christian Brothers, have bumped him off, and she did believe that Mr McCarthy's name had been mentioned. By all accounts, Mr Mulcahy had been a match for any of them, though. 'A tough man' had said the headmaster of Farranferris School. 'You wouldn't believe it, Reverend Mother, but he tried to get me to give him a cut-rate on the school fees on the grounds that he would be sending me ten boys. As if I could sell them or something! "Should be cheaper by the dozen, Father," he kept saying to me, with that laugh of his.'

'Everyone had great praise for the children,' she said to Bridie. 'All of them very clever, so I have heard. Their teachers think a lot of them.'

Bridie's thin, lined face lit up. There was a glow in her eyes and she straightened herself. Despite the blackened teeth, her smile was lovely. 'God bless them, the cleverest children in the world,' she said. 'Nothing is any trouble for them. Good children, too, just a bit of mischief from time to time, but very good children.'

'But Fred was always your favourite, though; still is, I'm sure, isn't he, Bridie?' The nuns in the convent used to tease Bridie about this, so the Reverend Mother thought that she would resurrect the old joke. The smile immediately faded from the woman's face and a hunted, worried look replaced it.

'I haven't had sight nor sound of him for months,' she said defensively. 'Never have a chance to say a word to him these days.' She took the lid off the aluminium teapot and stirred its contents vigorously. Then seizing a large knife, she started to chop the sandwiches in half, reducing them to a manageable size.

'He never comes near this place,' she said and the tone of her voice was still anxious and defensive. The Reverend Mother's heart sank. Bridie never could look you in the face and tell a lie.

'So Fred wasn't here on Tuesday, then, was he?'

'No, not at all, no, not a sight of him.' Now the knife chopped the sandwiches into dainty quarters and the eyes were fixed resolutely on the table.

'Wouldn't his father have welcomed a visit, do you think, Bridie? Were father and son at odds with each other?'

'Not a bit of it.' Bridie spoke with emphasis, but she still avoided the Reverend Mother's eyes. The sandwiches had been reduced to the smallest size possible, but now she started busily divesting them of their crusts. In the background, footsteps kept crossing the hallway and the front door opened and was closed again every few minutes. The Reverend Mother felt rather guilty. Surely these sandwiches and those pints of tea in the large teapot should be offered to the sympathizers.

Perhaps she was blocking access to the hospitality. She got to her feet and went towards the door.

'You must come to see us, soon, Bridie,' she said. 'Sister Bernadette was saying recently that you've become quite a stranger. And I'd like to give you a message for Fred, Bridie; I know that he always comes to you when he is in trouble.' That, of course, had been said by Bridie many years ago, but the memory of it was there and the woman flushed a rosy red and then paled. The Reverend Mother left a moment for that that to sink in and then said earnestly, 'Tell him from me that the truth is always the straightest way in the end. Tell him, that, Bridie, won't you?'

Bridie said nothing. She looked down and then looked up. There were tears in her eyes. Nothing more could be said, though, and there was a slightly relieved look on Bridie's face as the Reverend Mother left.

A thin woman in a black shawl was coming out of the front room and she rushed to open the front door for the Reverend Mother, accompanying her down the steep pavement once they were out of doors, grabbing her arm in a protective fashion when she wobbled a little.

'Take little small steps, Reverend Mother,' she advised. 'That's the way to do it. See the way that I do it. I've lived on Shandon Street all of my life. Was born here, married here and I suppose I'll be waked and buried here. Shandon Street people get good muscles in the backs of their legs, so they say.'

'I suppose that you know the Mulcahy family well,' said the Reverend Mother taking her new acquaintance's advice. The short steps did make her feel more secure going down this dreadfully steep hill. She was glad, though, for the steadying arm.

'Well, yes, and no. They kept themselves to themselves, the Mulcahy family. Very hard workers. The children, too. If they weren't doing their homework, they'd be grabbed to do something in the yard, so they didn't stint on the homework, easier than battering those skins with iron bars. Too young for hard work like that. My husband, God rest his soul, used to say that. You wouldn't see the Mulcahy boys much out in the streets or down the lanes, with the other boys larking around gas poles, "waxing a gazer" we call it, Reverend Mother. They'd be indoors and at their books. Very sad about young Fred. He was a great boy for the study, so they say.'

'He joined the Republicans, didn't he?' The Reverend Mother knew that there must always be two sides to a gossipy conversation.

'That's right, he did. Terrible trouble with his father, there was. He wasn't the sort of man who'd give advice and then tell a lad that he was old enough to make up his own mind. No, a dreadful row there was; *up and down the banks*, it was, I'll tell you that, Reverend Mother and not a word of a lie. Picked up a stick and hit the boy around the shoulders. You could have heard them at the bottom of Shandon Street. Well, they do say that Fred never spoke to his father again. Came to see his mother from time to time. Awful fond of her, he was. He'd come on fair days when he knew that his father would be out of the way. And, of course, once they cleared the furniture out of the last of the houses his father went off to live in the posh new house, in Montenotte, if you please, took Sally and the younger boys and so Fred knew he was safe then. Came and gave a hand to his mother and Susan, and poor old Bridie, of course.'

'But his father was here last Tuesday, wasn't he? Came to meet the auctioneer. So I heard,' said the Reverend Mother.

'That's right. I saw the auctioneer's car go up the road at about three o'clock in the afternoon. Mr Mulcahy would have been there to meet him. So you can bet a prayer on it that young Fred got well out of the way.'

The Reverend Mother thought about that last sentence. An empty house next door, and a back yard. Did Fred leave once his father arrived or did he lurk in the background, perhaps hoping for more conversation with his mother? She decided to change the subject.

'Was that man, Mr McCarthy, I think Mrs Mulcahy called him, was he her husband's partner?'

'Partner, not a bit of it. Not to say anything evil of the dead, but Mr Mulcahy wouldn't be a man for a partner. Liked his own way far too much, Reverend Mother, I can tell you that.

No, they were both in the same way of business, of course, Richard McCarthy was a good twenty years younger. There was talk about him marrying one of the twins one time, but it didn't come to anything. Not as far as I know, anyway. Terrible place for gossip, Shandon Street, you'd never credit it, Reverend Mother. People always want to know their neighbour's business.' The woman stopped beside a hardware shop and smiled up at the window above where a girl was holding up a baby. 'Well, this is my place, Reverend Mother, you wouldn't come in and have a sit down and rest your legs? A bit of a climb up the stairs, but then you could have a good sit down and a cup of tea, too.'

'No, I wouldn't, I must be getting back to school, but thank you for the offer.'

'Well, you're a great woman for your age! Imagine you walking all the way from Shandon to St Mary's of the Isle. Half an hour it used to take her to go and visit you at the convent, Bridie would tell me, but then she'd always have a couple of babies in a pram and another couple stringing after her. Poor woman!'

Poor Bridie, indeed, thought the Reverend Mother as she walked away, noting with relief that the pavement was less steep as she neared Pope's Quay. There was always a feeling of guilt in the back of her mind about Bridie. Should she have kept her? Could she have kept her? Could she have kept the baby a secret from the bishop? She had feared not. The chaplain, she had known, would have felt it his duty to remonstrate and if she ignored him, to take the matter straight to the bishop.

At least poor Bridie did not have to go to one of those Magdalen Laundries.

Many times during the last twenty years the Reverend Mother had wondered about the speed with which Bridie had found herself a live-in position with the Mulcahy family. The baby, apparently, was going to be no problem. The Reverend Mother had asked no questions, had not felt that she had any right to do so. She had contented herself with bestowing on the woman several sets of underwear, petticoats, a thick, warm shawl, an extra pair of good leather shoes, old sheets and even a couple of newish ones, and a promise that she would always be there if Bridie needed any help for herself or for her baby.

But the baby did not live. The poor little thing was born dead.

And was buried in the *cillín* at the top of Shandon hill, within the walls of the ancient *dún*.

NINE

St Thomas Aquinas
*'Ordina, Deus meus, statum meum et quod a me
requiris, ut faciam, tribue ut sciam; et da exsequi sicut
oportet et expedit animae meae.'*
(Oh my God, order my life, and grant that I may know
what Thou wilt have me to do; and grant that I may
fulfil it as is fitting and profitable to my soul.)

I t was after six o'clock in the evening when Susan Mulcahy
arrived at the convent. There had been no one to answer
the doorbell when she arrived so she had very sensibly
gone to the chapel where the Benediction hymns and solemn
notes of the organ rose through the foggy air. She had slipped,
unnoticed, into a back seat in a dim corner by the confessional
stall and had stayed there while the nuns filed out for their
evening supper and recreation time.

The Reverend Mother had delayed for a while to talk to the
elderly chaplain. Long experience had taught her that he worried
about little matters and if not given a regular opportunity to
ventilate them, then he would come and disturb her in the
middle of some task and, what between remarks on the weather,
apologies for interrupting her and comments on the latest
missive from the bishop, he would manage to take up a considerable portion of her valuable time. A quick word every morning
and evening worked out to be an efficient arrangement and she
did not grudge those few minutes from her busy day.

Nevertheless, she was quite distracted that evening.
Who on earth was sitting there at the back of the church,
waiting so quietly. Surely it was Susan Mulcahy. The Reverend
Mother's heart sank as she nodded and smiled at some story
about the Holy Father in Rome. A plain girl, nineteen years
old, may well have decided that boys were not interested in
her and now, in the grip of sorrow, mourning a father's violent

death, and perhaps feeling guilt that she had not loved him . . .
It was a familiar scenario and one that she would have to
discourage as forcefully as possible.

'You must go to Rome one day, Father,' she said, interrupting
the tale. 'Why not? It would be a wonderful experience. Of
course, we would miss you, but I'm sure that you would find
someone suitable to take your place while you were absent.
Think of the wonderful tales that you would have to tell the
children when you returned!' She beamed on him, wished him
a pleasant evening and walked briskly down the middle aisle
of the chapel.

'Ah, Susan, how kind of you to call to see me. Come into
my room, will you?' She betrayed no surprise, but adopted a
business-like tone which, she hoped, would make the subse-
quent conversation shorter and more fruitful.

The girl followed her in silence as she ushered her into her
room. She lacked the good looks of her brothers, took more
after the father. The faithful Sister Bernadette had made
sure to put the Reverend Mother's supper tray all ready by
the fire and the Reverend Mother took up the teapot with an
inquiring look.

'No, thank you, Reverend Mother,' said Susan. 'I've done
nothing but drink tea all day long and I'm sick of the stuff.'

Her voice and her manner were assured and matter-of-fact
and the Reverend Mother sat down with a feeling of thank-
fulness. At least she hadn't burst into tears. That was often
the first step in declaring a vocation, or a revelation sent
from Mary, Mother of God, herself.

'Take this chair, Susan, it's relatively comfortable. Now tell
me what I can do for you.'

'I came for a bit of advice, really, Reverend Mother. It was
Bridie that suggested it. I was wondering who I could talk to
and she suggested you. I hope you don't mind me coming
so late, but the burial is tomorrow and there'll be a lot to do
during the next few days. I'm afraid that if I leave this
business, I might be pushed aside.'

'Well, I'll do my best to advise you,' said the Reverend
Mother cautiously.

'I want to go to university,' said Susan abruptly. 'I could

do it, you know. I've gone on studying after my father made me leave school. I've used Fred's old books and I know that I could pass the matriculation examination as easy as anything. John, my brother John, he's helped me a bit. My father was happy for the boys to matriculate. He liked that, but he wouldn't hear of me doing that. Sally and I had to leave school to help our mother to look after the younger children. I do know that I could pass the examination, Reverend Mother. I have studied Latin until I was blue in the face. I could easily do Fred's Leaving Certificate paper. I've a very good memory and I loved translating Latin into English, it was just like working out puzzles. And I can do trigonometry and everything and once when John had a terrible headache I did an essay for him and he copied it out and gave it in and Father Duffy marked it as A+. Sent him down to the headmaster to show it.' There was a great note of pride in the girl's voice and the Reverend Mother smiled at her.

'So what would you wish to study at university, Susan?'

'I want to be a doctor. I've wanted it all of my life, as far back as I can remember. My father wouldn't hear of it, of course. All I was good for was saving him the price of a girl to look after the children. I didn't matter. I've never mattered.' The girl's voice was harsh and the Reverend Mother decided not to speak. Allow her to get the suppressed bitterness out of her system.

'And now he's dead and I can do what I like,' said Susan. There was a note of triumph in her voice and the Reverend Mother felt uncomfortable. Still she said nothing and now Susan appeared to notice her silence.

'You probably don't believe that I can study medicine, but I can,' she said passionately. 'I bought a book once from a second-hand bookshop down on Lavitt's Quay. I read it in bed at night. I know most of it off by heart. Some student sold it off, look at it. She fumbled in a shabby handbag and produced a dog-eared book with a large tea stain across its cover. *Anatomy for First Year Students* was the name on the cover. The Reverend Mother took the book and leafed through it slowly, not wanting, in any way, to denigrate the achievement of this poor girl and also to give herself time to think.

'I can get my mother to do anything I want. She's no bother. But it's that man, Reverend Mother. You saw him, didn't you, when you came to our house this morning. Richard McCarthy. Standing there like a black crow, pretending to be in deep mourning. He says that he is the executor. I don't know what to believe. I don't trust him. Ever since Fred left, he's had great influence over my father. He's the one that persuaded him to set up a yard on the Shandon hill, he and that auctioneer between them. My father had been going to keep one house, keep it as an office and a business place and keep the yard behind, also. But then he changed his mind. Mr McCarthy has his own place near there so he persuaded my father to buy that land, the *cillín*, from the bishop and upset poor Bridie and my mother too.'

'Your mother.' The Reverend Mother did not insert a questioning note into the words. They sounded, she knew, as a mere echo, but they kept the door open for more revelations if Susan wished to make them. After a moment, the girl spoke again, a monosyllabic answer.

'Yes.'

The Reverend Mother waited. And after a few moments' silence the girl twisted uncomfortably in her chair. 'I helped her. I was only fifteen. I had just been taken away from school. I didn't even know that she was expecting again. We were never told anything. She was lying on the bed, crying with a pain and then there was a lot of blood and . . . and he came out and it was a little boy, tiny, a tiny little boy. I can't help crying when I think about him and how small he was, tiny little feet. I was all on my own but she, my mother, kept telling me what to do, kept saying not to tell anyone, to get some old sheets, to get a bucket. She kept telling me things, making me do things and then Bridie came back and looked after her.'

'And the baby?' The Reverend Mother edged open the drawer in front of her, where she kept a clean handkerchief, but the girl was tearless.

'Bridie put him in a box, a shoe box. I took him away with me, into my room and I tried to warm him in my arms, but he was getting colder and colder. I knew, really, that it was no good. There was a mug of water there and I sprinkled some on his little head and I said, "I baptize you, Joseph, in the name of the Father and the Son and the Holy Ghost". I knew that the priest wouldn't do it, so I did it. And you're the only one I've told. I suppose it was a sin, but I don't care.'

'Christ, himself, said that the greatest sin is the sin against charity.' Not something that was always remembered by those who purported to speak in his name. The Reverend Mother sometimes wondered what Christ would have thought of the Church's rigid rule against baptism of a dead baby and against the burial of an unbaptized child in consecrated ground, but she added nothing to her comment. Let the girl finish her tragic little story.

'And that night Bridie and I went up to the *cillín*, Fred came with us and we buried the baby under one of the sally trees. They're all cut down, now. My father had them cut down when his shed was built.' There was another few moments of silence after she said that and then Susan seemed to shake herself as though pushing away the memories.

'You see the thing is, Reverend Mother, my father was a rich man. He's been making a lot of money, hand over fist. The war was good for him. He sold a lot of leather to the British army, for boots and belts, that sort of thing and wool too. I've helped with the books and I know how much has been coming in. And now lots of English firms trade with him. He ships stuff over to Bradford every few weeks. I've been sent down to the bank with a couple of hundred pounds stuffed into this handbag here. And then there's been the sale of those two houses, the second one should be sold soon if Mr Hayes stirs himself.'

'But, of course, the house in Montenotte . . .'

'That's been paid for. It's been bought and paid for. He's been putting money aside for years for that. Never even put it in the bank, kept it in a safe here and every time that he did a good deal, the extra cash went into that safe. It's been his dream since I was about thirteen or fourteen years old. He wanted to live in Montenotte, there side by side with the best of them. He used to say that. No, there's plenty of money now and I want to go to university. I'm tired of being a skivvy.

Any fourteen-year-old from an orphanage could do as well as
I could.'

'What does your mother say?'

'She says to ask Mr McCarthy. He's got the will. He says
he's an executor.'

'And did you?'

'No.' There was a pause for a moment. 'I know that it
would be useless. I know what he wants. He wants to marry
me. It was a stupid idea that my father got into his head.
They talked it over, the two of them, agreed a price, I suppose.
And then my father called me into his office one day a few
months ago and told me what had been settled.'

The Reverend Mother suppressed a smile. 'What did
you say?'

She shrugged. 'I said no. He blustered a bit.'

'Not too angry.' The scene between Fred and his father
came to her mind, but Susan shook her head.

'I just told him, "No, not in a hundred years" and he just
shrugged his shoulders.'

It sounded rather too simplistic, but the Reverend Mother
allowed the statement to pass.

'What about Sally? Was the offer passed on to her?' This
Mr McCarthy would have been more interested in the business
link than in the girl. She thought back to that man with the
heavy jaw and the bold, bright blue eyes.

'My father probably had other notions for her. Sally is
much prettier than I am. And not so awkward,' she added
defiantly.

The Reverend Mother studied the very white face in front
of her; every single blemish was standing out. The girl looked
at the end of her resources. Without asking, she poured a cup
of tea, added milk and put a small slice of cake on a plate.
This time Susan made no protest, but obediently nibbled and
swallowed.

'That's done me good,' she said when she had finished. 'I'm
making a mess of this explaining, didn't mean to talk about
the baby . . . Well, Mr O'Sullivan, the solicitor and Mr
McCarthy, Mr Richard McCarthy, the pair of them are hand
in glove, well, they say that everything is left to my mother,

but that there isn't much to spare and he'd advise her to keep on the house in Shandon, sell the business to him and sell the house in Montenotte. He says that if she doesn't do that, she'll have nothing to live on and that will be that. And as for there being money for me to go to university, well, he says that is nonsense.

'And what do you say, Susan?'

'Well, I say that he's the one that's talking nonsense when he advised her to sell the business. My mother is only forty-two years old. She could live another forty years. Is she going to be living on money from the bank all of these years? What if something happens to money, happens to the bank, it wouldn't be the first time. No, she should keep the business. It's a good one and she knows it inside out. Hire another man, but she could give the orders. And then there are all the boys growing up. John is like Fred, he's a scholar and he should have his chance, but Robert is seventeen now and he wants to leave school. He's clever enough and he has a good head for figures. But he likes to be doing things. And he's like us all, he knows what needs to be done. There's none of us that don't know how to run that business. And if Mr McCarthy wants to be helpful, he could put in the word of advice from time to time instead of trying to persuade my mother to sell him a business that's worth three times his own. He's just trying to turn my father's death to his own advantage, Reverend Mother.'

'I see,' said the Reverend Mother, looking at the resolute face in front of her and thinking of the frightened nervous face of the mother. 'I suppose that you wouldn't want to run the business, yourself, Susan, would you? Perhaps you and Robert between you.'

Susan shook her head. 'No, I wouldn't, not that I couldn't if I put my mind to it, but I want to start on my medical studies. It's a six-year course and I'm getting on now. I'm nineteen years old.'

'Have you seen your father's will?'

Susan shook her head, again.

'Do you know the name of the solicitor? You mentioned it, didn't you? What was his name?'

'He's a man on Pope's Quay. His name is O'Sullivan.'

The city was full of people of that name, but the Reverend Mother resolved, now that she had checked that it was O'Sullivan, to have a word with Lucy's husband. Rupert may have detested the father, but he would surely not refuse a word of advice for the sorrowing widow and her huge family if it came to problems with the solicitor. Things did not sound too good to her, though. It was obvious, even from that one short meeting that Mrs Mulcahy was unlikely to stand up to this forceful Mr McCarthy, or perhaps Mr O'Sullivan, either. Susan was under twenty-one and she had no rights to any of the money that her father had accumulated. She studied the girl for a few minutes. Clever, yes, she would take the girl's word for that. The Mulcahy children were all endowed with brains. From what she had seen of them she could be sure of that and Susan had, as a small child, appeared to be very advanced, reading fluently at an early age, she seemed to remember Sister Bernadette bringing her to display her achievement to the Reverend Mother. The Mulcahy children were, to Sister Bernadette, like Bridie's children and they were all praised and admired by the lay sisters in the kitchen. Susan, now that memories were coming back, had been as clever as her older brother Fred.

A very plain girl, though, and with an awkward stiff manner. Marriage offers might not come too easily.

'When it comes to it, a girl with a good manner will score over just good looks,' her cousin Lucy had declared when speaking of her granddaughters. She had poo-pooed the idea of brains. 'Brains are best kept secret until after the marriage,' she had said briskly. 'No, a good manner, reasonable looks and an ability to dress well, that's what will get a girl a good husband.'

The Reverend Mother debated the matter internally for a few minutes, looking across at Susan, dressed in the same style as her mother, almost ankle-length skirt, her hair bunched up under an oddly elderly straw hat. Virtually every girl of five or six years on either side of her age had shortened her skirt to such a degree that Sister Mary Immaculate had taken, at one stage, to pinning a flannelette frill on the bottom of any skirt which did not touch the ground when its owner knelt on the floor of the classroom. In Lucy's eyes, this girl would have little hope of many offers of marriage, her manner was abrupt and awkward; her looks were plain and her dress sense non-existent. And the one offer that had been mooted was distasteful to her.

'I suppose you have never considered becoming a nun, Susan.' The words were out almost before she realised what she was saying, but she went ahead with the proposition. 'Our order, as you probably know, deals with nursing as well as with teaching. I see no reason whatsoever why one of us should not go a step further and train to be a doctor. And, of course, the order would find the money for your training, just as it does to train nurses and teachers. Don't answer me now. Think about it. And, in the meantime, I would suggest that you urge your mother to see this solicitor for herself and to find out exactly how she is left. It would probably be wise for you and a couple of your brothers to accompany her.'

Susan said nothing. She had, thought the Reverend Mother, very intelligent eyes, pale grey in colour and fringed with straw-coloured lashes. They did not enhance her face, did not lend any beauty to her plainness, but no one who looked into those eyes could fail to see a potential.

'I'll think about what you said, Reverend Mother.' And then, half to herself, she muttered, 'I suppose that I would safe in a convent.' She gave a quick glance across at the nun. 'I mean that I don't suppose that Mam would make me marry Mr McCarthy if I was planning on being a nun.' There was a silence for a couple of seconds and then she rose slowly to her feet.

The Reverend Mother stood up, also. She liked this girl very much and was willing to do what she could for her, but safety had not been on offer. She said nothing, however, but pressed the bell for Sister Bernadette, sent good wishes and renewed sympathy to Mrs Mulcahy and then turned back to her work.

There had been, she thought, something very odd about that remark, 'I suppose that I would safe in a convent'. Was the reference really to a possible offer of marriage from her father's friend Mr McCarthy, or did it allude to something quite different. She thought about the matter on and off as she wrote twenty 'thank-you' letters, managing, with the ease of long practice, to make each one sound different and personal to the recipient.

After half an hour, she put down her pen and glanced at the clock on the mantelpiece. Nine o'clock. Not too late. Her cousin would probably not be going to bed for another hour or two. But how could she talk in privacy? She stood up, stretched herself and then decided.

'Thank you, Miss Clayton,' she said as the telephonist expressed a conviction that Mrs Murphy would still be up and would be delighted to talk to the Reverend Mother. She waited, holding the receiver to her ear, listening with interest to the background comments from the telephone exchange ladies: *'She's up late, thought they all went to bed at six o'clock . . . They'd be praying all night, that's what I've heard . . . Not a bit of it . . . how would they be fit for teaching those bold young rashers if they'd been up all night . . .'* and then there were a few clicks and Lucy came on the phone.

The Reverend Mother was ready, immediately greeting her in French. When she and Lucy were girls they had spent a year with cousins in Bordeaux and both still spoke fluent, idiomatic French. Miss Clayton may have studied French as a schoolgirl but she would be unlikely to be able to keep up. Nevertheless, the Reverend Mother persisted until she heard a click and the light buzzing sound disappeared from the line. Lucy heard it at the same moment.

'Thank goodness, I was beginning to run out of family news; my French is getting rusty. She did hang on for a long time, didn't she? Wonder whether she has a French dictionary. Now what have you really telephoned about?'

'I wanted to ask Rupert a question, well, to ask you to ask him.' Rupert, she knew, would probably be reading the *Irish Times* from cover to cover at this time in the evening. He was a man of regular habits. Read the *Cork Examiner* while digesting his meal and chatting to Lucy, then flicked through the *Law Journal* and, by this time of the evening, would have settled down to study the articles in the *Irish Times*.

'I'll try. You'd better make it interesting, though. He's reading an article about Stanley Baldwin, and shouting comments about it – don't know why he's so concerned.'

'I just want his opinion of a Mr O'Sullivan on Pope's Quay – one of his profession,' she added. Rupert tended to have a top-lofty view of the solicitors in Cork and might not easily recognize such a common name, especially one who was practising, not in the hallowed precincts of the South Mall, but from the obscurity of the north side of the river and on the fringes of Shandon.

She listened to the click of Lucy's heels and resigned herself for a wait. Rupert might well have fallen asleep, despite his interest in Stanley Baldwin, or he might prove recalcitrant about giving a view on a fellow solicitor, or he might, in a post-prandial haze, have difficulty in recollecting such an obscure personage. What she was not prepared for, however, was a masculine voice in her ear, saying, quietly, 'Good evening, Reverend Mother.'

'Good evening, Rupert.' The Reverend Mother did not waste time with meaningless apologies at having interrupted him. No point in saying what you didn't mean, she had decided a very long time ago and in general she kept to that resolution.

'As to your question,' he said, 'I would advise you to have nothing to do with the subject.' He spoke with heavy deliberation.

'I see.' The Reverend Mother followed his cautious lead.

'Certainly no investment.'

'I see,' she said again. The choice of the word 'investment' was an interesting one. Surely investment meant that money would be involved. This was unexpected and most probably very significant. Rupert was a cautious man. He would not use the word 'certainly' unless that word was the only one that served his purpose. She wondered how to prolong the conversation without alarming him.

'A young friend of mine has been thinking about training to be a lawyer,' she said. 'You have probably heard me talk of her, one of the cleverest pupils that I have ever taught. What would you say are the most important qualities that a lawyer, a solicitor, needs?'

'Probity,' he said without hesitation and she could hear the sound of relief in his voice. Her reference to Eileen had reassured him. 'You see, my dear Reverend Mother, a solicitor bears a great trust. If a house is sold, a house bought, in the main it is the solicitor who will hold that money. He will hold it in a special clients' account, that's if he is wise and honest, but if he is not honest, if he is easily tempted and lacks probity, then that money can sometimes be used for other matters. Mainly, I would say, with the intention of paying it back, but sometimes, unfortunately, with the intention to deceive and to defraud.'

'I see,' said the Reverend Mother thoughtfully. 'Well, I shall certainly have a chat with her about that point, though I would think that she is a person of high ideals. Her hopes would be to benefit the poor by the use of her professional knowledge.'

'That's good to hear.' Rupert was enjoying himself, she could hear the expansive tone of his voice and imagined him drawing on his cigar. 'Certainly ignorance and diffidence makes the life of an embezzler an easy one. Never be afraid to ask a question, Reverend Mother. If anyone has money belonging to you, then ask and ask again until you are satisfied with the answers. And, if I were you, I would give that advice to anyone you know. I don't believe in blind trust, you know. If ever you have trust in anyone, make sure that trust is built on a rock and survey it with a pair of binoculars from time to time. Myself, I don't believe in trust,' he repeated. 'I believe that the good Lord gave us brains to assess information, gave us a tongue to ask questions, and gave us friends and relations to point us in the right direction.' Rupert finished with a laugh and probably another quick puff on his cigar.

'Thank you, Rupert, that's extremely useful,' she said. As he went to call back Lucy to the phone she pondered on the position of Mrs Mulcahy. The house at Montenotte had been bought and paid for, according to Susan, but there was money from the sale of the house on Shandon hill, the sale of the furniture and the income from the prosperous business. This solicitor on Pope's Quay held the will, did he also hold the money?

TEN

Issue of General Order No. 14
'No man of any rank who is addicted to drink will be
permitted to remain a member of the Civic Guard.
This is a penalty which will be rigidly enforced.'

Patrick had made an appointment with Mr O'Sullivan for
nine o'clock in the morning so as to see the solicitor
before he left to attend the funeral of his client, possibly
one of his few clients, thought Patrick as he went down the
basement steps of an insurance company, following the sign
that said: 'Ignatius O'Sullivan, Solicitor'.

There were two rooms in the cellar. One door was firmly
shut, but the other stood wide open. Patrick went in there and
looked around. It was sparsely furnished with a couple of
chairs, a table and on the table was a hand bell, with a hand-
written notice 'PLEASE RING FOR ASSISTANCE' placed
beside it. No typewriter, no filing cabinet, no sign of a clerk.
Patrick gave a swift glance at the mould-covered window and
the dusty floor. In a very small way, this solicitor; perhaps
that was what had attracted Mr Mulcahy to him. Looked as
though he would not charge much. A man like the merchant,
who had made his money from the waste products of the meat
market, would not want to waste it on a fancy lawyer in South
Mall. Patrick picked up the bell, shook it vigorously and then
realized that the other door had already opened and a man
was standing right behind him. Surprisingly old; I had expected
him to be about my own age, at the beginning of his career,
thought Patrick. The voice on the telephone had been young,
slightly high pitched. Very assured, though, shaking hands in
a brisk but formal way.

'Good morning, inspector, you are very punctual, come into
my office.'

The office also was fairly bare. A chair for the solicitor, and

a couple on the other side of the table. An elderly typewriter
– so no clerk, no filing cabinet here either, but there were
some shelves that held five, rather battered looking black tin
boxes. There was a smell of paint in the air and Patrick could
see that one of the five had been newly painted, the white
letters slightly dripping down the black background. It bore
the legend: *Estate of Henry Mulcahy decd.* And he wondered
if that had been done for his benefit. The other four black
boxes preserved their anonymity, although they looked well
used and no dust had accumulated on them. The solicitor lifted
down the Mulcahy box and placed it solemnly in the centre
of the table, moving aside the typewriter to accommodate it.
Patrick took off his badge and held it out for perusal and Mr
O'Sullivan smiled politely.

'I know you well, by sight and by repute, inspector,' he
said, waving away the badge. 'Now what can I help you with?
What about a sherry. I won't tell anyone. I know that you're
human like the rest of us.'

'No, thank you, Mr O'Sullivan,' said Patrick politely and
then, almost without drawing a breath: 'You've heard of the
tragic death of Mr Mulcahy.'

The solicitor bowed his head in acknowledgement.

'From his widow?' asked Patrick with a slight degree of
curiosity. Among the wealthy families of Blackrock and
Montenotte, he had learned, the custom would be to summon
the family solicitor in the event of any crisis, a death, a robbery,
a problem with a recalcitrant son who was in trouble with the
police, an insurance claim or even an unexpected win on the
races. But amongst the denizens of Shandon Street, or Barrack
Street where he had been raised, this sort of professional help
would be fairly unknown, even in the case of those who had
money. The solicitor was unexpected, somehow. A man like
Henry Mulcahy who had risen the hard way, had been a barrow
boy at one stage, men like that didn't often go to the luxury
of having a solicitor.

'No, not from the widow.' There was almost a hint of a
. . . not exactly a smile, but a twitch of the lips. Mrs Mulcahy
would have not thought of sending for the solicitor. Patrick
could have betted on that. 'No, not Mrs Mulcahy, poor

lady. I heard it from Mr McCarthy, a trading partner of the deceased.'

'And when was that, sir?' Patrick had his notebook out. 'Trading partner' – he added a question mark at the end of the two words. *I must find out if that is true.*

'Must have been Friday evening,' said the solicitor after a moment's hesitation.

'Friday evening, you must have been working late, sir.' It would have been eight o'clock in the evening by the time that news had broken to the widow.

There was a moment's silence. 'He came around to my private residence.'

'I see.' Patrick made another note while he thought about this. Rather strange. It seemed as though the two men were on friendly terms. He must meet this Mr McCarthy. A quick word after the funeral, he thought. Half the business in Cork is done after funerals; he had once heard someone say that and he had often noticed the little clusters standing closely together, at a good distance from others, and speaking low and softly with many backward glances.

'And Mr McCarthy is an old friend of the Mulcahy family, I suppose.'

'That's right. And, of course, he is executor of Mr Henry Mulcahy's will.' The solicitor pulled the tin box towards him and took out an impressively large bunch of keys, very old keys. Patrick eyed them sharply, wondering whether he bought them as a job lot in the Coal Quay market. Many were quite rusted and looked as though they had not been near a lock in an age. Mr O'Sullivan selected one that was bright and shining and inserted it into the padlock on the tin box. He did not open it, though, just paused, looking enquiringly at Patrick and awaiting a nod from him before he clicked open the lock.

Brand new padlock, brand new key, recently opened, I could bet, thought Patrick. The room was full of dust, but the tin box was shiningly clean. He leaned forward as the lid was raised. Only one item within it, a parchment scroll tied up with a pink linen ribbon.

'The last will and testament of the late gentleman,' said Mr

O'Sullivan picking it out and seeming to check the box for any other contents.

'Last will?' queried Patrick.

The solicitor laughed gently. 'Just a legal expression, inspector. To the best of my knowledge and belief, the unfortunate gentleman made only one will and this is the one that I hold in my hand.'

'And the date when it was signed?' Patrick inserted the words 'will' and 'date' onto a fresh page of his notebook.

Mr O'Sullivan hesitated a little, glanced at the will and then back at the inspector. 'A week today,' he said and pursed his lips as though to whistle a little tune.

'A week today.' Patrick was startled. 'Last Tuesday. But that's the day when we assume that he was killed.'

'So I believe. But the body was only discovered on Friday. As I've been told,' he added quickly.

'And he came here to make his will.' Patrick gave a quick glance around at the empty shelves and the dust that lay thick all over the flat surfaces and even clung to draped spiders' webs from the pale green walls.

'I took his instructions here, but the will itself was, in fact, signed in his office in Shandon Street.'

'You had known the deceased, well? Or just recently? For how long?' Patrick stretched his legs beneath the desk and encountered an obstacle. He moved a toe carefully along the length between the legs of the table. A solid wall of tin boxes were piled up in there.

Mr O'Sullivan had considered this question for a long moment before replying, 'Mr McCarthy introduced him.' And then as Patrick still waited, he finished by saying, 'A few weeks ago, I believe. Mr Mulcahy wanted to make a will, mentioned the matter to Mr McCarthy who brought him to see me, on a Monday, I believe. We discussed the matter very fully and I arranged to bring it up to his house the next day once I had drafted it.'

'Could I see it?' Patrick held out a hand for the piece of parchment while his mind worked rapidly over this unexpectedly close link between the making of the will and the violent death of Henry Mulcahy.

'Certainly.' The solicitor unscrolled the document, placing the telephone on one corner and inkwell on the opposing corner. 'You will see that it has been signed, below Mr Mulcahy's own signature, by two people, Mr McCarthy, and Mr Hayes. They do not see the will, just testified that they have seen the testator, in this case, Mr Henry Mulcahy of Shandon Street and Montenotte, sign this will in their presence. I usually carry with me this piece of card which covers over the testamentary details of the document.' He produced it from the corner of the table in front of him. 'And you can see, inspector, that one of the witnesses is the executor to the will and the other is the auctioneer who was in the house at the time – it could, of course, have been anyone, a servant or anyone, even a passer-by on the street.'

Patrick read the will. It did not take long. Basically, it just left everything to his wife. He would have thought that a man like Henry Mulcahy would have wanted to control what happened to his fortune after his death. He turned back a few pages of his notebook where he had written down the details of the Mulcahy family, names and ages. In a few years' time, four of the twelve children would have reached the age of twenty-one, would be adult in the eyes of the law. There was no provision in this will for them, for any money or property to be left to them, nor were there any stipulations for the education and maintenance of the younger children. Henry Mulcahy had shown an enormous trust in his wife. Except that he had appointed this Mr McCarthy as his executor. Could that be of significance?

'I wonder whether I could have a copy of the will.' Patrick looked around at the bare office. There had been no sign of the arrival of a clerk and he guessed that the man worked on his own. 'Or if you would be kind enough to let me have a sheet of foolscap paper then I will just copy it out myself, if I may,' he continued. 'It's a short document from what you say; it won't take me long.'

There was an oddly reluctant look on the man's face. A slight hesitation, a certain stiffening of the posture, a moment's silence before Mr O'Sullivan opened the drawer in front of him and handed out a sheet of slightly crumpled paper. Patrick set to work immediately, rejecting the proffered pen for a soft, rubber-tipped pencil that he kept in his breast pocket. The contents of the will, the legalese, all this did not interest him so much as the man's signature. Patrick had a talent for drawing and he did his best with the signature, stopping, from time to time, to reverse the pencil and rub out a letter that did not appear to follow faithfully the shape of the original. Then he did the same with the signatures of the two witnesses, Mr McCarthy and Mr Hayes and held the result to the dim light from the very dirt-encrusted window. He looked with care at Henry Mulcahy's signature, comparing his version with the original written with very black ink on the parchment. He was reasonably contented with his work. He would, he thought, recognize the man's hand if he saw it again. Quite a strong, olden day style of writing, the 'H' had a distinctive curl that was almost a spiral, but the 'M' did not share this, but ended with an abrupt and very straight line. Odd that a man would do the one, but not the other. Patrick examined the other two signatures. The auctioneer's untidy scrawl, his signature Edward Hayes stretched across the page, but Richard McCarthy had written his name with great care. The handwriting of a man who did not do much writing; each letter carefully made as though in copying a headline from an exercise book. His had been easy to copy as, unlike the dead man's signature, there had been little individuality in the hand. Patrick carefully placed the sheet of foolscap paper into his attaché case and looked back across the table at the solicitor. Did he imagine it or was there a slightly uneasy look about the man.

'Did Mr Mulcahy ask for advice on the making of the will, sir?' he enquired. 'I suppose,' he continued, 'people do ask for your professional advice on a matter like this, don't they?'

'Some do, some don't. Depends on the person. Some know their own mind long before they approach you, others are still dithering weeks later. And of course there are some who are for ever changing their wills.' He smiled thinly. 'Now they are a boon to a hardworking solicitor, inspector.'

'But not Mr Mulcahy.' Drafted his will on Monday, dead on Tuesday, thought Patrick as the man nodded. There used to be a rhyme chanted in the playground when he was a small boy. What was it? *Solomon Grundy, Born on Monday, Christened on Tuesday, Married on Wednesday, Took ill on Thursday, Worse on Friday, Dead on Saturday, Buried on Sunday.* As a child he had always imagined that Solomon Grundy's early death was due to his early marriage. But Henry Mulcahy had married at the reasonable age of mid-thirties, had chosen a much younger wife who bore him twelve children. It was only after he made his will that his death occurred.

Patrick rose to his feet. 'Thank you for your time, Mr O'Sullivan. I shall see you, no doubt, at the funeral.'

'Yes, indeed, inspector. A sad occasion, very sad, indeed. All those fatherless children!' Despite his words, there was a relaxed note in his voice. The man was relieved that there were no further questions from the police. A smooth, anxious-to-please sort of fellow, thought Patrick, as he made his way up the cellar stairs. But if that relief was due to an impression that he had hoodwinked a young and inexperienced policeman, then it was premature. Patrick had a strong impression that something was wrong and that this solicitor would need an eye kept on him.

Quite a big funeral, but probably mainly neighbours, he decided as he stood looking around after the service had ended. Decidedly lacking in important civic dignitaries. The presence of a reporter from the *Cork Examiner* was due more to the notoriety of the murder rather than a desire to offer tribute. There were no long queues to shake hands with the widow and her children and he was able to pay his respects with almost no waiting time.

'A very sad and difficult time for you, Mrs Mulcahy,' he said, shaking hands with the woman and the two daughters. She had a black shawl around her head, though the two girls wore hats. He nodded at the boys. They all wore black blazers, Farranferris School uniform, he recognised, and black ties and black armbands. No tears, he noticed. Even the youngest boy stood silent and solemn, shocked but dry-eyed. All eyes swivelled, though, when a man in shiningly-new black clothes came across to them. A heavy man, his metal-tipped boots rang on the stone of the pavement, lending emphasis to each

step. Younger than he seemed at a distance, though. The dead
man's widow and children watched him impassively and
none took a step forward or offered to introduce him. Patrick
scrutinised the high colour of the face as the man shook him
vigorously by the hand.

'Good of you to come, inspector. I'm Richard McCarthy.'
He spoke as though he were a close relative.

'Ah, yes,' said Patrick. 'I understand from the solicitor that
you were a partner to the late Mr Mulcahy, a working partner,'
he added after a moment when the man looked taken aback.
One of the girls moved her head then and looked sharply at
the newcomer.

'Yes, well, I suppose we did work together, a little, on an
informal base.' The words were guarded. 'Nothing official,
though, no legal documents, nothing like that.'

'But you would know his business?' Patrick had an eye on
the girl, Susan, he thought, though he couldn't swear to it.
Mrs Mulcahy had not introduced any of her children to him.
Yes, he thought from Joe's description that this must be Susan.
She was looking scornful, he thought, her thin lips compressed
as though to hide a smile, her eyes sharp and intent on Mr
McCarthy's face.

'Pretty well.' The man was still cautious. He, too, glanced
towards the girl. Patrick took a few steps away from the
mourning family and, when the man followed, lowered his
voice to a confidential murmur.

'And he was doing well, was he?'

'Pretty well. But this death has come at a bad time for
him.' This time it was Mr McCarthy who moved. He walked
away, picked up a small paper bag that was lying on the
stone-flagged church yard, crumpled it up and then placed
it in a bin full of dead flowers. Patrick followed and stood
beside him. The unpleasant smell of decay reminded him
of the body in the trunk. Odd how badly flowers smelled
when they began to rot.

'A bad time,' he queried.

'The man was what we call a *chancer*, inspector. Things
happen in our way of business. Something goes wrong with
the mixture, the skins mightn't be good ones, and when you

buy in the thousands, just as Henry Mulcahy did, then you can't check every skin, and then there's the selling of them. There mightn't be a sale after all the hard work, all the money spent on them. Or something might go wrong with the delivery. He exported a lot of skins to England. That was his main market. Ships can sink; rats can get in among the goods; salt water can spoil the leather. But Henry never kept any money back, never made provision for losses. Make; spend, that was the way the man worked and sometimes "the spend" came before "the make". That bloody big house he built for himself on Montenotte, well, I can tell you straight, he couldn't afford it. There'll be a lot of debts to be paid once probate has been granted.'

Patrick nodded. *You know a lot about the man's affairs*, was his thought, but he did not comment. He would gather as much information as he could from this Richard McCarthy. His eyes went to the figure of Mr O'Sullivan. Odd the link between the young man beside him, uncouth, uneducated and the suave gentility of the solicitor who was at that moment shaking hands with Mrs Mulcahy. The word 'probate' and 'granted' had tripped fluently off the lips of the young merchant in front of him, though most of his speech was rough. Somewhere or somehow, the two had met and Mr Mulcahy had been intro-duced, had been persuaded into making a will, naming as executor, his young friend, business partner, rival – which was true, he wondered as he looked across into the graveyard. Soon there would be a move to carry the coffin down to that gaping hole that he could see in the distance. The grave diggers were used to waiting while the condolences were got through, but once the handshaking stopped then they would want to get moving on the main business of the day. Henry Mulcahy had been dead for almost a week. It was time that he was buried.

'So do you think that one of his business rivals might have killed him, someone that he owed money to, is that right, Mr McCarthy?'

'You'll have to give us the answer to that, inspector. I don't know nothing about it.'

Alarmed, belligerent? Patrick ran over in his mind the books on law that he had read for his examinations. He didn't remember anything about the duties and powers of an executor. Nevertheless, if an executor and a solicitor were in league with each other, and had only Mrs Mulcahy to deal with, then perhaps assets could be concealed.

But was the dead man rich enough to be worth a murder?

'Perhaps you could help me with your local knowledge, Mr McCarthy. Who else is in the hide and skin business in Cork?' Easy enough to find that out from Guy's Directory, but the man was anxious to appear helpful and he reeled off a list of names, including wool merchants and leather dealers among the tanners. Patrick listened and nodded. His face, he was sure, still looked attentive, but his eye had been caught by someone who had just walked jauntily up to the mourning family and was busily shaking hands, not just with the widow, but also with the family. Tall, long-legged, tweed breeches tucked into shining leather boots, jaunty cap perched on the top of the head. Some might have taken the latest arrival for a youth, but Patrick recognized the face instantly. He saw her head turn towards him.

'Thank you, Mr McCarthy, you have been very useful. Thank you for your help.'

The man took the hint and went off, leaving Patrick standing there. He frowned; there was something familiar about that jacket and those tweed breeches. But then he smoothed out his brows. Eyes would be upon him and he prided himself on showing the world a face that held nothing but polite neutrality. Eileen MacSweeney, what on earth was she doing here?

She must have felt his eyes on her, looked across, said a few more words to Susan Mulcahy and then came up to him and said in a rather informal way, 'Hallo, Patrick.'

He looked at her disapprovingly. He didn't like the way that she dressed in trousers and tweed jacket, her air nonchalant and self-confident. Even the deep shine on her boots annoyed him obscurely. Who did she think she was? Countess Markowitz?

'Good morning, Miss MacSweeney,' he said, and didn't trouble to hide the disapproval in his voice.

'Good morning, inspector,' she said and he wished that he had not noticed the mocking note in her voice. It made him feel awkward and ill-at-ease.

'You are well, I hope.' He remembered now. She was the

one who had rescued Fred Mulcahy, had been, he could guess, involved in all that business out in Douglas. He wondered where young Fred was now and had a strong suspicion that the girl in front of him knew perfectly well the whereabouts of a man who was not just wanted because of the Republican raid on the barracks of Douglas, but also because of suspicion that he might have been involved in the killing of his own father.

'You know the Mulcahy family?' he asked.

She raised a pair of strong black eyebrows as though slightly astonished at the question.

'I know Susan Mulcahy,' she said with the air of being obliging. 'We sat the Intermediate Certificate together. It was held at the high school for girls.'

Eileen would be a few years younger than Susan, he guessed, but he supposed that she might have sat for the intermediate certificate at an earlier age than the usual fifteen or sixteen. She had a name, he knew, of being very clever. His mother would know all about her; the whole of Barrack Street was a great admirer of Maureen MacSweeney's talented daughter. He found her immensely annoying, interfering with things that she knew nothing of. Putting her own life and other people's in danger.

'So Fred Mulcahy is here for the funeral of his father, is he?' he asked, casting a glance towards the sorrowing widow, surrounded by her two daughters and nine sons. Fine looking boys, he had heard a few whispers to that effect, but their presence made it even more noticeable that Fred, the eldest of the family, reputedly his mother's darling, was not present to support her during this terrible ordeal.

'Is he?' Eileen, to his annoyance, swung around and surveyed the mourning family, appearing to scan their ranks and then turned a pair of large, innocent, grey eyes upon him. 'Not that I can see,' she said, turning back to him.

Play actor, thought Patrick irritably. 'His mother could do with him here today, would welcome his presence,' he added, conscious that, despite himself, a measure of anger had come into his voice. He thought of his own mother and knew that he could never have allowed her to parade in front of the curious glances of the whole city of Cork without the support of a son by her side. He thanked his lucky stars that he had never been tempted to join in with the Republicans. Stupid enough four years ago, he thought, but idiotic now that a treaty had been signed and the majority of the country only wanted to settle down and live their lives in peace. Who cared about the six counties of Northern Ireland? Let them sort matters out for themselves.

'Perhaps he didn't think that it would be safe.' There was an ironical note in her voice and he had an uneasy feeling that she thought herself twice as clever as he was, and that she was probably correct in that.

'Perhaps he's right.' He endeavoured to copy her tone of voice, but only succeeded, to his own ear, in sounding bad-tempered. She looked at him for a long few seconds, almost as though she were weighing him up.

'What exactly is Fred Mulcahy wanted for, Patrick?' she was trying to sweet-talk him, he felt. There was a persuasive note in her voice, but he wished she did not sound as though she were older and wiser than he. 'There's no real evidence, is there, about the Douglas business? And he had nothing whatsoever to do with his father's death. The man was dead and crawling with maggots when Fred shot him. He just did that because he was a bit upset.'

'If you are in touch with Fred Mulcahy,' said Patrick trying to preserve a tone of remote authority, 'then the best service that you can do for him would be to tell him to report to the police and to give his explanations to them in person, not to send messages by a girl, by a third party,' he amended and added, 'I wouldn't like to see you waste your time.'

'Oh, that's all right, Patrick. I don't mind. I wouldn't like to see you make a mess of this case, wasting your valuable time over someone who had nothing to do with it, while the real murderer gets away with it,' she said sweetly. 'Now I'd better be getting back to work. We're very busy at the printers, today.' She turned and scanned the small crowd of sympathisers that still lingered in the churchyard.

'And if you want a bit of advice, Patrick,' she said, 'I'd turn my attention to someone who actually gains from Mr Mulcahy's death, someone who could quickly pick up some contracts while the widow, poor woman, is sorting herself out.'

ELEVEN

Kevin O'Higgins, Minister for Justice
'The internal politics and political controversies of the
country are not your concern. You will serve with the
same imperturbable discipline and with increasing
efficiency any Government which has the support of
the majority of the people's elected representatives.
Party will, no doubt, succeed party in the ebb and flow
of the political tide. New issues will arise and the
landmarks of today will disappear, but you will remain
steadfast and devoted in the service of the people, and
of any government which it may please the people to
return to power. That is the real meaning of
democracy, Government of the people by the people
through their elected representatives. It is the only
barrier between mankind and anarchy.'

Patrick arrived at the convent just after four in the
afternoon. He was apologetic and slightly shamefaced
when Sister Bernadette showed him into the Reverend
Mother's room.

'I'm interrupting you, Reverend Mother. I should have
telephoned,' he said. 'But it wasn't planned. I just met Dr
Scher and he told me that he was going to drop into the convent
to see Sister Assumpta and so I thought, well, I thought that
I might come along and perhaps . . .'

'You are very welcome, Patrick,' said the Reverend Mother.
He didn't look well, she thought. There were dark shadows
under his eyes. This case was a difficult and unpleasant one
and had huge coverage in the papers who were running per-
mutations of lurid headlines ranging from: 'GRUESOME
DISCOVERY'; 'MACABRE FINDING'; 'BODY IN
TRUNK'; 'CORPSE DELIVERED TO CONVENT', accord-
ing to the style of the newspaper or periodical. She felt very

sorry for Patrick. Life had not been easy, never was easy for
these children from the slums. Many slipped into despair,
dissolution, prostitution and crime; some emigrated and some
ended up drowned in the River Lee; very few struggled through
to success in their native city. And those who did, in her
experience, mostly bore the scar of insecurity and took life
with intense seriousness. Would there be a new world now
that Ireland had got its freedom? So far, there seemed little
sign of it. She sighed and turned her attention to this puzzling
case. There was, as she often reminded herself, limits to what
she in her convent could achieve, but sometimes a listening
ear could be important.

'And what about Fred now, Patrick?' she asked.

In answer, he took from his pocket an envelope. He smoothed
it carefully and then handed it to her.

'Read that, Reverend Mother,' he said.

The envelope had been professionally slit with a sharp
paperknife and she edged the sheet out carefully. It had rough
edges and looked as though it were torn from a child's school
jotter. She held it for a moment, listening to the voices outside
in the corridor and then turned to Patrick.

'It's Dr Scher,' she said. 'Have you any objections to him
seeing it?'

He shook his head. He looked more relaxed when the door
opened and the small, round figure bustled in, placed his bag
on the windowsill and went straight to the fire, holding out
his hands to warm them and then fiddling with the damper,
and embarking on a vigorous riddling of the smouldering coals.
Somehow the atmosphere in the room had lightened with the
arrival of Dr Scher. Patrick was, she thought, completely at
ease with him and trusted him implicitly.

'Just been having a chat with Sister Bernadette, Reverend
Mother,' he said. 'Fear not, you haven't been forgotten. Sister
Bernadette had delayed your tea because she knew how much
you would like to share it with me.'

Probably been stewing the tea on the stove to get it strong
enough for Dr Scher's taste, thought the Reverend Mother, but
aloud she said, 'How is Sister Assumpta?'

'Passing gently and slowly to a better world,' he said with

the kindness that she admired in him. It had often taken her aback that such a bustling, energetic man with a sharp tongue could show such compassion and patience towards elderly and senile patients.

She bowed her head and allowed a moment to pass before turning to the letter in her hand. 'Patrick wishes us both to read this letter,' she said. 'Shall I read it aloud?'

She read it carefully, first to herself and then to both of her listeners.

> To whom it may concern: I, Frederick Mulcahy, wish to inform the Civic Guards that I was the one who killed my father. I swear that no other person was involved in this deed. By the time that you read this confession I will be on my way to a foreign place and will be beyond the reach of the justice system of the corrupt government which has betrayed its citizens, the people of Ireland.

'A confession. Well, these lads and lassies of the IRA do like to make life easier for you lot at the barracks, don't they? Up the Republic,' said Dr Scher flippantly.

'A confession is not too much good without an arrest,' said Patrick grimly.

'Doesn't go into any detail about the actual means of death, does he?' said the Reverend Mother. 'What is the position about that, Patrick? Who does know how Mr Mulcahy was killed?'

'Only myself, the superintendent, my sergeant, Joe and Dr Scher.'

'And God in his heaven, and, of course, his deputy down here, the Reverend Mother,' said Dr Scher.

She gave him a reproving glance before saying, 'I find it of significance that Fred did not say how he killed his father.'

'Do you think he is really on his way to foreign parts, Patrick?' asked Dr Scher.

'There's been a bit of violence in Douglas,' said Patrick. 'You may have heard of it. The Republicans smuggled in some guns and a gang came over from Passage West. The army were over there pretty quickly. Came down from the Victoria

Barracks, five or six lorry loads of them. Took a few prisoners, though not Fred Mulcahy. But I'm not sure about this "foreign parts" business. There's been no sightings of any foreign ships as far as I know. The navy put a barricade across the mouth of the harbour, down there by Carrigaline.' He hesitated for a moment and a tinge of colour crept into his pale cheeks.

'There's something else, too. I was at the funeral of Henry Mulcahy this morning and a friend of Fred Mulcahy turned up. Apparently she is also a friend of Susan Mulcahy. This young lady came up to me. You know her, Reverend Mother; she came to school here; it's Eileen MacSweeney from Barrack Street, well, she spoke to me of Fred Mulcahy, tried to persuade me that he had nothing to do with the murder of his father.'

'Sweet on him, is she? Pretty girl, that little Eileen.' Dr Scher gave a sentimental sigh.

'Well, I don't know about that.' Patrick's flush grew to a deeper red. 'All I know was that I got a strong impression that she felt he was in danger of being arrested by me. I don't think that she would have bothered if he were on his way to America. I certainly got the impression that Fred Mulcahy was in hiding somewhere and that she was trying to persuade me to take up a different line of enquiry, that she was trying to see whether it would be safe for him to come out of hiding.'

'So you think that, when he wrote that confession, wrote that letter that he "jumped the gun" as our American friends would say. What do you think, Reverend Mother?' Dr Scher looked from one to the other and then his head swivelled and he looked expectant as there was a sound of trolley wheels from the corridor. He went across to the door, flung it wide open and stood there, beaming.

'You're an angel straight from Heaven, Sister Bernadette. I'm just dying for a decent cup of tea. You should taste the stuff that they dole out in the police station. Not fit for man or beast.'

'A very melodramatic young man, Fred Mulcahy,' said the Reverend Mother, taking care to pitch her voice beneath the clamour made by Dr Scher, so that her words were heard only by Patrick. She returned the letter to him and tucked her hands into her sleeves while she brooded on this strange confession, accepting the cup of tea from Sister Bernadette, but shaking her head to the offer of cake.

'I'll help myself to some bread and butter in a little while, sister,' she said and Sister Bernadette, taking the hint, vanished from the room.

The Reverend Mother swallowed a little tea and then looked across at Patrick.

'I suppose you sometimes get false confessions at the barracks, don't you?' she queried, a tentative note in her voice.

'Occasionally, perhaps.' Patrick sounded dubious. 'There's a drunk old man who keeps coming and asking if we want him for a shooting. He spent a night in the cells once and he liked the breakfast that they gave him – the superintendent didn't fancy his fried egg and rasher that morning and so they gave it to the fellow in the cell and he's never forgotten how good it tasted. But apart from that . . .'

'I see,' said the Reverend Mother. Her cousin had lent her a few of the Sherlock Holmes novels by Conan Doyle. There seemed to have been many false confessions in them, but perhaps the people of Cork lived such dangerous lives that they did not run unnecessary risks for the sake of drama.

But for the sake of a very dearly loved mother? That was possible. And Fred Mulcahy had seemed like a very melodramatic young man. What was it that the boy had muttered so savagely? Once again she recalled his words. He had felt that his mother had led a life of slavery. Had he feared that she had lifted an iron bar in a moment of desperation or a fit of anger and had struck her husband with it? And, in a state of panic, had hidden the body in an old trunk. Had that fear, that suspicion, worked on him to the degree that he had written out a confession before leaving the country?

'You think that Fred Mulcahy might have suspected someone else of doing it? One of his young brothers, his sisters or his mother even?' Dr Scher chewed vigorously on the currant cake which Sister Bernadette made every week to feed important convent visitors, like the doctor, the bank manager, and, of course, the bishop or his secretary. 'Who was in the house that afternoon when Mr Mulcahy was last seen alive, Patrick?' he said, once he had swallowed his mouthful.

Patrick produced his notebook.

'Well, apart from Mrs Mulcahy and Susan, there was the servant, Bridie and Mr Hayes the auctioneer. He and Mr Mulcahy went from top to bottom of the house – it was crowded with furniture as the two houses that the family had formerly occupied had been cleared out once the sale of one had gone through.'

'Must have been a lively set of houses with twelve children running around upstairs, crossing from one attic to another,' commentated Dr Scher with a smile while the Reverend Mother brooded on some of the numerous children from her school, occupying only one room or two rooms, but where the family was often as large. The Mulcahys were lucky that their father's business successes enabled him to purchase first a three-storey house and then a second house as more children came along. She wondered whether Fred Mulcahy had ever thought of that.

'And then when they had looked at everything and notes had been made, Mr Mulcahy went into his office with the auctioneer. That was just about when a man knocked on the door and said that he was Mr O'Sullivan, the solicitor. Bridie, apparently, showed him into the office and she overheard something about a will. By the way,' said Patrick, looking up, 'all of this was corroborated in my interview with Mr O'Sullivan, the solicitor, when I saw him this morning, before the funeral.'

'O'Sullivan, I haven't heard of a solicitor of that name. I thought that I knew all of the South Mall crowd,' said Dr Scher.

'Pope's Quay,' said the Reverend Mother briefly. 'Go on, Patrick.'

'And Mr Richard McCarthy arrived soon after the solicitor. The will was signed and the signatures were witnessed by the servant and by Mr Hayes the auctioneer.

'How long did they stay?' she asked.

'Apparently at that stage, Mrs Mulcahy sent the servant, Bridie, to ask if they wanted a cup of tea, but that was refused. Soon afterwards Mr Hayes, the auctioneer, left. They thought the solicitor, Mr O'Sullivan, perhaps accompanied by Mr McCarthy, went about five minutes after that, but they were a bit vague about whether they had heard the door slam or not. They did think that when the three men had gone, that Mr Mulcahy went upstairs by himself and that was all Mrs Mulcahy knew. She said she was sure that it was just one set of footsteps on the stairs. She imagined, when she didn't see her husband later on that he had gone back to Montenotte. Oh, and a neighbour gave evidence that she thought that young Fred Mulcahy had been there earlier, but she knew nothing about when he had left. She said that he often came to see his mother at times when he knew his father would not be there. So he may well have been around the house earlier, but would probably have slipped out when his father arrived.'

'So when Mr Mulcahy met his death only the three women were present. Is that what you're saying, Patrick?' asked Dr Scher.

'Well, that's the way it looks,' said Patrick. 'But if I've learned anything over the last couple of years, it is that people are very unreliable about this sort of thing. These three women, the mother, the daughter and the servant, were all very busy. They were sure about Mr Hayes, as he came into the kitchen to say goodbye and to tell them that the men would be around in about half an hour for the furniture. They actually heard him go out of the hall door and heard it close behind him and Susan heard him cranking up his car, and drive off, but they were a bit vague about the solicitor and about Mr McCarthy.'

'And, of course, they said nothing about Fred, I suppose, did they? Poor things! Well, the mother and the sister, anyway. I don't suppose the servant would be too bothered lying for him, though, would she, Patrick?'

'That's where you are completely wrong, Dr Scher,' the Reverend Mother put in. 'Bridie had a lot to do with the up-bringing of Fred. His mother had four other children by the time that he was six years old. There were the twins, Susan and Sally. And the two next boys, John and Robert. Bridie loved all of the children, but Fred was her darling. She would,' said the Reverend Mother with great deliberation, 'give all to shield him, at all costs.' Even life itself, she thought and hoped that she was not becoming melodramatic in her old age. Her mind went back to Bridie and the poor dead baby, who had died even before it could be baptized. Fred, she had often thought, had almost taken the place of Bridie's own child.

'And he loved her, did he?' asked Dr Scher. 'I suppose that he did. It cuts both ways, usually. If she adored young Fred, then he probably kept a great affection for her, even when he had grown up. And, he hated his father. No one empties a revolver into a dead man's chest unless there is a lot of pent-up anger. If he had seen this Bridie pick up an iron bar and strike the man across the head, he might have helped to hide the body and then wrote that false confession when he knew, or thought he knew, that he was on his way to America, is that what you're thinking, Reverend Mother? You have to admit that there is something rather fine about a young man making a false confession in order to shield a servant in his parents' house.' There was a note of enthusiasm in his voice. A very sentimental man, Dr Scher, she thought, but she shook her head.

'No, I don't think that he knew anything about the body in the trunk, even if he had known that his father had been killed a few days earlier. I think that he genuinely thought that it would be full of guns. I was present and I know that once I lifted the lid that he shrank back. He gasped. He said something. I think it was, "I know nothing about this, nothing whatsoever." I may not have got the words quite right,' said the Reverend Mother, 'but the tone of utter horror in his voice is engraved on my mind.'

'And the shot, the way that he emptied his pistol into the body of his father?' Patrick, on the other hand, had no trace of sentimentality in him. Life had been too hard a struggle. He had never, even as a small child, liked stories. Sums, numbers and facts, these were what interested the seven-year-old Patrick Cashman.

'Pure melodrama,' scoffed Dr Scher. 'That didn't kill the man. Might have relieved the boy's feeling, but it didn't kill his father. Didn't even draw an ounce of blood from him. The man was already dead, for a couple of days at least.'

'And what about the blood on the breast of his coat?'

'I've been waiting for you to ask me about that, Reverend Mother. But the answer is that I'm not sure. It was old blood, a few days old, but it didn't come from the fatal blow which cracked the man's skull. That was the back of the head. Whether it was his blood, or someone else's blood, well, I can't tell you that. Someone else's, I would hazard a guess, but that is only because there seemed to be no opened wound on the man. Lots of old scars, but nothing that recent. Of course, he could have had a nosebleed and then cleaned up his nostrils carefully, afterwards. I did look, but saw nothing to indicate a nosebleed. Still, it's not something that I can rule out. And noses do bleed a lot.'

'Indeed,' said the Reverend Mother, thinking of the school playground and the nosebleeds which resulted from children running into each other or crashing against railings. 'I still think that Fred did not know his father was dead, or at least knew nothing about his body being put in a trunk. It might, of course, have been possible that he knew of the death, but did not know of the disposal of the body and that was what gave him the shock. However, if you were to ask my opinion, I would say that my impression was that he knew nothing of the killing of his father until that moment.'

This was greeted by a respectful silence which made her feel slightly conscious-stricken. Not a good thing for her to be so assertive. Patrick had to make up his own mind. She finished the tea in her cup and brooded on this murder. She hoped that the obvious solution was not the true one.

'I've got it,' said Dr Scher suddenly. 'Came to me in flash as soon as I had finished that second cup of tea. Great stuff, that tea. Well, this is what happened. After the three men had left the house, old man Mulcahy started throwing his weight around, shouting, being abusive to, say the daughter, Susan. She picks up an iron bar, hits him over the head, he falls to the ground, young Fred, who was hiding in the attic or something, comes running into the room to find his father stretched on the floor. His mother, protective of her son, as mothers are, tells him to get out, to get out quickly or he will be blamed. He goes, not knowing whether his father is unconscious or dead, perhaps believing that he is unconscious. He's what? About nineteen or twenty? It's an optimistic age. I see nineteen-year-olds up at the university who believe that they can cram a year's work into a week of black coffee and all-night study. As soon as the boy is gone, the three women examine the body. They find that he is dead. They don't know what to do. They lift the body into a trunk that that is lying there, wedge it in with skins and then allow it to be taken away by the auctioneer's men.'

'And, of course, nothing was heard for three days until the auction took place when it was sold and delivered to the convent,' said Patrick. He looked thoughtful. 'It's possible,' he admitted.

'Possible; it's brilliant,' said Dr Scher. 'And now I am going to have another finger of cake to revive me.'

The Reverend Mother handed him the plate. It was, she had to admit, a possible explanation. Fred was young; Dr Scher was right. The young are optimistic. He could have told himself that his father had a hard head, would wake with nothing but a headache and, hopefully, no memory of what had happened. In any case, he might have been hustled out of the house before he had a chance to even touch the man.

And then when he saw the dead body in the trunk, he had taken fright, he would have realized that one of three women dear to him would be hanged for that murder. He did the stupid thing of attempting to take responsibility by shooting the dead man, and then, later, when he had read the newspaper accounts and realized that his father had been killed probably days earlier, well then, he once again tried to take responsibility by signing a confession.

Unless, of course, it was all an elaborate double bluff by a young man who had, reputably, a brilliant mathematical brain.

TWELVE

St Thomas Aquinas
*'Et ideo actus iustitiae per comparationem ad
propriam materiam et obiectum tangitur cum dicitur,
"ius suum unicuique tribuens"* . . .'
(Therefore the act of justice, in relation to its proper
matter and object, is indicated in the words:
"rendering to each his right" . . .)

'It's Bridie, Reverend Mother,' said Sister Bernadette, closing the door firmly behind her and standing with the knob in her hand as she spoke. 'I keep on telling her that you are very busy this morning. "Reverend Mother has the bishop's secretary with her and they are going over the accounts, Bridie." I said that to her. I kept on telling her. "Sit down, Bridie, sit and have a cup of tea." If I said that once, I said it forty times, but she just wouldn't. Up and down every minute, that's the way she's been. "Surely, he's gone now." That's what she kept saying to me. "Perhaps that bell is not working", that was the next thing. Of course, I guessed that you showed him out yourself. You always do.'

The Reverend Mother sighed. Yes, she had showed out the bishop's secretary, and yes, she always did do that. It was, she had found by experience, the only way to get rid of him. Whenever she proposed to ring for Sister Bernadette, he told her not to trouble, that he would see himself out, and then he would start talking again, airing his views on the best use of diocesan funds, on the way that economies could be made, on the uselessness of lighting stoves in classrooms where active children could easily be kept warm and other economies which occurred to him. However, if she got to her feet and went towards the door while arguing, then he would follow her like a dog so that he could interrupt with his own views. In that way she usually managed to get him to the hall door and to let an icy breeze play over him until he departed hurriedly.

'Send Bridie in, Sister Bernadette,' she said. 'I'll see her now.' She cast one more glance at the document that the bishop's secretary had left behind, pages full of empty boxes with minus and plus symbols and daunting looking percentages on the outer margins. Planning of money resources, she had found by experience, was not of much use when crises happened on a regular basis. She preferred to put her energies into raising money when it was needed. The bishop, according to his secretary, was unhappy about the frequency with which she applied to prominent businessmen for funds, had even overheard that her visits were dreaded by the wealthy. The bishop, apparently, was so upset about this that he was even willing to give her the help of his secretary, a person who understood economics. Or so the rather overweight and self-satisfied young man, sitting opposite to her, had said. Carefully she tucked the useful pieces of paper into an overflowing drawer at the bottom of her desk. It bore no label, but in her mind was catalogued as 'Rubbish from the Bishop'.

'Yes, send Bridie in now, Sister Bernadette,' she repeated as, with difficulty, she managed to get the drawer closed. She moved away from the desk and took a seat by the fire. Bridie would not have been so insistent if she had not had something serious to talk about. She was owed all of the Reverend Mother's attention when she came to the convent for counsel. She had been one of the flock and the bond had never been broken.

Bridie had entered the convent as a fourteen-year-old orphan more than twenty years ago. She had been brought up by an aunt, not very kindly treated, according to her parish priest. A good girl, he had said. Would make an excellent lay sister, was sensible and hardworking, anxious to please. Could read and write a little. Would be grateful for any kindness. Lay sisters were the backbone of convent life, the people who washed, scrubbed, cleaned, cooked and shopped. Those not educated enough to engage in teaching or in nursing, women who had neither fortune nor education, according to the founder of the order. Originally they had been the maidservants of wealthy women who entered into the religious life, but by the middle of the nineteenth century they were mainly from small, impoverished farms and from the families of farm labourers hit by the recurring potato famine. Nevertheless, they took the same vows of chastity and obedience. The new recruit was placed in the kitchen, working under the benign rule of Sister Bernadette.

Bridie had been most obedient and most hardworking. A model lay sister in almost every way. Yes, obedience came naturally to her.

Chastity, however, was a problem. Bridie liked men. In the beginning it had been just flirtations with delivery boys, something that Sister Bernadette dealt with firmly. But then Bridie had taken to slipping out at night when the nuns were all in their beds. Sister Bernadette was forced to report her to the Reverend Mother when she found, for the second time, that the person-shaped lump under the blankets of Bridie's bed was, in fact, a pillow and a nightgown. Bridie received a warning and then another warning and then came a threatened scandal. Bridie was pregnant. Sister Bernadette, in tears, reported the matter to the Reverend Mother.

Bridie looked nearer to forty than to thirty now, thought the Reverend Mother as the woman came into the room. She was looking smarter than usual, wearing a red coat that seemed slightly too small for her and a black straw hat crowned with an ornate flower. She didn't look well, looked a lot older than her years could be. A pretty girl she had been when she had first come to the convent, with a fresh complexion, dark blue eyes and thick black hair. The fresh complexion was now weather-beaten and coarsened and the hair, beneath the incongruous hat, was turning grey. A sad-looking woman, locked into middle-age, with nothing much to show for her life.

'Come in, Bridie, come in and sit down. Sit there by the fire. Would you like tea?'

The Reverend Mother allowed a few moments to elapse after the invitation, but since nothing but silence followed it, she said quietly, 'No tea, thank you, Sister Bernadette.' Very unlike Bridie who adored endless cups of tea and slices of cake. What had brought the woman here? It was also very unlike her to insist on waiting to see the Reverend Mother, though hearing that she was busy with the bishop's secretary, rather than her usual practice of having a confidential chat with Sister Bernadette and allowing the news to be spread second-hand.

But the Reverend Mother said nothing, asked Bridie no questions. After the door closed behind the lay sister, she bent over the fire, endeavoured to stir it into a livelier state and then leaned back. Bridie, she thought, should be allowed to take her time; should be allowed to think through the implications of what she wished to say. Even when the silence was eventually broken, it took a while to come to the point. But after a long session of remarks about the weather, appreciation of the fire and excuses about her visit, Bridie gathered her courage together.

'Have you read today's *Cork Examiner,* Reverend Mother?'

'Not yet.' Obligatory reading for most Cork people, but the Reverend Mother left it in the nuns' refectory until after the hour of dinner. By this stage, Sister Bernadette would have informed her of most of its contents, but she still flicked through it while she had her tea.

'It's Freddie,' said Bridie with a choke in her voice. 'It's Freddie, Fred Mulcahy. They've got him up there in the barracks. They found him hiding out in the marshes at Passage West. They say that he has confessed to his father's murder. But he didn't do it, Reverend Mother. I know that he didn't do it.'

The Reverend Mother sat very still and looked across at her visitor. There had been a ring of sincerity in the voice.

'You think that he is unlikely to have done it, that he is not the sort of person who would have been able to murder his own father?' As she spoke the memory of young Fred Mulcahy firing repeatedly at his father's inert body came vividly to her mind. It takes a certain nature, a certain aggression to do something like that, was the thought that occurred to her, but she said no more, just waited to hear what Bridie had to say.

'I'm not saying that. Anyone is capable of anything when it comes to it.' This was unexpected from Bridie. Bridie was always so tentative, always so anxious to agree and to try to guess at a response before giving her own opinion. Sentimental remembrances of Fred's babyhood, of his good nature as a child, of the impossibility of a boy like Fred bringing himself to murder his own father. All that would have been more in the usual mode from Bridie, but now she made no exceptions, made no excuses. After that bleak assertion, she said no more, but seemed to be thinking hard. In the silence of the room the clock ticked and the Reverend Mother watched the hand jump to eleven o'clock. The clock chimed and Bridie sat up very straight.

'I know he didn't do it, Reverend Mother,' she said as though the clock had given her the signal to speak. 'I know it because I was the one that did it. I was the one that killed Henry Mulcahy.' And then, quite abruptly, the frozen look on the woman's face broke up and she began to cry.

'They won't hang me, Reverend Mother, will they? I'd hate to be hanged. I'd kill myself first. Could you just tell the guards for me and let me just go off down to the river before they come for me. I'd prefer to do it that way if I was going to be hanged. I'm frightened about that now.'

'Tell me what happened, Bridie,' said the Reverend Mother. 'Here, take my handkerchief. Don't cry, just tell me calmly what happened and allow me to sort it out.' There was an untouched cup of tea that she had left on the mantelpiece while the bishop's secretary had gorged himself on cake. It would be cold by now, but she stirred two heaped spoonfuls of sugar into it and stood over the woman and saw that she swallowed a few gulps before she returned to her chair.

'Now, Bridie, tell me sensibly. What did happen?'

'He was up in the back attic when I went up there. He was standing there. Just standing in front of the trunk, looking through one of the windows. There wasn't much light up there, the front attics get light from the street, but the back ones don't. I didn't see him at first. I had just come up for a bucket, but then he started pulling at me, the way he always did and I pushed him away. Told him I wanted nothing to do with a man who could build a tannery yard on top of the body of his own dead child. And then he went across and put a chair under the handle of the door. Just so that no one could come in. He knew that I would never be able to escape him. That I wouldn't try. He knew that I was scared stiff of him.'

'What happened then?' There was something very artificial about this account. Would Henry Mulcahy really have bothered with Bridie, looking the way she did now? Twenty years ago, it might have been a different story.

'I killed him; I thought that it was the only way that I could ever be rid of him . . . So I killed him.'

Bridie had left a long moment of silence between her last sentence and the one that had gone before. It was almost a response to the silence that had greeted her confession. The Reverend Mother studied her carefully while Bridie lifted the cup and swallowed some more of the cold tea. Their eyes met over the rim of the teacup and then Bridie sat back and waited with an expectant air. The Reverend Mother thought about it for a moment. Bridie, she remembered, was not from the city of Cork. A country girl, she had never had the fluency and the stream of words that came from the true city dwellers. And yet there had been quite a flow of words to describe the scene in the attic. Almost as though she had rehearsed the story.

'Tell me, Bridie,' she said eventually, 'how did you kill Mr Mulcahy? What did you do?'

This detail about the death being caused by the blow of an iron bar or cudgel to the lower back of the skull was, she knew, known only to the Civic Guards, to Dr Scher and to herself. Patrick had told her that they were keeping it a secret for the moment. There had been no trace, in the house at Shandon Street, of any instrument that might have caused the death of the merchant.

It was a simple question, but seemed to be an alarming one. Bridie endeavoured to put the empty cup back on its saucer, but her hand trembled and the cup slipped to the floor. Not broken, the rug had saved it. But Bridie spent some time apologizing, exclaiming about her carelessness and taking the cup to the window to make sure that there was no crack in it. The Reverend Mother waited patiently until the woman ran out of words and then repeated her question.

'Well, that's my business, Reverend Mother,' said Bridie

flushing a dark red, and then, aghast at her own temerity, she began to cry again.

'Mr McCarthy said that they wouldn't hang me. He said that to tell them Mr Mulcahy put me in fear of my life. He told me to tell the Civic Guards that it was self-defence. He said that he knew a clever lawyer that would get me off. Susan and the Missus said that they would be witnesses for me. We've been talking it over this morning. It was Mr McCarthy who came in with the paper. We hadn't got ours, yet. Susan is going over to Montenotte to talk to Sally and the boys. I said I'd go straight to the barracks and sign a confession and . . .' Bridie ran out of words and started bleakly through the window pane at the fog outside.

'And so you decided to drop in to see me and to get a second opinion on this very serious matter, Bridie.' The Reverend Mother made her voice sound bracing and Bridie nodded obediently.

'What do you think, Reverend Mother?' she asked pathetic-ally. 'Will I just get a few months in gaol? I wouldn't mind that. It would be a good rest for me and meals regular, they say. Just a few months. That's what Mr McCarthy thought. That's what he said to Susan. He said that he had been talking to a solicitor and that was his opinion. Susan wanted to go with me, to make sure that I was all right, but he said that I would be better on my own. What do you think that they'll ask me? My head is in such a muddle ever since that evening. I couldn't remember a thing about it much. I remember putting him in the trunk, of course. The auctioneer has been up, telling us all about that.'

'Excuse me, Reverend Mother.' Sister Bernadette put her head around the door after a perfunctory knock. 'Mr Hayes, the auctioneer is here. He'd like to have a word. He said to tell you that it will only take a minute of your time, but he has a van waiting at the gate and he's due himself in Ballinlough in ten minutes' time. Got his own car, parked behind the van.'

'Very well.' The Reverend Mother rose to her feet. She felt slightly annoyed at the way that Sister Bernadette graded the social status of her visitors, was willing to interrupt a conversation with poor Bridie, whereas wild horses would not have dragged her to knock on the door while the bishop's secretary was closeted in the Reverend Mother's room. Nevertheless, it mightn't be a bad idea to give Bridie a few minutes to think matters over and perhaps to find a way to climb down from her dramatic purpose.

'Take Bridie into the kitchen will you, Sister Bernadette? Give her a fresh cup of tea from the stove out there. I'll be back in a couple of minutes, Bridie, and then we can finish our conversation.'

'Reverend Mother! I won't keep you half a second.' Mr Hayes on his rubber-soled shoes swept into the room on a flood of words. 'Busy, I'm sure! Well, don't I know it! You're always busy, Reverend Mother. Everyone knows that, God bless the work that you do. Now, you'll be wondering why I come here bothering you and I wouldn't have thought of it, wouldn't have dreamt of it, but for that terrible business last week. I'd have just sent one of the lads over with a note or had a word on the phone with your good sister. But after what happened the last time! Never will I forget it! I said to Jack; my right-hand man, you know. Been with me for more years than I like to think of. I said to Jack, the Reverend Mother of St Marys of the Isle will like these, but I daren't send them to her unless I'm by her side when she opens it. Come and see it. I'll guarantee that you'll be pleased with it. Out-of-date, but good stuff. Do come and see, Reverend Mother. I'll not have an easy moment until you approve.'

Mr Hayes fidgeted around the Reverend Mother like an over-active sheep dog and she allowed herself to be escorted up the corridor and into the convent hallway. There was a trunk lying there, placed on the sturdy wooden seats of three chairs. And on either side, with the appearance of a guard of honour, were two of the auctioneer's men, clothed in well-brushed green leather aprons and standing stiffly to attention.

This was a very different trunk to the other one. It was a good quality heavy leather trunk and plastered all over with travel labels. 'Calcutta', she read on one, 'Marseille', 'Bristol', 'Singapore', 'Southampton' on others.

'Open it up, boys,' commanded Mr Hayes and obediently they flung back the lid.

'There you are, you see, children's clothes. Stuff left over from the Major Heffernan sale. No buyer for them, but very good stuff, Reverend Mother. Feel the thickness of that little coat. Hardly worn. And all those shoes. Look like they've come straight from the shop, don't they? Never wore a passed-down item in their lives, Reverend Mother, did they? New clothes every day of the week; that's the way it would have been,' said Mr Hayes, his excitement leading him into a pardonable exaggeration. 'Look at those lovely little jumpers. Jaeger wool, I'd be bound. And the thick woollen socks. Your little boys and girls would be snug in those, wouldn't they? And those rubber boots, look at them, Reverend Mother! Brand new! Just out of the shop, clean as a whistle.'

'Oh, the pretty dresses and the little frilly aprons!' Curiosity and the raised voices had brought Sister Bernadette peeping out from the kitchen and now, in answer to the auctioneer's beckoning arm, she joined in the hymn of praise. 'And the lovely flannel nightdresses and petticoats! Oh, Reverend Mother, just look at those little Chilprufe vests and not a moth hole in one of them!'

'Well, I must say that these would be very useful to us, Mr Hayes,' said the Reverend Mother cordially. 'You were very kind to think of us.'

'Not – at – all!' Mr Hayes gave an expansive wave of a hand. 'Only too glad to do something. Salt of the earth, salt of the earth, the people around here. Only too glad to do something for them. They may be poor, but what of it, I say. Our own blessed Saviour was poor. Nothing wrong with being poor. Poor and honest, that's what they say, don't they?'

Not always, thought the Reverend Mother. Mr Hayes, she noticed, cynically, had carried his starting handle into the convent with him in case one of those poor, but honest people took a fancy to his motor car.

'Do I owe you anything, Mr Hayes?' she asked politely. Another one of those meaningless phrases with which she oiled the wheels of charity. Still this was Cork and these little rituals had to be gone through. If a Cork person tells you that they don't want a cup of tea that means they are absolutely dying for it and would be most offended if you took them at

their word, her father had once explained to a confused over-
seas relation.

'Not a penny, not a penny!' said Mr Hayes, warmly. 'You'd
be surprised, Reverend Mother, at the stuff that gets left over
after a sale. Very bad times, these days. Don't like to say it
but we haven't had a day's luck in this city since the boyos
started waving the green flag, and not a word of a lie. No,
these would be thrown out, thrown out, Reverend Mother.
Look here. I'll show you the sale bill and you can see for
yourself. He moved aside his auctioneer's hammer and gavel
and took out a heavily bound book. 'On my way up to a
house sale in Ballinlough,' he said by way of explanation
of the hammer. 'Look at that, Reverend Mother, there it is,
bottom of the Major Heffernan sale. "TRUNK OF
CHILDREN'S CLOTHING, UNSOLD".' He put a stubby
finger under the bold capital letters. 'Not much call for these
sort of out-of-date things from the crowd that we get in for
an auction of stuff from a place like Fota House, Reverend
Mother. Fussy! Lord, Lord! I could tell you some tales!' Mr
Hayes raised his eyes to the ceiling above and then fastened
up his bag again. He waved aside her thanks. 'Now don't let
me keep you another minute. I know that you are busy. The
good sister here will tell these lads where to put the trunk,
and then they have another delivery to do, but I'll be off
now; that house sale is in twenty minutes' time. Got my own
little Ford now, you know, Reverend Mother, support local
industry, that's me. Ford has brought a rack of jobs to Cork,
you know. Well, Reverend Mother, I'm off now and will
leave you to get on with the good work that you do. God
bless you, Reverend Mother.'

'Thank you again, Mr Hayes,' said the Reverend Mother.
Quickly she went back down the corridor. The man was
actually opening the front door and she would not delay him
another minute.

'Oh, there you are, Reverend Mother.' Sister Mary Immaculate had been attracted by the boom of Mr Hayes' voice,
trained to reach the furthermost corners of his large auctioneering hall. The Reverend Mother suppressed a sigh. It was
no good brushing past the woman. She would only be tearful

and suffering from a headache for the rest of the day, if she felt that she was being denied her true status as invaluable assistant to the Reverend Mother.

'Yes, sister, did you want me?' she said with as much patience as she could command. 'Perhaps we could have a chat just before dinner if that suits you.'

It was no good, though. Sister Mary Immaculate was in full flow. 'No, need for that, Reverend Mother. I just wanted to explain that I was passing by the back door, and the phone rang, so I picked it up because I could hear that you and Sister Bernadette were busy at the front door and it was the bishop's secretary. He told me to tell you that he was in the process of drafting some of those documents that you felt would be so interesting to see and he would be sending them down to you this afternoon, by a special messenger.'

'Oh, good,' said the Reverend Mother. Her mind was on the woman waiting patiently for her in the kitchen. She had to make sure that poor Bridie did nothing stupid. It seemed to her that there was something very odd about that discussion that had taken place in the half-empty house up in Shandon Street. Had Bridie and her devotion been sacrificed by mother and daughter to save Fred? Sister Mary Immaculate, though, was not easily escaped from. She stood right in the middle of the corridor and it was obvious that she had something of vital importance to say.

'I must tell you, Reverend Mother,' she said with one of her annoying little titters. 'This will amuse you. You won't believe it, but the bishop's secretary was surprised that you had not confided in me your plans for the reform of the convent finances. Most astonished, these were his words. "I am most astonished, sister, that you don't know about my method. I had assumed that the Reverend Mother would have talked it over with you, her second-in-command, before now." That's what he said to me, Reverend Mother.'

There was more to come. The Reverend Mother resigned herself to a further delay. Better to let Sister Mary Immaculate get it off her chest out here in the corridor, rather than have her coming into the kitchen where that poor woman was dealing with much more serious matters than hurt pride or the bishop's secretary's view on how finances should be handled in order to avoid any waste of the diocese's money.

'Of course, sister, I always value your advice,' she said evenly, doing her best to recollect the wise words, uttered by the foundress of the order, on the subject of unity among sisters. Sister Bernadette, she could hear, was no longer receiving the full flow of the auctioneer's oratory as she lingered by the doorway, but now she was chatting with the removal men, debating about the size of a trunk and the feasibility of standing it on one end. In the meantime, poor Bridie was alone in the kitchen, alone with her sad and dark thoughts. 'We'll talk about it afterwards; but now I must go,' she said decisively, but then hesitated for a moment, looking appraisingly at her assistant.

A brilliant thought had just come to her. Why not let Sister Mary Immaculate deal with the bishop's secretary and the pair of them could work away and together create a vast pile of documents which it would be unreasonable to expect her to read too quickly. She could always find another drawer or a box or something.

'Sister,' she began, 'I hate to overburden you, I know that you are very, very busy, but I have long felt that your abilities are not properly used here in the convent . . .'

She did her best to be concise, but the matter took longer than she had imagined as Sister Mary Immaculate made so many interruptions, and insisted on sharing so many of her ideas, that in the end the Reverend Mother had to make a pretence that she needed to visit the bathroom and even then had to lurk inside the stony cold of the white-tiled room for an extra few minutes to make sure that her zealous assistant had taken herself off to the classroom where, in all probability, a crowd of active ten-year-olds had started to have noisy fun in the absence of their teacher. She emerged cautiously, but the back corridor was empty and she hurried down to the kitchen. Her mind was now completely focussed on Bridie. She really must question the woman about the role played by this Mr McCarthy in the family councils. At the sight of the chaplain coming down the stairs from distributing Holy Communion to the sick and elderly nuns on the top floor of the convent, she took out her rosary, slid the time-worn beads through her fingers and walked away from him with what she hoped was an enigmatic look on her face. She did not pray, though. Her mind was busy with arguments which would weigh with Bridie.

By the time that she opened the kitchen door, she had decided on a course of action. At least Bridie had been warm during her fifteen minutes or so of absence. The kitchen was the most inviting place in the convent, she had often thought. The enormous black stove glowed and flickered, bunches of herbs and sides of bacon hung from the ceiling beams. Pots of blackberry jam and crab apple jelly gleamed from the dressers. The well-scrubbed long table in the centre of the room shone golden under the light from the overhanging oil lamp.

But there was nobody there.

She hesitated for a moment and then a young lay sister came through from the scullery, a sharp knife in one hand and a half-peeled potato in the other.

'Sister Bernadette has gone to the door, Reverend Mother,' she said respectfully.

'I was looking for Bridie, sister.'

'Oh, she said that she had to go, Reverend Mother. She passed me a minute ago. She went out through the back yard.'

'Go after her, Sister Imelda,' said the Reverend Mother urgently. 'Go after her and bring her back.' The young lay sister, though hampered by heavy skirts, was only fifteen years old and would be faster than Bridie who was riddled with rheumatism. When did the woman leave? She herself went to the door and stood there, as the girl flew across the wet yard and went to the gate.

In her anxiety the Reverend Mother ventured out herself, treading carefully on the slippery flagstones. She reached the gate and stood there, looking up and down. The convent yard entrance was only a few yards down from the road on one side and on the other, the narrow laneway led only to the river. There was a slight fog, but it was almost noon and a faint silver warmed the clouds above their heads. There was enough light for her to see instantly that the lane was empty except for the flying skirts of Sister Imelda.

'Bridie! Bridie!' She feared that the shrill shrieks would surely bring Mr Hayes back down upon them, but fortunately there was no sign of the auctioneer. Once released from human company, his Ford car had borne him away swiftly to his house sale in Ballinlough. The Reverend Mother looked up and down the lane and suppressed an urge to join in Sister Imelda's shouts. She forced herself to remain still and to say calmly when the young lay sister returned, 'Just walk down towards the river, sister, will you? Perhaps Bridie went to get some air.'

She stood very still and waited until Sister Imelda returned, slightly scared, slightly apprehensive. Only fifteen, but already well aware of the reputation of the two-channelled river that encircled the city of Cork.

'There's no sign of her, Reverend Mother, no sign.' She half-whispered the words and looked apprehensively into the face of her superior. And then, hesitantly, faced with silence, she said, 'Should we get someone? Get the guards . . .?' Her voice tailed out.

The Reverend Mother pulled herself together. 'You go back in, child,' she said. 'Sister Bernadette will want those potatoes peeled by the time that she gets back, won't she?'

She waited until the scullery door had crashed closed behind Sister Imelda and then, tentatively, she made her way down the laneway. Several tiny tumbledown hovels, many of them still occupied, lined the right-hand side of the little roadway. She had been told that the building stone, blocks of red sandstone and gleaming white limestone, for the convent had been brought up the river and then taken on carts up this lane. She had often wondered whether the people living in these one- or two-roomed hovels had marvelled or sworn at the ornate building, three stories high, that was raised to house some holy women.

But now her thoughts were all on poor Bridie. Always a victim, she thought, as she picked her way carefully among the puddles. A victim of the false prudery of the convent, who should have sheltered her in her time of need, a victim of the man who had made her pregnant, and now a victim of her own love for a boy who had taken the place of her dead baby in the poor woman's lonely heart. She stood for a moment looking up and down the river. Low tide; the shoreline was exposed, raucous seagulls pecking vigorously among the malodourous deposits on the bank. She looked up and down, as far as her eyes could reach, but she had little hope that she would see anything more than Sister Imelda's young eyes had done. And then she trudged wearily back up the steep slope of the laneway, went into the back hall of the convent and unhooked the phone.

THIRTEEN

St Thomas Aquinas
Et ideo tristitia potest esse de praesenti,
praeterito et futuro, dolor autem corporalis, qui
sequitur apprehensionem sensus exterioris,
non potest esse nisi de praesenti.'
(Consequently sorrow has the power to be of the
present, past and future: whereas bodily pain, which
follows apprehension of the external sense, can only be
something of the present.)

'Patrick said that you sounded worried,' Dr Scher's arrival
had frightened her for a few moments, and even now
she scanned his face for any sign that he had been sent
to break bad news.

'I merely wondered whether a visitor that I had an hour ago
had dropped into the barracks to give him a message.' The
Reverend Mother had formulated her query to Patrick carefully
during her return journey back up the lane and even now, to
her own ears, it sounded innocuous, the sort of question that
could have been put with regard to a visitor who had left an
umbrella behind, she had imagined. Patrick, however, had read
more into it, and so, apparently, had Dr Scher. For one of the
very few times in her acquaintance with him, he had turned
down the offer of a cup of tea and politely but firmly closed
the door on Sister Bernadette who was doing her best to urge
him into partaking, what she termed, just a small sup.

He poked the fire, more as a ritual performance than because
it really needed it. Sister Bernadette had made it up to a roaring
blaze while exclaiming with horror at the Reverend Mother's
damp muddy shoes and the stained hem of her skirts. He
carried over her chair, placed it by the blaze, stood over
her while she sat down and then placed himself opposite
to her and waited for her to speak.

'So Bridie didn't arrive at the barracks.'

Somehow she was not surprised. There would have been plenty of time for Bridie to have gone to the barracks. If she had not arrived by now, there would be little chance of her being still alive. She would not have gone back up to Shandon Street and confessed that she could not bring herself to make a sacrifice for a boy who had been like a son to her.

'Did she tell you that she was going to confess to the murder?' he asked.

She did not answer that. Bridie had spoken to her in confidence. She just looked across at him and he nodded gently. 'Don't worry. Don't bother answering. She was one of your flock at one stage, wasn't she?'

'How did you know?' Sister Bernadette she supposed and did not probe him for an answer. He, like she, had a right to professional silence.

'Is there anything that I can do?' she asked.

His eyes went to her soaked shoes and he shook his head. 'Nothing really. You've been down to the river, I see. But it would have been no good, you know. It's hard even to save someone that has gone over a bridge in front of your eyes. The tide flows rapidly, the water is not exactly crystal clear and it's chock full of rubbish. Very unusual to get anyone alive out of it. You can only pray that her mind did not turn in that direction. She's in the hands of your God now, Reverend Mother. You pray to him.'

She sighed wearily. *I'm not sure that I am too good at praying these days, I'm not even sure that it works.* She thought the words, but she did not say them aloud. It would be a very shocking thing, she thought, if she, Reverend Mother Aquinas, should express any doubts about God's listening ear; if she allowed her experience of death, starvation, abuse of small children, suicides, murders – all everyday occurrences in this city of Cork – to make her wonder about even His very existence. Not all of these horrors should destroy her faith in God, if she were a true *religeuse*. Aloud, she said merely, 'I'm sure that you're right, Dr Scher.'

'Of course,' he said in an off-hand manner. 'I'm always right.' And then with a return to seriousness: 'I am guessing that she was on her way to the barracks, to confess to the murder of Henry Mulcahy. And yet, she was not sure that she was doing the right thing, she was apprehensive about it. And what's more natural than she should call into the convent to discuss it with her former mother superior, who may well have been a guiding light to her through the years.'

'I stupidly left her in the kitchen with Sister Bernadette while I went to see Mr Hayes, the auctioneer, who brought me a trunk-load of children's clothing, very good quality, I have to say, but I wish that he had not come at that moment,' said the Reverend Mother wretchedly. 'And then, of course, Sister Bernadette had to come out to see . . . and Bridie just went . . . left by the scullery door.'

'Do you think that she did kill Henry Mulcahy?'

The Reverend Mother shook her head firmly. 'No, I don't. She refused to tell me how she did it. She was flustered and taken aback when I asked her that question. She said that it was her business, but, of course, that was a ridiculous answer when she had just told me that she had killed him. And, as you know, Patrick has told me that they were keeping the method a secret for the moment, so perhaps only the murderer knows how it was done. Have the police found anything to match what you felt was the murder weapon? An iron bar, I think you said.'

Dr Scher shook his head. 'No, nothing was found that matches what I had in mind. I had a wander up around Shandon myself yesterday. There was a death, a suicide, I suppose, poor woman, in Cattle Mart Lane – took poison, poor thing. I went to see if I could save her, too late, of course. She was dead when I arrived. So I went out and bought some sweets for the children. They were being taken off to an orphanage by a neighbour. I saw the sign, "Mulcahy and Sons" so after I handed over the sweets, I had a look around, then went up to the cathedral, met the verger, and he showed me the new tanning yard. Plenty of long bars, iron rods up there, used for stirring and lifting the skins and hides, but they weren't what I had in mind. I was thinking of something shorter, though. You see, the nearer you are, the greater the force. A short iron bar or a very hard solid piece of wood. Could be anything,

something heavy – I've seen a wound like that from a very
thick glass bottle in a public house, broke the skull in just the
same way . . .' Dr Scher fell silent.

'Did the verger tell you about the *cillín* when you went up
to the cathedral? Mr Mulcahy roused up a lot of ill-will when
he built his tanning yard on top of the graves of those unbaptized babies.'

He nodded, but said nothing and she was grateful for his
silence. It was difficult for her, even within her own mind, to
explain why the church put this additional burden on a
sorrowing mother when they denied her a Christian burial for
an unbaptized baby. To these poor women, these little *cillín*
graveyards, always on the site of some ancient settlement, had
to be very sacred places.

'No need to answer, but I guess Bridie's baby was buried
in that little place,' he said. Then he added, gently, 'That
would give a good motive in the eye of the law, perhaps a
better motive than any that the young lad, in the cell, might
have had.'

'Yes, I had forgotten about Fred.' The Reverend Mother
roused herself. 'Now, since we are in this confessional mode,'
she said, purposely introducing a tart note into her voice, 'and
since the door is shut and we have decided to trust each other's
discretion, perhaps you could tell me whether Fred Mulcahy
has been able to tell the Civic Guards how he murdered his
father.'

'Well, strictly between ourselves, talking within closed doors
and windows, and having complete reliance on your discretion,
I can divulge to you that Fred Mulcahy killed his father by
shooting him three days earlier. This accounted for the blood
on the man's coat front.' Dr Scher kept a deadpan expression
on his face as he gave the fire another poke.

'But that's nonsense.'

'Interesting, isn't it? First the boy empties his pistol into
the man, saw the blood on the chest, I suppose. His young
eyes would be sharper than yours, Reverend Mother. He
probably saw it instantly, thinks that his mother or sister,
perhaps, had killed the man, though where they would have
got a gun, no one knows – still there are lots of guns floating

around in this city of ours. In any case, he wanted to take responsibility.'

'And not realizing that his father was killed by a blow to the back of his head.' Talking and thinking about Fred took her mind a little off wondering whether the woman in the river was Bridie, and so she encouraged Dr Scher with an interested look.

'He wrote a confession, as you know,' said the doctor. 'Wrote to the superintendent at the barracks. Told them that he had killed his father, but that by the time the letter was received that he would be on his way to America. That didn't work out; this America business. The army arrested him and handed him over to Patrick, once they heard he was looking for Fred Mulcahy. Found him lying out in the marshes. Always difficult for them, I understand, to be sure who took part in a fight and who was just a bystander. Much easier to have him hung for the murder of his father, especially when he was so obliging as to confess to it in writing.'

'I've been turning over in my mind the three women in the house,' admitted the Reverend Mother, 'but now I think that I have reduced that to two women. If Bridie had been responsible, there was no reason why she should not have told me how she killed the man.'

'The mother and the daughter,' mused Dr Scher. 'Quite a hard blow, I would think. Not as easy as shooting a man. Would they have been strong enough?'

'I understood that both did quite a lot of work in the tanning yard,' said the Reverend Mother, thinking back to past gossip when Bridie had visited with the children. She stirred restlessly. Why, on earth, had she not quickly gone to the root of the matter with Bridie as soon as it was apparent that the woman had not been responsible for Mr Mulcahy's death? That would have been the right thing to do. She tightened her lips with exasperation at the thought of Mr Hayes and his never-faltering flow of talk, and then Sister Mary Immaculate, another one where it was almost impossible to stem the flood of words. Restlessly, she got up and went to the window. The bell had sounded for dinner time. Some of the children would be collected by their parents to be taken home for a meal,

while the nuns had their own meal, but others would be left
in the school playground, the lucky few with a slice of bread
and jam, the others hungry. By her orders a basin of potatoes
from the convent garden were scrubbed and placed in the
bottom of the kitchen range first thing each school day. By
noon, they were hot and tasty and filled the empty stomachs
of these thin children. She would have to go and see about
the serving of them. She rose to her feet.

'You've been very kind, Dr Scher,' she said formally.
'I mustn't keep you any longer. I know that you are a very
busy man.'

'Sit down again, Reverend Mother,' he said gently. 'Sit down
and let me go and see.'

And then she heard what he had heard. Beneath the sono-
rous clang of the convent bell, calling the nuns to their meal,
there was the lighter sound of the front door bell, fixed to
ring in both the corridor and in the kitchen. She ignored his
outstretched hand and went to the door.

'Thank you, Dr Scher; I must answer that,' she said.

Sister Imelda was emerging from the kitchen when she
went out, her plump young cheeks distended with food.
'You go back and finish your meal, child,' she said. 'Oh, and
Sister Imelda,' she called after the girl, 'would you ask Sister
Bernadette whether you could distribute the potatoes to
the children, today, when you have finished your own dinner,
of course?'

The front door to the convent was panelled with glass,
garishly coloured and set in lead-lined, diamond-shaped panes.
Nevertheless, she had seen the outline of the figure and of the
cap that crowned it and she knew who it would be, and knew
that she would be preoccupied during the next half hour or
so. Little Sister Imelda would enjoy that task. Deftly she undid
the lock and opened the door.

'Come in, Patrick,' she said. 'I have been expecting you.'
She did not invite him to take off his coat, but took him
straight down the corridor. Dr Scher was standing at the
door and he stood back when he saw Patrick, holding
the door open for them and then shutting it when all three
were in the room.

'I'm very sorry, Reverend Mother,' said Patrick and she wondered how often he had to say those words to grieving relatives and friends.

'You've found her,' she said instantly.

He bowed his head. 'We've found her, we think. Just five minutes ago. A messenger boy on his bicycle. He came straight to us, sensible lad.' He hesitated for a moment, looking past her at Dr Scher.

'You want me?' Dr Scher's face was sombre.

'I'd like you to look at the body before she is lifted from the river.'

'The river,' said the Reverend Mother. 'Near us, Patrick, down our lane.'

He shook his head. 'Not there, Reverend Mother. She went over the top of the old weir, down near the brewery stables. The body . . .' He hesitated looking from her to Dr Scher.

'I'll come immediately.' Dr Scher was already buttoning himself into his heavy woollen coat.

'You go back, Patrick. I must fetch the priest.' She took down her cloak and put it around her shoulders and went to the door. The elderly chaplain would not be too pleased to be called away from his midday meal, but it would do him no harm. Like most of the chaplains that she had known in her years in the convent, he had put on a considerable amount of weight after a couple of years of easy living and an abundance of treats from the kitchen. 'We'll go with Dr Scher,' she added.

Patrick bowed his head obediently, but Dr Scher immediately protested. 'No need for you to come, Reverend Mother.'

She ignored him. 'You go and get your car started up, Dr Scher. We'll join you in a minute.'

The chaplain was halfway through his dinner when she knocked at his door. He had a napkin tucked into his round collar and a slight smear of gravy at one corner of his mouth.

'There's been an accident, Father,' she said. 'It's Bridie, a former member of our community, before your time, of course. She appears to have fallen over the weir.'

'Fallen over the weir.' He stared at her suspiciously. 'Not suicide, I hope,' he said with a longing glance at his dinner which rather belied his expression of hope. There would be no need for prayers or for extreme unction for a suicide. Suicide was a sin against the Holy Ghost and would merit nothing but a place in hell; no priest could gainsay that.

'Not for us to judge, Father,' said the Reverend Mother coldly. 'I would suggest that you wear a warm coat and take a scarf as well as your hat. It can be cold by the river. Dr Scher is waiting, so please be as quick as you can.' And with that she turned her back on him. She did not return into the convent, but walked through the church gate and up the lane, passing the other convent gate, the one that led to the yard outside the back scullery and washhouse. Bridie had come out of there while she had been delayed with the auctioneer and Sister Mary Immaculate. The Reverend Mother found it hard to forgive herself for that, but quickly moved her mind onto other matters.

Bridie had not gone down the lane, then, but had turned up and gone onto the main road, meaning, perhaps, to go up the hill to the barracks. And then, she thought, as she watched Patrick execute a neat turn, swivelling the Ford's steering wheel before driving away, and then, perhaps, Bridie changed her mind. The woman had a mercurial temperament. Up one moment, down another. At one stage she would have persuaded herself that a merciful court would sentence her merely to a few months in prison, but, at another moment, darker thoughts would come and she would live through the horrors of death by strangulation.

And so she had headed towards the certain death of throwing herself over the weir and into the river.

'Hope that your car is going to start,' she said to Dr Scher as he swung the starting handle with no visible effect.

'Now, Reverend Mother, have faith,' he panted.

'Difficult when there is nothing to see or hear,' she retorted. Her session with the chaplain had brought back her courage. She had failed Bridie, but failure, she had found, was a part of her life; had been as long as she could remember. Failure had to be overridden; had to be put aside. Now she had an ordeal ahead of her, but it was the least that she could do.

'The point of faith is believing in things that you can't see or hear,' he pointed out and at that very moment, the engine spluttered into triumphant life.

'I stand corrected,' she said as the chaplain came panting up and then humbly chose the back seat for himself. She would have faith, she thought, have faith that Bridie was now to be welcomed by God to a heaven, have hope that it might recompense for the hard purgatory of her life on earth.

But she found it very hard to find charity in her thoughts for those who had driven the poor woman to this last act of desperation.

And then she moved her mind in a different direction, looking across at Dr Scher as he pulled out from the pavement and drove in his usual erratic style along the road and then turned down towards the river.

Why had Patrick wanted the doctor to come to the river? The usual procedure, surely, was that the Civic Guards would take the body to the mortuary at the barracks. There must be something that he wanted a professional opinion about. She thought about it, looking down at her hands, puzzling over the problem and then was distracted by the vehement sounding of an angry horn. She looked up to see a van take evasive action, dodging out of the way of Dr Scher's Humber and noticed, coming out of a hardware shop, Mr McCarthy, erstwhile partner of the dead man and potential suitor for the hand of Susan Mulcahy. Perhaps he had been sent by the family to make sure that Bridie went to the barracks. Otherwise, why should he be shopping for tools down here when Shandon Street had a perfectly good hardware shop of its own. Or could there be a more sinister reason for his presence down here on St Mary's Isle?

She got briskly out of the car when they arrived, not waiting for Dr Scher to come around and help her out. It was quite some time since she had been here and she thought that the place was even more derelict than when she had last seen it. The original wall, built from blocks of sandstone, was now half demolished by the action of water, wind and rain. There was a narrow path, overhung with willows, and covered in moss, leading out towards the weir. Patrick stood on it, but she did not go and join him. She could see from where she was and she did not want to get in the way.

The weir beside St Mary's Isle was an ancient structure, known, when she was young, as the salmon weir. Her father, who had been a great antiquarian with an enormous interest in the history of his native city, had told her that the weir had been built by the monks who had owned the island before the nuns had taken it over. They had been an industrious crowd of monks, of the order of St Dominic, and they had constructed near to their monastery a water mill as well as the salmon weir. But the weir was now the only trace of their habitation and that had lapsed into a state of dereliction, with rotting timbers of the gate hanging loose and moss-covered rocks tumbled in crazy abandonment beneath the stream that ran down the slope towards the fast flowing south channel of the River Lee. The fog had lifted and a few gleams of sunshine lit the scene very clearly.

Amongst the silver foam of the tumbling water, the vivid lush green of the mossy stones and the broken chunks of water-worn wood, there was something red. Just a bundle, not like a person, just a crumpled shape. Quite near was a boat with a couple of civic guards. She could see how the sun caught the metal badges on their caps and the buckles on their belts, but they remained at a distance, resting on their oars and looking up to where Patrick stood.

He came back to them now. A pair of binoculars were slung around his neck and he undid them, handing them to Dr Scher.

'You'll need to adjust them, doctor,' he said. 'I'm very long-sighted.'

Dr Scher took a long look, twisting the centre wheel from time to time. And then he shook his head.

'Impossible to tell anything,' he said. He looked at Patrick. 'Do you want me to go down there,' he said.

'Would it help? You know what I'm wondering.'

'I suppose it would help,' said Dr Scher with a sigh. 'Time you got yourself an active young surgeon for this business. I could recommend you a few likely lads from the university.'

Patrick did not reply, nor did he smile. He just raised one arm and beckoned to the boat. The men rowed back to the bankside with tremendous vigour, glad to be moving, she thought. There was another boat there, a boat with just two men in it. That stayed in its position.

Dr Scher handed the binoculars to the Reverend Mother. It took her a moment or two of fiddling but then she was astonished at how the detail of the scene in front of her sprang up, almost causing her to flinch. She lowered the binoculars and looked back again. She had guessed at the truth without them, but now she knew.

'Is it . . .?' Dr Scher was looking at her.

'Yes,' said the Reverend Mother steadily. 'Yes, that is Bridie.' The colour of the coat had seemed to match, even without the aid of the binoculars, but the presence of a small dark object, crowned with an incongruous flower, wedged in between two rocks, had told the rest of the story. It was Bridie's hat, or perhaps the hat that was lent to her, along with the coat, in order to make a decent appearance at the barracks.

Dr Scher said nothing, just walked down the bank, and allowed himself to be assisted into the boat. The Reverend Mother raised the binoculars to her eyes again. The second boat, the boat that remained, now sprang into view in every detail. There was an ominous hook, a hook with a long handle and a tarpaulin stretched across the bottom of the boat. She controlled a shudder and forced herself to watch.

The young Civic Guards pulled hard at their oars and Dr Scher was beside the body within minutes. One of the men in the second boat raised the hook, but then replaced it after a shout. They were not using oars to propel the bigger boat to a position close up beside the body. A rope had been thrown over a high water spar and two men hauled slowly on that while a third knelt in the bows and shouted orders.

Bridie's body had landed among a heap of fallen stone. Dr Scher half stood, and then sat down again quickly as the boat rocked violently. Then he just sat while the men steadied the boat. Studying the body, studying the angle of the head, she thought suddenly. That was the point of this journey. She raised the binoculars again. Dr Scher had seen what he needed to see. She saw him sit back. Now began a slow and careful reclamation of the body. The Reverend Mother turned towards the chaplain.

'You have your prayer book with you, Father?' she queried in a steady voice and then took her rosary beads from her pocket.

FOURTEEN

Patrick raised his eyes from the page on his desk and looked thoughtfully across at Dr Scher. By now he was experienced enough to read between the lines of an official medical report of an autopsy.

'You think that she might have had her neck broken before she went down the weir,' he mused, returning again to his perusal of the summary. It was not a question. He knew that Dr Scher would not have welcomed a direct question on this matter. 'Not enough for you to swear to in court, but enough to give me a few ideas.'

'Possible' would be a word that he would be looking for at this stage, 'probable' would be even better, but certainties, Patrick thought, were to be distrusted until tried and tested.

'And the young fellow, young Fred Mulcahy, he's still tucked up in his cell, is he?' Dr Scher gave a half nod to Patrick's words. He wore a slightly puzzled air.

'Might as well stay there for the moment,' said Patrick. He understood the doctor's puzzlement. After all, Fred Mulcahy could not have been involved in this second murder, if the death of Bridie was a murder. And as for the first murder, well, that was a very strange confession. Nevertheless . . .

'The superintendent wouldn't like him released after a signed confession, not for something that can't be sworn to, can't be seen to be a certainty,' he explained. 'In any case, I would probably just have to hand him over to the lads up in the army barracks, and that while they're all still angry about the skirmish in Douglas. No, I'll keep hold of him. Officially, the woman went over the weir and broke her neck; that's all we need for the moment. It will make the real murderer relax and that must be a good thing.'

'So you don't think that Bridie did the murder, do you?' Dr Scher turned the question back onto Patrick. 'But she could have, couldn't she? It's a possible story. I've seen it happen myself. A woman who has put up with injustice, abuse, even serious violence, over the years, put up with it patiently and silently, can suddenly go over the edge for something small. This business of turning the *cillín*, that little unofficial graveyard for the poor little unbaptized babies, into a tanning yard, that might just have been the trigger for a poor woman like Bridie.'

'And then why was she not willing to tell the Reverend Mother how she killed the man?' said Patrick.

'It seems strange, doesn't it? It was only one small step forward, wasn't it? She could have just said, quite simply, "I took up a bar" or "I took up something heavy and I hit him across the back of the neck when he was bending down to pick something up". That would have been easy enough to say. Nothing to shock the Reverend Mother in that.'

Patrick nodded. 'And the Reverend Mother was never one to show any appearance of shock. I've known her all of my life and never seen her to be shocked. After all, she had just listened to a confession of murder, why should she be shocked at the method. And she's always been a person who listens very carefully, an easy person to talk to. Even when I was a child, I found this. Other nuns, like Sister Mary Immaculate, would shout you down, but she listened.'

'So you are inclined to think that the Reverend Mother is correct. Bridie did not kill Mr Mulcahy. But, of course, that doesn't mean that she did not commit suicide,' pointed out Dr Scher. 'She had been persuaded into confessing, but then panicked. Perhaps she saw no future for herself with the Mulcahy family and she didn't know what to do or where to go.'

'But you don't think so, do you? Medically speaking. Not after the autopsy. Not even before. I saw your face in the boat when you were looking at the body. Even then you were suspicious that it might not have been suicide.'

'It's very difficult to tell,' confessed Dr Scher. 'She fell down over those rocks; that you saw. But somehow I think that she was dead when she went over the edge. Just something about the angle of the head as though it had been loose as she tumbled down. And the body, too, when I got her on the table. There was a certain amount of bruising all over the body, but to my mind, it looked more like post-mortem, than ante-mortem bruising, all except for the neck; that could have been done before death. Something about the location of the bruises, also. Just a feeling that I have that an inert body tumbled down.'

'But if she had resolved to kill herself she might have just let herself go . . .'

'I have a theory that, even in suicide cases, at the last moment, it's human nature to struggle, to grasp at a tree stump, or a rock. There were no marks on the palms of the hands. Not anything that I could swear to, certainly not any fresh mark, lots of old scars. I suppose that it could have been suicide.' He brooded on this for a moment and then said decisively, 'No! I don't like it; don't think that it was suicide.'

'I'm sure that you're right. I thought that all along. It just doesn't make sense for the woman to commit suicide. Even if she lacked the courage to say no, she could always have just gone away, even taken the boat to Liverpool. She lived free in the Mulcahy household. She probably had a few shillings put away somewhere, enough for the fare, but if not, well, she need not have stayed with them. And she was accustomed to bringing her troubles to the convent which would surely have sheltered her in an emergency. No, I think that she was on the way to the barracks to save Fred Mulcahy. Before her courage failed her or before she was persuaded out of it. I know she mentioned suicide to the Reverend Mother, but that was to be after confession was made to the guards.'

'So, let's plump for murder,' said Dr Scher. 'Why should anyone murder her?'

'I wonder did this woman, Bridie, pose a threat. Did she know something?' Patrick stirred restlessly. 'But that doesn't make sense. If she knew something then all that she needed to do was to come and see me. I might even have released Fred within days if the story was tested and found to be true. But then, perhaps, she didn't know that she knew something.' Patrick mused on that for a few moments, bending a thin metal ruler into a hoop-like shape and then allowing it to spring

back. 'But our murderer suspected her,' he continued energetically, 'and followed her, followed her to make sure that she did
go to the barracks, saw that she went into the convent, instead,
and stayed there for some considerable time. And perhaps
when she came out, this person joined her, somebody that she
knew. Accompanied her, perhaps, and then told her that this
was a quick way to the barracks, something like that, strangled
her and pushed her body over the weir. The confession had
been made to the Reverend Mother. Our unknown assailant
could have made sure of that, could have questioned her and
got it out of her. Might have realized that she knew something
that would be dangerous to him or her. Suicide could have
been a likely scenario in preference to a trial and death by
hanging. This would have been believed by the coroner and
his jury and the hunt for the real murderer could have been
abandoned.'

'Who could it have been?'

Patrick was silent for a moment. 'According to the Reverend
Mother, three people knew that Bridie was on her way to the
barracks to see me and they were Mrs Mulcahy, Susan Mulcahy
and Richard McCarthy. Mr McCarthy, I gather, was the one
that assured her that she would get regular meals and would
only spend a few months in prison. A solicitor advised him
of that, according to the Reverend Mother's account of the
conversation with Bridie.'

Patrick got to his feet and took his coat and cap from its
stand. 'I think that we need the body to be officially identified
now. I'll go up to Shandon Street and get hold of the mother
and daughter, both if possible.'

'Interesting to watch their reactions, but at best they must
be a cold-blooded pair to force poor Bridie into that confession. That poor woman worked in their house, probably
slaved for them for over twenty years, apparently. Do you
want a lift?'

'No, thank you, Dr Scher. The walk will do me good, clear
my head.' He didn't like to say that Shandon Street was
somewhat steep for Dr Scher's elderly Humber. He would
be quicker walking.

'Joe!' He gave a quick knock on the sergeant's door and

then put his head inside. 'Joe, I want you to get hold of Mr Richard McCarthy, I want to have a word with him about the Mulcahy murder. His place of business is up on Shandon Street, quite close to the cathedral. Take a guard with you in the car and bring him back here. I'm off, but I will be back within the hour.'

'Yes, inspector.' Joe was on his feet, looking slightly astonished. 'What shall I do with him if I'm back before you?'

'Put him in a cell, no, that won't do. Put him in room eight. No cups of tea or anything. Just tell him that I will be back shortly.'

Room eight was probably worse than a cell. It was very damp with one small, barred window that faced onto a fifteen-foot high wall. It was seldom used because of the problems of damp and lack of sunlight, but it had a couple of chairs and a desk with three sound legs that was propped up by a wooden box. Mr McCarthy could brood on his story while he waited there.

Susan came to the door to answer Patrick's knock on the Shandon Street house. He thought that she looked at him expectantly, but otherwise could read little from her face. She wanted to be a doctor, according to the Reverend Mother. A strange occupation for a girl, he thought disapprovingly. Probably showed that she was a bit cold-blooded.

'Good afternoon, Miss Mulcahy,' he said politely. 'Could I come in, please?'

She led him into the office and found him a chair and then seated herself opposite to him with her back to the window that overlooked Shandon Street. Plain-looking girl, he thought. Wonder what Richard McCarthy sees in her. Still, perhaps, he had wanted to cement the alliance with her father. But what about now? Did he still want to marry this tough-looking young lady who wanted to go to university instead of settling down to have a family? And, even if Mr Mulcahy had left plenty of money behind him, it would soon shrink once shared out between a widow and twelve children.

'Could you call your mother, please,' he said aloud and watched her frown.

'My mother is not well, inspector, she has gone to lie on her bed. She has a bad headache.'

'Nevertheless, I would wish to see her, Miss Mulcahy.' Firm and polite. He was well-practised in this voice by now.

'Why?' And then when he did not respond to that monosyllable, she added, 'Is it something to do with Bridie? If so, I can assure you that I know all about that business.'

'What business?'

She eyed him angrily. 'I know that Bridie has confessed to you that she was the one who murdered my father. And let me tell you, inspector, that I am not surprised.'

'No.' He leaned back a little in the chair and watched her as well as he could. The room was lit only by the light from the street window and even in the early afternoon, it was quite dim. She showed no impulse to hide her face or to look down but opened her eyes at him defiantly.

'My father, inspector, was not a man who treated women well. My mother had a lot to put up with, and so had Bridie.'

What was she implying? He lacked the finesse to put that question to her. After all, she was an unmarried girl.

'What made Bridie decide to go to the barracks and to confess to murder?' he asked. The woman must have a surname, but no one had mentioned it. Even the Reverend Mother, meticulously polite, had never called her anything other than Bridie.

'I don't know, inspector; what did she say to you?' A tough girl, he thought. By all accounts the poor woman had brought her up. Surely she should be showing a bit of concern, a bit of compunction that she had been one of the persuaders. Unless, of course, that concern for her brother had overridden any feeling for her nurse.

Or concern for herself.

Patrick found himself considering the girl opposite to him. Sturdily built, quite tall for a girl, probably helped in the tanning yard from time to time. Women, he knew from his upbringing, could be as strong as men when they needed to be. She would have developed good muscles over the years, would know where to find a weapon and where to conceal one. He remembered the tenement that sheltered himself and his mother and remembered how the women, in the absence of men, coped with seeming impossible feats of strength. His own mother had by sheer force of will and determination, once held up the collapsing timbers of an abandoned coal house so that she and he could escape with their meagre bag of nuggets.

But was it possible for a daughter to murder her own father? Would that be possible? He almost laughed at the question that had come into his mind. He must be getting soft. In his experience people often hated members of their own family more than strangers. His eyes wandered to a basket placed beneath the counter. A large cabbage, a bottle of Jeyes Fluid and a tin with 'Beamish & Crawford' printed on it. It would be yeast, of course, yeast from the brewery. Yeast-baked bread, always a great treat for those who had an oven, after weeks and weeks of griddle-baked soda bread. The Jeyes Fluid and the cabbage could have been bought locally on Shandon Street, but for the yeast, she would have had to go right down to the river, down North Main Street and South Main Street, almost as far as St Mary's Isle, itself, where the Beamish & Crawford brewery sold off yeast at a low price.

'You've been shopping, Miss Mulcahy,' he said.

He saw her glance hastily at the basket and for a moment could have sworn that she paled slightly. But then she faced him courageously. She had been quick-witted enough to see the implication of the yeast.

'Yes,' she said. 'I walked down with Bridie. She asked me to come with her. I did some shopping on my way back.'

'But you didn't accompany her to the barracks.' He watched her carefully as he said that. Would there be a hesitation, an acknowledgement that the woman had gone to the convent.

'No,' she said. And yes, there had been a slight pause before the word. But that could be explained. It was a bit cold-hearted not to accompany the woman and to sit by her when she confessed. Especially if Bridie were just doing it to save the girl's own brother.

'You didn't think that you would have been a support to her?'

'No, she didn't want me to come any further. We parted at Hanover Street. She went off towards the barracks.'

He considered her for a moment and he didn't like what he saw. A tough young woman, he thought. Surely any decent girl would be showing signs of anxiety by now.

'Bridie was found dead in the river, just by St Mary's of the Isle, about an hour ago, Miss Mulcahy,' he said and purposely made the words harsh. 'What do you know about that?' The second sentence came out from him like a follow-up punch, but he wasn't sorry. If this girl had killed her own father; induced an unfortunate woman, a woman who had brought her up, to make a false confession, and then pushed her into the river, well, then, it wasn't safe to leave her at liberty. Those who have killed once, will kill again, was his experience.

And she didn't bat an eye, didn't show any surprise, any horror. Didn't ask any questions. She looked at him steadily, but almost as though she were not seeing him, just turning matters over in her mind.

'I'm not surprised,' she said after a long moment.

'Not surprised! Do you think that someone pushed her over the bridge, then,' he queried and then waited to see the effect of his words. Would she show alarm? Would she introduce the idea of suicide?

'Was that what you meant?'

'Was what?'

'I thought, originally, that you meant that she committed suicide,' she said and there was almost an air of relief about the words that puzzled him.

Perhaps, though, to give Miss Mulcahy her due, the girl was thinking about Bridie's immortal soul. There was a belief in Cork that, although someone who committed suicide would go straight to hell, that the victim of a murder would have all of their sins forgiven – on the vague grounds, he thought, that they were not given time to make a last confession. He had never heard a priest endorse this viewpoint, but, nevertheless, had always been glad that the relatives of those mutilated bodies in the barracks' mortuary would have that means of consolation. Nevertheless, this girl was a cool customer. He made up his mind instantly.

'I'm afraid that I must ask you and your mother to make a formal identification of the body, Miss Mulcahy,' he said.

'What about Fred?' The words came out in a slightly faltering tone.

'Not possible by the rules,' he said curtly.

You make the rules in your own department. The superintendent had said that to him after a few drinks to celebrate Patrick's appointment as inspector. The man was quite drunk at the time, of course, but Patrick had stored up the words at the back of his mind. He scrutinized the girl's face. Tough and all as she was, this had disconcerted her. Boldly he swung open the door and walked out into the hall.

'Mrs Mulcahy,' he called up the stairs. 'Mrs Mulcahy, I'm sorry to disturb you, but I'm afraid that I need your presence. Could you come down, please?'

He stood in the hallway, waiting. In a moment the girl came out. Without saying anything, she took a coat from the hallstand and put it on. There were two coats there, both black. Once she had buttoned up her own coat and pulled on a hat, she took the second coat and held it; held it oddly, almost as though she nursed it within her arms. There was a sound of footsteps from overhead and then the opening and closing of a door.

Mrs Mulcahy was very white. Patrick knew a moment's compunction as he watched her come down the uncarpeted stairway. She moved heavily and slowly, almost like an old woman. She did not look at him, but at her daughter, and there was a measure of fear in the gaze. She said nothing for a moment, just turned her back and held out her arms, rather like a child waiting for an adult to dress her. It was only after she had buttoned up the coat that she spoke, and then it was to her daughter rather than to him.

'Is it Bridie?' she asked and Susan nodded.

'She threw herself over the bridge at St Mary's Isle, Mam,' she said. There was a warning note in the girl's voice, almost as though she wanted to forestall a comment, or a question from her mother.

Interesting, thought Patrick. Susan had gone back to the suicide idea. And yet he had said nothing to deny that she might have been pushed, rather than have jumped. The bridge leading to St Mary's Isle was a populous one. There would have been many witnesses to any suicide from that place. The matter would not have been in doubt. The lonely, derelict and deserted weir upstream from the river was a different matter.

'I want you and your daughter to come and identify her body, Mrs Mulcahy,' said Patrick. He felt another moment's compunction as he saw how her face paled even more, but he eased his conscience with the thought that he would get Joe to make them a cup of tea and then drive them back up the long steep hill to Shandon. Somehow, he felt that he would get more of the truth out of Mrs Mulcahy than from her taciturn, clever-eyed daughter. He went to the front door and held it open and they passed through without a word to him or without another glance at each other.

Their appearance on Shandon caused a certain amount of excitement. Women in shawls clustered in small groups, eyeing the trio and whispering to each other. Upper windows were darkened by figures peering down onto the street. Doors opened and women with mops, women with bags for the rag-and-bone man, women feeding babies, women throwing the contents of buckets into the gutter, appeared and even the pawnshop owner came to the doorway, an old-fashioned bellows in one hand and a customer at his shoulder. Patrick felt rather sorry that he had not brought the Ford. He had wanted to think, wanted to work out the implications of Bridie's death, but this was hardly fair on the women. He thought that perhaps he should engage them in light conversation, make some remarks about the weather, perhaps, but a glance at the two aloof faces made the words die on his lips. In any case, the pavement was very narrow, very full of holes and very slippery between the holes. One needed to pay attention and to look for a safe place to step. And so they walked in silence, the two women ahead and he behind, all the way down the street until they reached the quay. Neither asked a question as they crossed the first bridge, and then the second bridge, but when they came to Clarke's Bridge, only a few minutes away from St Mary's Isle, Patrick saw the two women look at each other and then Susan glanced at him. A very rapid glance, but he had been waiting for it and without turning his head, had kept her face within his vision.

She didn't look enquiring, he thought. Didn't look as though she were going to ask a question of him. The fleeting look was appraising, the look one gives when summing up the opposition.

Joe came to the door of his room once he heard the voices in reception.

'Key to the morgue, please, sergeant,' said Patrick. He saw old Tommy at the desk shoot up his eyebrows at this abruptness. Usually witnesses to identify dead bodies were handled with kid gloves, spoken to in soft, reassuring voices. The word 'morgue' was never mentioned in the normal way of things.

Patrick, however, said no more. Just cocked an eyebrow when Joe came back. His assistant responded with a slight inclination of his head towards room eight and Patrick was satisfied that his third victim awaited his interrogation. But first of all he would see what the women had to reveal.

'Come this way, please,' he said and led them down the passageway towards the building at the back of the barracks.

There was one gas lamp lit when he pushed open the door. It shone down on the table beneath it and the rest of the room was in darkness. Dr Scher must have left it on, not liking, perhaps, that the dead woman be left in the dark. A white sheet covered the body and Patrick moved across to the stone table and then stood and waited for the two women to come also. They tried to stand next to him and adroitly he moved to the opposite side and then pulled the sheet down from the woman's face.

Mrs Mulcahy gave a gasp and turned her head away, but Susan looked steadily and silently down on the body. The neck had been made visible by his action and he thought that he could see her look there. He moved the sheet just a little lower and watched her carefully. She bent slightly forward, scrutinizing the dead woman. He saw her nod.

'She broke her neck,' was what she said and he was repelled by the almost interested tone in which she spoke the words.

'You are not surprised?' he asked. Mrs Mulcahy had pulled

out a handkerchief and held it in front of her face. He had not
heard a sob, though, and the handkerchief, under the white
light of the gas fitting, seemed to his eyes to remain dry. Susan
did not answer his question. Her eyes were on the dead woman
and he wondered whether she was praying, or whether she
was thinking of what to reply.

'I'm interested in anatomy,' she said stiffly and the mother
drew a little to one side as though to dissociate herself from
her daughter's answer.

'Anatomy!' he echoed the word. It had been unexpected.

'I suppose that the act of striking against the water might
be enough to break the bones of the neck,' she said, half to
him and half to herself.

They mostly die with their lungs filled with water, thought
Patrick, thinking of all the dead bodies that he had seen in his
time in the Civic Guards, and of all the coroner's court hear-
ings that he had attended. He said nothing, however, just stood
very silent, as though waiting for the women's next move.

'Poor Bridie. She wouldn't have known what she was doing.
She'd be thinking of something and then she'd step into a
puddle without even seeing it ahead of her. Do you think that
she could have just fallen in?' Mrs Mulcahy ventured that
supposition. Her daughter gave her an exasperated look, but
Patrick seized on the remark. Get them talking and you'd never
know what they'll come up with. That had been the superintendent's advice to him when he had first become a sergeant.

'You would think that it might have been an accidental
death, Mrs Mulcahy, would you?' he asked.

Her gaze avoided his. 'Well, what else could it be? No one
was putting any pressure on her; I can swear to God about
that, inspector.' And then she said no more, silenced by a quick
swing of her daughter's face towards her. The interested,
contemplative look on the girl's face had changed to a look
of almost savage exasperation. She controlled herself with an
effort, though. A clever one, thought Patrick. Her mother had
recourse to the handkerchief, again, but Patrick thought that
he would push the question a little.

'Putting pressure on her?' he queried, looking directly at
the older woman.

'It wasn't any of my doing?' Mrs Mulcahy sounded defensive, almost belligerent.

'Who do you think was the one that put the pressure on, then?' The girl made a sudden, impatient move and Patrick felt slightly ashamed of himself. If there had been a solicitor present he would have been forced to withdraw this question.

'Not me,' she said stubbornly.

'Your daughter?'

'No, no.'

'Who else was present then, Mrs Mulcahy.'

'My husband's friend. Mr McCarthy. He came about the will.'

'And he tried to persuade Bridie to confess to the killing of your husband?'

'I'm not saying anymore,' she said then and turned to her daughter, clutching at the girl's sleeve as though for comfort.

'You've said enough,' said Susan grimly. She faced Patrick angrily. 'Should you be asking her those questions in here, beside the body?'

He decided to ignore this. If this was murder, murder of an unfortunate defenceless woman, it was his duty to get at the truth as quickly as possible. There was nothing in the police handbook which forbade what he was doing. He kept his voice soft and meticulously polite as he said, 'This is something that you will be asked in the Coroner's Court, Mrs Mulcahy. Was there, in your mind, any reason why Bridie might have wanted to commit suicide?'

She gave a little shriek, but said nothing, just looked sideways at her daughter. After a moment she began to get a little courage. 'She was a bit upset, like, wasn't she, Susan, that Fred was being blamed for the death of his father, that's right, isn't it, Susan?'

'Yes,' said Susan and closed her lips firmly on the monosyllable.

'I think that I should tell you, Mrs Mulcahy, that Bridie visited Reverend Mother Aquinas shortly before we found her body,' said Patrick. 'She told the Reverend Mother that you, your daughter and Mr Richard McCarthy had persuaded her that if she confessed to the murder then it would be judged to be self-defence and that she, Bridie, would only get a very short sentence, "be out in a few months" were the words that she used, I understand.' Patrick waited for a response, but Mrs Mulcahy had recourse to her handkerchief again. 'Perhaps you could answer that question, Miss Mulcahy,' he went on with an even more marked degree of politeness in his voice. He saw the girl look at him with intense dislike but stayed very still and kept his eyes fixed on her. I wonder did she do the two murders, she has that look about her, very sure of herself, very sure of her own cleverness. She thinks that she is going to get away with this. These were his thoughts, but he knew that his face would remain inscrutable.

'Both my mother and I were fairly sure that Bridie killed my father,' said Susan in a clear, confident tone. She looked at him across the dead body, but did not glance down at the inert form. 'She had gone upstairs after him. We heard a bit of shouting and then no more. And when Bridie came downstairs eventually, she said that *himself* had gone back to Montenotte and so we could all have a bit of peace. These were her words, inspector.'

'I see,' said Patrick. 'And why did you not tell me that before now, Miss Mulcahy?'

'I didn't want to get Bridie into trouble.' The words came very readily to this young lady. 'I thought that justice would prevail, that it would be found out that my brother had nothing to do with the murder of his father. But time has gone on, inspector, and my brother has now been four days in your custody. If Bridie had decided to confess, then all we could do was to make the best of it and hope that our evidence of mistreatment, of provocation, would be taken into account.'

'Well, in that case, Miss Mulcahy, I'll take a statement from you in my office. And then, Mrs Mulcahy, I'm sure that you could do with some tea and my assistant will look after you.' He bent over and drew the sheet back to hide the poor battered face again and escorted the two women from the room.

FIFTEEN

Michael Staines, First Commissioner of the Civic Guards
'The *Garda Síochána*, (guardians of the peace), will
succeed not by force of arms or numbers, but on their
moral authority as servants of the people.'

'Strange girl, that Susan Mulcahy. Do you know her at all, Reverend Mother?' For once Patrick helped himself to a cup of tea. He looked worried and frustrated, thought the Reverend Mother.

'Just a little,' she replied. 'I knew her as a child, of course, when Bridie used to bring the children to see Sister Bernadette. But yes, I met her recently.' She thought about it for a moment, but could not see any harm in divulging the reason for Susan's visit to her. 'She came to see me, she is keen to attend university and to study medicine,' she said. 'I think that there might be some argument over whether finances are sufficient for that. She is very keen. She had a first-year university student's book on anatomy, Dr Scher. She bought it second-hand and she said that she had memorized every word and every drawing in it.' She decided not to bring up her own offer to the girl. That, she felt, had probably been turned down and she was glad of it. Let Susan Mulcahy make her own way without hindrance of religious or family expectation.

'She should do well at university, then, this Susan Mulcahy,' commented Dr Scher. 'Most of these rascals just pick that book up a few weeks before the exams and as for memorizing the drawings! Well, you should see their efforts in the exam papers! And she wouldn't be the first woman to become a doctor from Cork University; we're much more liberal here than they are in England. It's only recently that they have admitted women to a medicine course in Oxford and we had our first woman doctor nearly twenty years ago. Yes, she should do well, any girl that can plough through that book on anatomy on her own and without the benefit of my illuminating lectures or instruction must be very dedicated and want to become a doctor very badly.'

'Badly enough to get rid of her father who was standing in her way,' said Patrick quietly. He sat back and looked at them both.

And then when the Reverend Mother and Dr Scher looked back at him, both slightly startled by his words, he said, 'Didn't care for her much. I talked with her for a long time. Joe fed the mother with tea and cake and I talked with Miss Susan Mulcahy. She gave nothing away that would in any way incriminate either herself or her mother, but she struck me as very clever, very determined. A bit-coldblooded, not at all moved by the sight of the dead body of a woman who had brought her up, very fluent in quoting Bridie's words now that the woman is not around to contradict her. I'm not sure whether she had any feeling for her or not, but there's no doubt but that she had a glib tongue in her mouth, as they say,' added Patrick. He had a slightly shame-faced aspect after that outburst, thought the Reverend Mother. She knew him well. A girl like that would bring all Patrick's insecurities about himself to the surface.

'You didn't like her, Patrick.' Dr Scher made the statement while pouring himself a third cup of tea. He held the pot aloft, but Patrick shook his head impatiently.

'It's not a question of like or dislike. It's a question of who might seem likely, who might fit the pattern of a secret killer. I didn't think that the mother would have had the nerve, to be honest. She might have picked up an iron bar or a pole and knocked her husband on the head, by all accounts he was fairly unpleasant, both to her and to Bridie, but I think that she would have gone to pieces afterwards. I can't see her shutting the body in a trunk and calmly allowing the auctioneer's men to cart it off to the auction.'

'Unless that was Susan's idea,' put in the Reverend Mother.

'Perhaps. Well, yes, I did think that she was a devoted daughter, to her mother. But putting Susan aside, and thinking about Mrs Mulcahy . . .' Patrick thought hard for a moment and then shook his head. 'She is certainly a possibility if she had been badly treated and was filled with resentment against her husband. But no, I don't see her killing him, I don't think so. But in any case, I'm pretty sure that she wasn't the one who followed Bridie down to the convent and then knocked her over the weir, breaking her neck first. Mrs Mulcahy might be quite strong, but I didn't get the impression that she was too agile. She stumbled a few times going down Shandon Street, and after all, she must know that place like the back of her hand. I was walking behind them and I noticed that. After a while Susan took her arm and seemed to support her. The weir, that slippery path, all those tumbled stones; that would have been difficult, whether she had a live woman, or a dead woman with her. No, I don't see Mrs Mulcahy as the person who killed Bridie. After all, the woman had twelve children, one after the other, and I wouldn't say that there was much care taken of her, either.'

Thirteen children, at least, thought the Reverend Mother, and a motive, she supposed, for hating her husband if he had built a tanning yard on top of her dead unbaptized baby's grave. Still Patrick was right, it took a certain amount of quick-wittedness to have popped the man's body into the trunk and closed the lid over. Even the macabre business of packing the body around with old skins showed a measure of fore-thought. And, as for the murder of poor Bridie, well that took strength as well as quick-wittedness. Mrs Mulcahy, she thought, recalling that prematurely aged, black-garbed figure that she had met in Shandon Street, Mrs Mulcahy was not a likely suspect.

'Could it have been both?' asked Dr Scher. 'The wife killed him in a fit of rage and the daughter, protective of her mother, engineered a cover-up. Hoped that the recipient of the trunk would be blamed.'

'Possibly even the auctioneer,' put in Patrick.

'Very likely,' said Dr Scher and the Reverend Mother allowed a thought to cross her mind of how the interrogation of Mr Hayes would progress between a laconic young policeman and the very fluent auctioneer.

'Perhaps, Miss Susan Mulcahy only thought of the involvement of Bridie when the news of her brother's capture

and incarceration arrived at Shandon Street. She seems from
what you say, Patrick, to be a very cold-blooded young woman,
but possibly she is fond of her brother.'

'It's possible.' The Reverend Mother brooded on Susan.
Was she cold-blooded enough to have carried out this murder
of a woman who had brought her up and lavished affection
on her and her brothers and sisters?

'Yes, indeed. She's a very cool young lady, indeed,' said
Patrick, almost as though he had read her thoughts. 'I was
taken aback when I pulled the sheet back from the body and
all that Miss Susan was interested in was in looking at the
neck for signs of broken bones. I must say that I mistrusted
her. I couldn't see an ounce of horror or even of ordinary
mourning in her.'

'How did you get on with Mr McCarthy, Patrick?' asked
Dr Scher. The Reverend Mother heard him, but was more
interested in turning over her thoughts about Susan, while
Patrick gave an account of his interview with the man who
called himself a business partner of the late Mr Mulcahy.
Patrick would have found the cross-examination of Mr
McCarthy easier than interrogating Susan. An intelligent girl,
a girl who was clear-minded about her own potential, her own
possibilities. Possibly a gifted girl. The gifted, she had often
thought from her reading of lives of great men, were often
single-minded, determined on a goal and ignoring or oblite-
rating all obstacles that got in the way of that goal. Could the
removal of a father, determined to reduce her to a servant or
a pawn in his business matters, could that, for Susan, have
been merely a matter of removing an obstacle to her goal of
qualifying as a doctor? She had been in the house, she had
been one of three people still remaining within the house in
the late afternoon, when her father, it was presumed, had been
killed. Unless, of course . . .

'What time did Mr McCarthy say that he left the house,
Patrick?' she asked. She had been watching him while her
mind sifted through the evidence against Susan. Patrick had
taken out his notebook and was scanning through its
contents. He read it through carefully, twice, she thought,
before putting it to one side. Even as a child, in the infant

classes of the convent school, he had been the fortunate possessor of an excellent memory. That, and his tenacity of purpose had been his two gifts and they had carried him further than others who had possessed more brains. The Reverend Mother thought fleetingly of Eileen and all her gifts, and heaved a slight sigh. But then she turned her attention back to Patrick.

'Mr Richard McCarthy said that he left about half past four,' said Patrick, 'and that he was, to quote himself, on the heels of Mr Hayes. He saw the auctioneer's Ford car go up Shandon Street and turn down one of the lanes. He went home then to have his supper. He lives up on top of the hill, himself, alone, he is unmarried and does not have anyone living with him, so there is no evidence that he did as he said. I got Joe, my sergeant, on to it, but it's a busy place and he's a man that goes up and down the street, quite a bit, so people don't take notice of his presence in the way that they would if a stranger passed them. No one could remember seeing him or they were so unsure that they would be no use to us or to him in court. His manner,' said Patrick, 'was very belligerent and aggressive. I made a note of it at the time. He kept emphasizing what a busy man he was and that he had spent a lot of valuable time assisting the Mulcahy family during the last few days.'

'And the proposed marriage with Susan, did he mention that?' asked the Reverend Mother.

'I asked him about it. He brushed it aside, said that it had been an idea of the father, but he didn't think that the girl was keen. He said that in a completely indifferent way.'

'Had he anything to gain from Mr Mulcahy's death, do you think?' asked Dr Scher.

'Get rid of a rival businessman. Possibly, probably, buy the business off the widow.' Patrick began to count on his fingers. 'Expand his own business. He may have been the one who persuaded Mr Mulcahy to build a new yard quite near to his own yard and the two businesses could now be very easily amalgamated into one. Nothing to stop that, once he persuaded Mrs Mulcahy to sell. And it wouldn't take too long an acquaintance with that poor woman to see that he could name his own price. There would be nothing stopping him.'

'Except Susan,' said the Reverend Mother and she felt a qualm as she said the words.

Patrick looked across at her.

'Susan, the girl,' he queried.

'Women aren't the same as they were when you and I were young, Patrick,' said Dr Scher shaking his head sadly. 'Shortening their skirts, cutting their hair, riding motorbikes, toting guns, as our friends the Americans say.'

Patrick ignored Dr Scher's teasing. His face darkened a little. 'I know,' he said. And then, after a moment, 'I wouldn't be surprised if Susan had something to do with her father's death. Is that what you were thinking, Reverend Mother?'

'No, not really,' said the Reverend Mother. 'I was thinking that she might be in danger. The young can be very confident, very sure of themselves, very sure that they can outwit enemies. Dr Scher is right. Freedom, to a certain extent, is rushing in very rapidly for these young girls. I often think of it. I see a big difference between the older girls that we have here in our school and their mothers, not so long ago. These girls speak their mind more readily, make more judgements, take more risks, ask advice less of the older generations.'

Patrick thought about this for a moment. He had an enormous respect for the Reverend Mother's judgement, but her words only made grow an inner conviction that Susan Mulcahy might have something to do with her father's death. Her stony face had held no sorrow when looking down on the dead body of the poor unfortunate woman who had been her nurse. A pity he could not confront her with her father's corpse, but it was a bit late for that now. The man was dead and buried.

'It might be good to keep an eye on her, Patrick,' said the Reverend Mother. 'She's had a big struggle throughout her life to get her brains acknowledged. It has probably made her value intelligence rather too highly. Myself, if I had a few fairy godmothers under my rule, I'd prefer them to hand out the gift of common sense to the little princesses of the future.'

Dr Scher laughed, but Patrick thought that the Reverend Mother had spoken with her usual good sense and felt obscurely comforted by her words. He took out his notebook again and scrutinized it.

'The women in the kitchen saw Mr Hayes leave, he came in and said goodbye to them and then they saw him go out, heard him crank up his car, so he did leave about half past four, and Mr Mulcahy was certainly alive then, but there is no real evidence of when McCarthy left the house, is there?' he said slowly.

'Didn't he leave shortly after Hayes?' asked Dr Scher. 'I thought that he said he saw him.'

'He *said* that he saw Mr Hayes's car. I'll send Joe to check, but I don't suppose that Mr Hayes saw him. Mr McCarthy would have been on foot and well behind the car. You don't go looking over your shoulder when you are driving.'

'The women heard Henry Mulcahy stump up the stairs, though. You said that, didn't you, Patrick. Wouldn't they have noticed a second pair of footsteps?' asked Dr Scher.

'Not necessarily,' said Patrick slowly. 'Mr Mulcahy was an elderly man and he was also very heavy. I remember noticing his weight in your autopsy report, Dr Scher. Mr McCarthy is thirty years younger and a much lighter man, very agile, I thought. If he went upstairs with Mr Mulcahy, behind him, probably, up those very narrow stairs, I think that the noise of one set of footsteps would have blocked out the other set. The question is, did he have enough of a motive for murder.'

'With a blow like that, I would, personally, never rule out either self-defence or accident,' said Dr Scher. 'Different with poison, different on the whole with a bullet or a knife. We're all more primitive than we think. It comes easily to a man to snatch up a stick, after all it's what people have been doing since back in the Stone Age. Whenever you see a picture of a man from those days, what do you notice about him? He's dressed in animal skins and he has a club in his hand. And, now that we've progressed beyond the Iron Age, well that club or stick might well be an iron bar.'

'So the two men might have an argument, a fight, tempers were lost, a blow, a fatal blow and then McCarthy, Mr McCarthy, decided to cover his tracks. He put the body into the handy trunk, slipped out into the back yard, fetched some skins – though perhaps they might have been in a bag, ready to be taken up to the tanning yard – anyway, he wedges the body in with them, closes the trunk and then slips quietly away, probably through the back door, would you say?' Patrick brooded on that for a moment, gave a nod and made a few notes, headed with the word 'CHECK'.

'What did you think of him, Patrick, when you interviewed him?' Dr Scher asked.

'I thought he was a good-looking fellow. Smart, too. One of those fellows that like to guess why you've asked the question, almost before it's out of your mouth.' It had been quite an unpleasant interview. Patrick very much disliked being rushed and this man McCarthy had seemed to be rushing him, continually interrupting his question before he finished and continually saying, 'I know why you asked that.' He had wished to find a reason to detain the man a bit longer, but had run out of questions.

'Quite good-looking and quick of wits.' Dr Scher seemed to muse over that for a moment. 'Odd that Miss Susan was so against the match that her father made for her, wasn't it? What do you think, Reverend Mother? You know a lot about these young girls.'

'I wouldn't think of Susan Mulcahy as a young girl, more of a woman,' said the Reverend Mother. 'She's nineteen years of age, almost twenty, intelligent and determined. As to why she did not acquiesce to her father's choice of husband for her; well, there are two reasons against it. The first should be sufficient. She didn't love, didn't even like the man, if she spoke the truth, and the second is that she has a different vision in front of her.' The Reverend Mother thought about this for a moment, tried to put herself in the place of Susan Mulcahy and then shook her head firmly.

'Marriage: to be a wife, under the complete power of a husband; children, perhaps one baby after the other for the next twenty, twenty-five years. Like her mother she could end up with a very large family. And her other choice . . .' The Reverend Mother paused for another moment. Patrick wondered whether she was thinking back to over fifty years ago, to her own choice. Had she ever regretted it? The answer, he thought, was probably no. And somehow it seemed impossible to even think of St Mary's Isle and the south side of Cork city without her presence. He listened respectfully as she continued firmly, 'Her other choice was to use the gifts that God had given to her, the gifts of intelligence, tenacity, perseverance and to train these gifts so that they could be used in the service of mankind. Susan would, I feel, make a successful doctor and the world needs doctors of all sorts, women and men, all people who can empathize with their suffering brothers and sisters and who can help to alleviate their pain.' She finished firmly, feeling slightly amused at the two respectful faces before her.

'Doesn't mean that she didn't murder her father, though, does it?' said Dr Scher breaking the moment's silence. Patrick looked dubiously from one elderly face to another. What would the Reverend Mother say to that?

'That, indeed, is quite possible,' she said calmly. 'She may well have thought that it was her only way forward. She may have become desperate. What do you think, Patrick? Does desperation play a part in murder, or is anger more of a factor.'

Patrick thought carefully about this, reviewing in his mind the murders that had occurred during his time in the Civic Guards. 'I think that the murders committed because of anger are usually easier to solve,' he said slowly. 'Murders where someone is frightened, fear and anger, these ones are done without too much thinking about it.' He struggled to express his feelings in the clear, succinct form that the Reverend Mother valued. He remembered when he was a child how she had told the class that he had something important to tell them about ants and how good he had felt, standing out there in front of everyone and seeing her go to the back of class and stand there, looking so interested. He had never forgotten that.

'Of course,' he went on, 'a lot of deaths occur after closing time of the public houses. People drink and then . . . but, often when someone is desperate, they brood on things for a long time and they plan. Especially women. Women are great planners. Poison, mostly, that's the easiest way to get rid of someone. Very hard to know who gives poison. They could be out of the house at the time, it's a difficult one to convict on. Some murderers are very clever, some are stupid; some plan and some do it on the spur of the moment.'

The Reverend Mother, he thought, was thinking hard, but she said nothing.

'And this hitting a man on the back of the neck with a heavy club of some kind, or an iron bar, what would say about that, Patrick. Does it seem like a "spur of the moment" murder or a planned murder?'

'I'd say "spur of the moment" murder,' said Patrick. Suddenly his mind seemed to have cleared. 'It all fits,' he said. 'The man said something, refused something, perhaps Susan asked again about going to university. Her father said no, told her to put it out of her head, once and for all. He turned aside, that would fit the character of the man, wouldn't it? He said *no* and then turned aside to show that he was not even going to discuss it any longer, perhaps he went to pick up something from the floor, after all they were cleaning the place out, getting it ready to be auctioned with vacant possession, so he could have bent down to put something in the trunk or to throw it into the fireplace and she was so furious that she snatched up a bar or a stick of some sort and hit him hard, may not even have meant to kill him. But she's a cool type. Once she saw that he was dead, perhaps felt his pulse, well, then she decided to cover up the murder, get rid of the body. Mr Hayes had told them that the men would be around in half an hour to collect the stuff for the auction so she would have to work fast.'

'What about the skins packed around the body? Where did she get them?' asked Dr Scher.

'From the yard, of course. They were clearing up there, herself and Bridie. If she is as clever as you seem to think, Reverend Mother, then she would work out that she couldn't afford to have the body roll or move in the trunk. So she rushed down, got a few skins, crept up the stairs again and then packed him in solidly, wrote a label saying "Old School Books" and then went back downstairs again to join Bridie and her mother.'

'You've questioned the mother, of course?'

'Joe did that, on the first evening. According to their report, they stayed together, all three, in the kitchen, until the auction-eer's men arrived. Then Susan took them upstairs and showed where everything was. It had been all labelled.'

'And the handwriting on the trunk label?' asked the Reverend Mother.

Patrick shook his head, glad that she had asked that. It reminded him of how thorough he had been.

'That's the trouble. That doesn't fit. Doesn't match anyone's handwriting. I've taken samples from the five people who were in the house at the time. But it looks like an assumed hand. That very fancy full stop with an empty space in the middle of it.'

'And the dead man, Henry Mulcahy, himself?' asked Dr Scher. 'Could he have written it?'

Patrick shook his head. 'No, it wasn't his. There are plenty of account books in the office in the front room. No resemblance at all. I've even sent Joe down to the auctioneer's place to get samples from him and his foreman. It doesn't match any of them, no resemblance.'

'And the brother, young Fred?' the Reverend Mother put the question in an absent-minded way. She appeared to be thinking hard.

'No, Reverend Mother, no, it wasn't Fred's either. It's a strange, fancy sort of handwriting and that full stop, like a little circle, with a dot in the middle of it. You'd think that handwriting like that could have been identified, but we haven't managed to do it. None of the women remember any talk of school books, in fact . . .' Patrick leafed through his notebook again. 'Yes, here it is, something Joe told me, he asked about the label and Bridie said the master would never have sold them school books with all the young ones still to be educated. "Never, in a month of Sundays". That's what she said to Joe.'

'You said something like that to me, didn't you, Reverend Mother?' said Dr Scher.

The Reverend Mother said nothing. Her face bore the expression of someone who is thinking hard, thought Patrick. Perhaps she was impatient at all this talk about labels. What did the label matter? What mattered was hard evidence. He had a moment's regret that so far his conclusions, his gut instinct, seemed to be leading him to Susan. He would have much preferred it to be McCarthy. He didn't like having a woman found guilty of murder. There was something horrible about it.

Still, as the superintendent often said to him, he wasn't there in the Civic Guards to pick and choose, he wasn't there to be popular either. First thing to get out of your head, the superintendent told him cheerfully on his first day at the barracks, was that you'll keep any friends. He was there to make sure that the law of the land was kept. And when there was a crime, he was to gather evidence, 'without fear or favour' was the superintendent's expression. He was to weigh up that evidence carefully and then hand it all over to the lawyers and forget about it. Give his evidence and let the judge make the decision.

Nevertheless, he thought, he would once again send Joe up around Shandon Street and try to find evidence that McCarthy had been seen coming out of the house at a later hour, then he had said. Not half past four, but later, even five minutes later, would be enough to cast suspicion on him. The women, all three of them, had said that they heard Mr Mulcahy go upstairs, almost straight after the auctioneer had closed the front door behind them. None of them had heard the door close again, but they had reckoned that Mr McCarthy had gone out with Mr Hayes. That had not been his story, though. And Mr Hayes said that he had been alone. And, according to Mr McCarthy, himself, he stayed behind for a few minutes to have a quick word with Mr Mulcahy and then he had left. He had seen the Ford car turn a corner, that's what he had said.

'About two minutes to start up the car and get it going up that steep hill, what do you think, Dr Scher?' he said aloud.

'More or less. Yes, you could say that,' said Dr Scher after a moment's thought.

Patrick turned over to a fresh page.

'Mr Hayes leaves at half past four, according to the evidence of the three women, the solicitor leaves a few minutes later, Mr McCarthy, by his own evidence, leaves about twenty-five or twenty to five, the three women in the kitchen go on scrubbing out the cupboards and wooden presses, and the big table, all ready to be taken to the auction. They say that they were busy and they didn't hear anything after they heard Mr Mulcahy go upstairs. Susan said that there was a lot of noise going on. They were in the washhouse, off the kitchen, pumping up water from the old well so as to scrub the place out. I suppose that there would have been the noise of scrubbing brushes and the sound of the water filling up. They have a pump to an old well in that washhouse, although they have running water in the kitchen and upstairs. It's an old house. All three of them were built about a hundred and fifty years ago. Susan said that.'

'And what time did the auctioneer's men arrive?' asked Dr Scher.

'A bit late,' said Patrick. This time he did not bother going through the ritual of consulting his notes. 'They didn't come until about ten minutes past five and they went straight up to that front room, the one where the trunk was lying and they took out the windows. They had ropes to lower the furniture and the trunk, of course, down onto the lorry. They were about an hour at it, in and out of the house.'

'So the murder took place between half past four, approximately, and about quarter past five. And this means that one of four people must have done it. It must have been either one of the three women in the kitchen or Mr Richard McCarthy,' said Dr Scher. 'You're very quiet, Reverend Mother.'

'I was just thinking about handwriting,' said the Reverend Mother.

SIXTEEN

Patrick Pearse
'The Republic guarantees religious and civil liberty,
equal rights and equal opportunities of all its citizens,
and declares its resolve to pursue the happiness and
prosperity of the whole nation and of all its parts,
cherishing all the children of the nation equally . . .'

Eileen knew who it was as soon as she came into the outer office of the printing works. She couldn't see the face very well as the room was very dim and the windows covered in grime. When Eileen had first started work, in an excess of enthusiasm and determination to make a success of her first job, she had offered to wash the windows, but had been greeted by a shocked refusal. Later she understood. Many strange people came to the printing works, some smelled as though they had been lying out in the fields, some had a noticeable revolver bulging out a pocket, but all approached the door with great caution, wore their hats well pulled down over their eyes and did not remove them. Even when safely inside, they continually gave furtive glances over their shoulder. None of them wanted to be seen through a crystal clean, well-polished window. Nevertheless, she immediately recognized this visitor, the dowdy, old-fashioned skirt, the long hair bunched up behind the neck. At the funeral, she had thought that Susan was dressed as if she were one of her mother's generation.

Susan was sitting very still, sitting with her strong chin propped up on one hand while she stared at the floor. Even when Eileen came in, she did not stir for a moment. But then she looked up and got to her feet and came to meet her. 'I thought that I'd like to talk to you,' she said. 'Well, when I went to see Fred in the gaol, he mentioned your name and where you worked. He didn't say any more, but I guessed that he meant me to ask advice and help from you. There's not much that you can say, is there, when a warder is listening in?'

Not much you can say, either, when your boss is in the back office, screened only by a four-foot high counter. The owner of the printing works steered a narrow course between running a legitimate business, producing posters, leaflets and tickets for small businesses and the more furtive printing of political pamphlets and polemical essays. He deprecated any open conversation on political or illegal matters in the confines of the business and most affairs were conducted with a traditional nod and wink, or else printer and customer went for a walk beside the river where all was wide open and no one could lurk in doorways and overhear a conversation.

Well-versed in the ways of the business, Eileen gave a furtive look around and murmured, 'Let's have lunch; will you wait? I'll only be about five minutes. I just have to finish off something.' She didn't delay for a reply, but escorted her visitor back to her chair, found the *Cork Examiner* and pressed it into her hands and then returned rapidly to her desk. Too late, though. The boss was there, talking to Jack, the compositor, who stood holding a rod full of upside-down and back-to-front letters, nodding his head wisely. They both looked at her as she went to sit behind her typewriter and then the boss disappeared hastily leaving her to Jack.

'You're not planning anything, are you, Eileen?' said Jack. He was an elderly man. She got a bit irritated with him sometimes when he tried to pretend that he was her grandfather and was the one to give her advice on all subjects, but mainly she liked him. Now, however, she did not look at him, but began to roll a new sheet of paper onto her typewriter, taking meticulous care that the edges were straight. It didn't work, though. Jack was a persistent man.

'No' planning daring raids on Cork Gaol or anything like that, are you?' he said. 'No' dragging your boyfriend out, dressed up as a girl, are you? I suppose there'll be no holding you now that you have your own motorbike. You'll be up there in *Dáil Eireann* waving a pistol at them. But I'd leave Fred Mulcahy alone. You may love him dearly, but he'll be very well guarded. You haven't a chance of getting him out of gaol.'

'Don't be stupid, Jack,' snapped Eileen. 'Fred Mulcahy is nothing but a nuisance to me. He's certainly not my boyfriend.'

'One of them, I should have said; I suppose the queue would stretch down the length of Patrick Street if you were to put all your boyfriends edge to edge.'

'You've dropped a piece of type, look, there it is, under your chair,' pointed out Eileen and began to pound on her noisy typewriter at full speed. This was the trouble about Cork. Everyone knew everyone else's business. Susan had probably been recognized the minute she set foot in the printing works and the mention of Fred had been enough to set alarm bells ringing. The proprietor steered a careful path between Republican interests and the mechanics of running a profitable business to feed his family. He had been dubious about employing Eileen after her spell of notoriety, but he had given her a trial and had been pleased with her. She had even received a rise in her wage packet recently.

'I'm not going to risk the job just for Fred Mulcahy,' she said to herself as she mechanically typed out yet another list of furniture, bric-a-brac and framed pictures for Hayes' auctioneering rooms. Fred was not worth it. She was sorry for him. He was obsessed with his father and how much he hated him and she had often suspected that he had joined the Republicans just in order to infuriate the old man, but that did not make him an admirable person. He had none of the quiet determination and dedication that characterized Eamonn and Danny and most of the other boys that she had known. Fred, she thought, is always trouble, no matter where he goes. She had been lucky to escape with her life and her liberty from that business in the harbour.

When she finished the job and came into the outer office, Susan was still sitting in the very same position, half turned towards the window; her eyes fixed on its grimy surface.

'Let me just drop these off at the auction rooms and then we'll have lunch,' said Eileen. It was an indulgence to go out to lunch. She had a sandwich in her bag and normally made do with that, unless Eamonn came to take her out. But she would treat herself and Susan today. There was a very nice place in Cook Street. A good place to talk secrets if you went upstairs and took a seat beside the back window. The stairs were very steep and, during the week days, not many people bothered to climb them. And the tables were far apart.

'I'll pay for the lunch, Susan,' she said when they got outside. She had thought that Susan looked a little worried when she had mentioned lunch. The girl was carrying a handbag, a very old and very old-fashioned handbag, large enough to be a shopping bag, but the possibility was that she might have no money in it. 'I've had a rise in salary,' Eileen said chattily as they walked along the South Terrace. 'It's a lovely feeling.' And then, a little curiously, she asked, 'Did you ever think of getting a job, Susan? It's nice to have your own money coming in. I could teach you how to use a typewriter. It's easy to get the hang of it and after that, well, you just need practice.'

Susan shook her head. 'I don't want a job; I want to go to university and this is where I need your help.'

'I wouldn't know much about that,' said Eileen. She surveyed the girl dubiously. Susan was clever. She knew that. She and Eileen had sat the Intermediate Examination at the same time and had divided the top honours of Cork city together. Eileen had scored the highest mark in most subjects, but Susan had mostly come second to her. And when it had come to mathematics, Susan had easily beaten her. Yes, she would have the brains, but could her mother afford the fees? University cost pots of money and Susan looked poor. In fact, she looked very poor. Her clothes were terrible. Not just dreadfully out of fashion, but just plain awful. They looked as if they might have belonged to her mother. They didn't even fit correctly. Eileen sent a few quick, surreptitious glances at her as they walked side by side. The coat was far too wide on the shoulders and its sleeves drooped down over her fingertips. And that skirt that she wore seemed to be dipping to one side where it appeared below the hem of the coat. She was a very thin girl, with a small waist and could look great if she had the money for new clothes and a decent haircut. A short skirt, knee length, or above if possible, one of those up-to-date, hip-length cardigans and her hair shingled, then she could look quite fashionable and attractive.

That, as Eileen knew well, would cost a tiny fraction of the termly fee at university.

'Can your mother afford university for you?' she asked bluntly.

Susan looked at her sideways. 'The money could be found,' she said obliquely and then turned to look at the river. Her air was that of someone who wanted to say no more for the moment, and Eileen did not press her and talked a bit more about typing and how she had practised and practised, typing the sentence 'The quick brown fox jumps over the lazy dog' over and over again and thereby acquiring the skill to hit the key of any letter of the alphabet without even looking.

Susan, however, did not appear to be listening, but when they came out from the auctioneer's place, she stopped and looked at Eileen.

'Would you mind if we skipped lunch and went up to Pope's Quay. I have an appointment with my father's solicitor and I'd like a bit of company. I'd like someone that I could talk to afterwards and see if I am imagining things.'

'Imagining things?' queried Eileen.

'Imagining if we are being cheated out of my father's money,' said Susan, bluntly. 'I think this solicitor, who is supposed to be looking after our affairs, I think that he might be cheating us.'

'I'm not too good at the figures,' said Eileen doubtfully. 'I only got through the Intermediate because of the geometry and the algebra. I liked those, but I hate adding up. It bores me stiff and whenever I try to check, well, I keep getting different results.'

'Don't worry about the figures; I've got them all here.' Susan patted the large handbag. 'I just want you to watch his face, and perhaps ask a question if it occurs to you, sort of innocent-like, and then we can chat about it afterwards on our way back to your workplace.'

'Oh, I can do that.' Eileen gave a giggle. 'I love asking awkward questions. What's the name of your father's solicitor?' Did the girl miss her father, she wondered. She had not shed a tear at the funeral, but that just might be Susan. Never one to talk very much; she remembered that from the far-off days

when they had both sat the Intermediate Examination at the
Model School. All the other girls had been excited, nervous,
exhilarated, all talking away while Susan sat quietly in the
background studying log tables.

'It's a Mr O'Sullivan,' said Susan. 'I think that he is cheating
us. He says that he hasn't the money from the selling of the
two houses. But he must have. The bank doesn't have it, well,
so Richard McCarthy says. They won't talk to me at the bank;
I even dragged my mother down there but they wouldn't talk
to her. Just a lot of *plámás* – a lot of the old "How are you,
Mrs Mulcahy? I'm sorry for your trouble." All that sort
of thing, but no solid facts. They advised her to get Mr
McCarthy to talk to her. Said that he is the executor of the will,
so he's the one that she should be dealing with. Mam wants
me to talk to him.'

'And did you? I saw him at the funeral,' added Eileen.

'I did, but I might as well be idle. He's not telling anything,
just going on about how complicated everything is and how
we should leave everything to him.'

'What did your mam say to that?'

'She doesn't want any trouble. She'd prefer to let Richard
McCarthy handle everything.'

'But you're not happy.'

'No, I'm not.' Susan's voice was firm and downright. 'I've
been over and over the accounts; I know them well. And I
just think that nothing makes sense. Where is the money if
it isn't in the bank, that's what I want to know? I asked a
neighbour and she told me that the money is paid to the
solicitor who holds it until everything is fixed up. My father's
house was sold by auction, but I don't suppose that makes
any difference.'

Eileen thought about it. It did seem reasonable that if a
house was sold then the money for it should be somewhere.
And then she thought about something else.

'What about the house in Montenotte?' she asked. The whole
city was aware that Mr Mulcahy, Hide and Skin Merchant, if
you please, had built himself a large and fashionable house
in the exclusive territory of Montenotte. 'Wouldn't he have
spent the money there?' she asked.

'No,' said Susan. 'No, he would not. That house was budgeted for years ago. It was all bought and paid for and reckoned up, long before the house in Shandon Street was sold. I could show you the figures.' Once again she touched her enormous handbag. 'They are all here, all in this accounts' book. I've spent enough time on it. Reckoning up the credit and the debits, writing out cheques and reconciling the figures. There's nothing that I don't know about these accounts. In the last few years, my father has left them completely to me. I remember telling him that I had struck a balance, that everything for the Montenotte house had been bought and paid for. He was very pleased. He didn't have much education, my Pa, he told me once that he had come to the city as a barefoot-boy, but he had a good head for figures.'

'You take after him, I suppose,' said Eileen. She felt sorry for this poor girl. Susan was a daughter of a prosperous merchant, and she, herself, was the illegitimate offspring of a fifteen-year-old girl. Nevertheless, she knew that in the amount of love and of attention that she had received, she had been very much superior to poor Susan. Her mother thought the world of her, had always done so; had been amazed and noisily celebratory of her achievements from as far back as she could remember. The whole of Barrack Street had been informed of Eileen's cleverness. And she knew full well, that if there had been any remote possibility that Maureen MacSweeney could have funded a university education for her daughter, that she would have lived on dry bread in order to fulfil that ambition.

'I always liked figures,' said Susan.

'What do you want to study at university?' Eileen asked. The Reverend Mother had wanted Eileen to go to university, had wanted her to stay on in school for another year; had wanted to coach her for a university scholarship, a scholarship that would fund fees, books, and living expenses for a degree. She had been tempted. Had thought about it very seriously. Had known deep within her that the Reverend Mother's faith was not unfounded, had known that with hard work and the Reverend Mother's guidance, she would have a good chance.

But she had thrown it up; thrown it up to join the Republicans
who were fighting against the ignoble treaty which allowed
Britain to retain the north and to retain the important ports,
such as Cork Harbour. Still, some day, some day when Ireland
was a true republic and when Patrick Pearse's pledge that all
children in the land would have equal privileges, when that
day came . . .

'Not maths, is it?' she said aloud.

'No, I want to study medicine, to be a doctor,' said Susan.

'That would be brilliant. A woman doctor. That's what this
city needs. That would shake everyone up a bit.' Eileen was
immediately enthusiastic and began to walk faster. 'Let's see
what this solicitor has to say for himself,' she said.

'I can't possibly show you the will,' said Mr O'Sullivan. 'You
don't understand the law, young lady. The will has to go to
probate before it can be shown to anyone.'

'In books they always show it to the family straight after
the funeral,' put in Eileen.

'Oh, books!' The solicitor gave a light laugh and then put
his hand in front of his mouth and gave a hollow cough into
it. 'Don't you worry about the will, Miss Mulcahy. Myself and
Mr McCarthy, your father's executor, we'll look after it. These
matters are very, very complicated, you know. I don't suppose
that either of you have heard of such a thing as probate.'

'Yes, of course we have,' said Eileen stoutly, her mind flit-
ting through the pages of *Bleak House*. Surely that word,
'probate' had been mentioned somewhere among the eight
hundred pages of that huge novel. The Reverend Mother had
lent it to her from the series of classical novels kept in the
nuns' refectory and it had been an unspoken secret between
them that Sister Mary Immaculate would never know that
those sacred books, which reposed, mostly untouched, on their
well-dusted shelves had been lent to one of the girls. In the
secrecy of her room, the Reverend Mother had overseen the
making of a brown paper cover and Eileen had carried it home
reverentially.

'I'm thinking about becoming a lawyer myself,' she said
carelessly. 'So, of course, I have to study things like Probate

and Affidavits and Chancery and the Michaelmas term and all that sort of thing.' She finished with a light laugh and stared confidently across the empty desk at this solicitor. He had an uneasy look, she thought, although he was hiding it under an assumed manner of patronizing ease.

'And, of course, you do have to give Miss Mulcahy an idea of what her father's estate is worth. Just a round figure,' she said airily. 'Don't worry about the shillings and pence. Just how much did he leave in pounds?'

She saw how the solicitor's eyelids flickered and said the word 'crooked' to herself. It would be good to have someone like Tom Hurley here to interrogate him. She leaned slightly forward, just in the way that Tom Hurley would have done, shoulders squared, hand going to pocket as if ready to produce a gun at a moment's notice.

'As I say, probate . . .' His eyes went to the door a few times and now he almost seemed as though he were listening. And yet there had been no one in the other basement room when they had arrived.

'You've been expecting me, Mr O'Sullivan,' Susan put in. 'I've arrived at the time that you appointed. I'm surprised that you are not more prepared for my visit. I did tell you that I wanted to know about my father's will.' Susan was, of course, only trying to back up her friend, but Eileen wished that she had kept quiet. The girl's voice was rough with nerves and it shook badly. She was just giving this crooked-looking solicitor a chance to despise her.

'My client is, of course, very worried and anxious about this matter,' she said aloud, doing her best to try to imagine how Mr Tulkinghorn in *Bleak House* would have handled this conversation. 'She finds it most odd that there seems to be this veil of secrecy over affairs which concern her and her sister and brothers so closely.'

'Oh, don't concern yourself, Miss Mulcahy. You'll be fine. The house in Montenotte may have to be given up to pay the costs *et cetera, et cetera*, but you'll all be snug in the house in Shandon Street. You and your sister will probably be getting married soon. And your brothers, well, you know, Miss Mulcahy, some of those older boys might be best off going to Liverpool or London and looking for work there. This is a dangerous city for young lads and they, as you know to your sorrow, I'm afraid, they do get into trouble with the police. Bad company leads them astray,' he said, complacently smoothing his greasy, too long, greying hair behind his ears.

Eileen knew a moment of indignation and camaraderie on behalf of Fred Mulcahy and even more so on behalf of the boys with whom she had shared a life of exile and self-sacrifice. She opened her mouth indignantly and then shut it again. No point in being diverted by a man who knew how to pronounce *et cetera*, a word that, up to now, she had only imagined as a one syllabled *etc*. She would be suave and confident in everything that she said. By now she had thought herself thoroughly into the role of Susan's legal advisor. She could see the girl fidget with her handbag and sent her a warning glance. This was not the moment to produce the accounts book. Let him give the information first and then refute it if necessary.

'You're going off the point, Mr O'Sullivan,' she said doing her best to make her voice sound light and slightly bored, the voice of a person with superior brains and superior knowledge. 'Miss Mulcahy just wants to have an indication of the worth of her father's estate, before legal costs,' she added hastily, thinking once again of *Bleak House* and of how the entire Jarndyce fortune had been used up in paying legal costs. She wouldn't put it past this greasy lawyer to help himself to any money that was going. One of the lads out in the safe house in Ballinhassig had been studying commerce at the university before he joined the Republicans. She might try to get in touch with him, if they could only get hold of this will. 'Just stick to the figures, Mr O'Sullivan,' she said and hoped that her voice sounded patronizing. 'Make them lose their tempers,' that was Tom Hurley's method of questioning. 'Words come out, when tempers are lost,' had been his motto.

Mr O'Sullivan, though, did not seem to be taking too much notice of her. His head was turned towards the door, his ear noticeably cocked for a sound. Eileen saw Susan turn also. Definitely there were steps, heavy steps, coming rapidly down the uncarpeted stairs leading to this grubby basement. Very assured sound to those steps. No hesitation at the door or in the outer office. A perfunctory knock and then the door was flung open.

Richard McCarthy. Eileen recognized him instantly. He had been at the funeral, standing officiously beside Mrs Mulcahy, almost elbowing the boys away. Susan's intended husband, at least intended by himself, and possibly by her mother who seemed to be the sort of woman who would always take the easy way out. A lot too sure of himself. A quick glance at the solicitor, a smile and a nod at Susan and a suspicious glance at herself.

'Sorry, I'm late. Got delayed. A consignment of hides arrived hours too early. Good morning, Susan. And who is this?' He looked straight into Eileen's face, though his words were addressed to Susan.

'Miss MacSweeney,' said Eileen promptly. He wasn't going to be allowed to call her by her first name as though she were a child. 'We met at the funeral of the late Mr Mulcahy.' She decided to take the bull by the horns. 'Miss Mulcahy is very worried about her father's estate. She feels, probably wrongly, that you implied that there might be financial problems in the way of her pursuing her education. She has asked me to look into the matter.'

That would be enough for him to be going on with. She faced him, keeping her expression as cool and calm as she could manage and feeling pleased that she was wearing her new skirt.

'Don't know what you mean by "imply" or what business it is of yours, but I suppose that Susan brought you here and she must regard you as a friend and tell you her affairs and so I suppose, Susan, it doesn't matter if I tell this young lady, what I told you, does it?' He rounded on Susan and she stared back at him with, Eileen noted approvingly, an expression of contempt. She herself gave a pitying smile.

'My knowledge of the law, Mr McCarthy, would indicate that you, as executor, should be informing the wife and adult children of the financial position in which they find themselves. That would be your duty.'

Was this true? Surely it must be. After all, they had a right to know. Especially if someone was pressurizing them to sell the house that Mr Mulcahy had so recently purchased.

'Miss Mulcahy,' she bit back the words, 'my client', this man might just laugh at her, but she tried to sound very at ease as she finished, 'Yes, Miss Mulcahy, is anxious to see whether the figures that she has in her possession agree with the figure mentioned in the will.'

To her slight annoyance, Susan opened her bag and produced the well-used, slightly battered accounts book. That, she thought, should have been kept in reserve. Perhaps he might snatch it from her. Deliberately she got up from her chair and went across to stand beside Susan.

He stared back at her with a wide blue stare. His beard seemed to jut out a little more, almost as though every hair in it was alive. Suddenly he looked quite dangerous. His eyes went to Susan's account book and then back again to her and she saw those eyes narrow. There was an appraising look on his face, just as though he were weighing up the risks of disposing of the two girls in order to get his hands on the accounts book.

Was he a criminal? Or more exciting still, was he a murderer? He could be, she thought. He had the look of a murderer. Looked as she would imagine Bill Sykes in *Oliver Twist* to look like. That stupid Fred. Why did he have to muddle things? First shooting a dead body, covered in maggots and then posting a confession to the guards' barracks. This man, she thought, looking at the hard eyes, would probably have killed without compunction. And he could quite well be the murderer of his business rival. How he must have laughed contemptuously when he heard of Fred's confession. Somehow, or other, he had got his hands on Mr Mulcahy's money, knew that he could bamboozle the widow and was prepared to marry Susan in order to silence her.

But he had reckoned without Eileen MacSweeney. She turned back to the solicitor. 'A round figure, Mr O'Sullivan,' she said. 'That is all that Miss Mulcahy wants at this stage.'

'He could even round it up to the nearest hundred,' put in Susan and Eileen gulped.

To the nearest hundred, she thought. Susan's father must have been incredibly rich.

'No,' she found the courage to say. 'I'm sure that a solicitor should do better than that. You must have the figures, by now, Mr O'Sullivan. The bank have told Miss Mulcahy that they gave them all to you.'

For a moment she thought that she had won. The two men looked at each other, almost as though they were exchanging information with that glance. Mr O'Sullivan half-opened his mouth, but then Mr McCarthy swung around at Susan.

'You'll have to come back on another day, Susan,' he said roughly. 'There's no way that I can talk to you without your mother's presence. She's named under the will, but you are not. You have no right whatsoever to any legal information. You are a minor, you know. And you can leave that account book behind, too. That should have been handed over to me as executor of your father's will. Give it here, now, please.'

'No,' snapped Susan, hastily replacing the book into her bag. 'No, I won't.'

'Give it here!' He reached out a hand and seized the strap of the handbag.

'Don't give it to him, Susan!' yelled Eileen. 'That's assault and battery. Don't you lay a finger on her, my man!'

This would not be enough; she knew that. She peered up through the bars of the grimy basement window and saw a pair of dark blue trouser legs walking briskly past.

'Help!' she screamed, running to the door. 'Help! Susan, there's a policeman up there. Help. My friend is being attacked. Help! Get the guards!'

Quickly she seized Susan's arm and dragged her to the door. McCarthy had released the handbag and turned towards the window. She slammed the door in his face as soon as they were over the threshold. No key, otherwise she could have locked them inside. As it was, she contented herself by continuing to scream, 'Get the guards!' as they both rushed up the steps, through the hallway and into the streets.

An elderly postman was standing near to the building, looking at them in a concerned way.

'Are you all right, ladies?' he asked.

'Yes, we're fine,' said Eileen hastily. 'A couple of men tried to get fresh with us. It's all right now. Don't you worry!' She waited until he had gone on his way and then said, 'Let's go across the bridge and then up to the barracks, Susan. I think that we should report this pair to the guards. There's something very fishy going on.'

SEVENTEEN

St Thomas Aquinas
*'Da mihi, Domine Deus, cor pervigil, quod nulla
abducat a te curiosa cogitatio: da nobile, quod nulla
deorsum trahat indigna affectio; da rectum, quod nulla
seorsum obliquet sinistra intentio: da firmum, quod
nulla frangat tribulatio: da liberum, quod nulla sibi
vindicet violenta affectio.'*
(Grant me, Lord God, a watchful heart which shall be
distracted from Thee by no vain thoughts; give me a
generous heart which shall not be drawn downward by
any unworthy affection; give me an upright heart
which shall not be led astray by any perverse intention;
give me a stout heart which shall not be crushed by
any hardship; give me a free heart which shall not be
enslaved by passion.)

The Reverend Mother very seldom made social visits. Her time was normally fully occupied with her duties as a superior of a convent of nuns, a headmistress of a school – and a teacher – an organizer of hundreds of charity appeals, a counsellor and confidante for the unfortunate of the parish.

However, today she had telephoned her cousin Lucy and proposed visiting her for supper.

Lucy had been most enthusiastic. The chauffeur would be sent to collect her cousin, would be available to take her back at any hour of the day or night. They would have a splendid supper and she would, personally, do the flowers on the table.

'Don't go to any trouble,' said the Reverend Mother. 'A chat with you and a chat with Rupert. That will be enough for me.'

There was a silence for a moment while Lucy digested that and then she said enthusiastically, 'Won't that be lovely! No troublesome convent bells ringing and no interruptions from people urgently wanting your presence.' And with that insult to Sister Bernadette, who would not have dreamed of allowing any interruptions while the Reverend Mother was chatting to her cousin, Lucy put down the phone. No source for gossip from that conversation, thought the Reverend Mother and smiled to herself at the thought of Miss Clayton informing the other ladies that the Reverend Mother was going to have an evening out, visiting her cousin in Montenotte, if you please.

The chauffeur called for the Reverend Mother punctually at six o'clock. There was a stir of interest in the convent at their Mother Superior going out so late in the day. Sister Mary Immaculate waited on her for last instructions with the martyred air of one who is left to bear a heavy burden, alone and without support, and Sister Bernadette assured her that she would position herself by the doorbell during the evening so that the Reverend Mother would not be left to wait for more than a minute or two on her return.

'You will make sure that the chauffeur comes to the door with you, Reverend Mother. The streets are not safe at night,' she said earnestly.

The Reverend Mother thought that, Cinderella-like, she should promise to be home on the stroke of midnight, but then repressed the temptation. It was very kind of dear Sister Bernadette to be so concerned and so she assured her that her cousin's well-trained chauffeur would always accompany her to the door and ring the bell for her. The entire convent, she knew, was seething with something like indignation at the late hour appointed by Mrs Murphy for her cousin's visit. Hopefully it would not come to the ears of the bishop, but she feared that in a city that lived on gossip, it would not be too astonishing if the matter were not brought up at the next diocesan convention. A family anniversary, she decided, as she repinned her veil to her wimple. Yes, short answers were always best. *'A family anniversary, Your Excellency'*; then a slight tightening of lips and an obvious change of the subject. The bishop would, of course, have access to knowledge about her own date of birth and the anniversary of her entrance to the convent, and she wouldn't be surprised if he knew all about Lucy, also. But a family anniversary was good. Even the bishop would not press for further details if she bore the air of one who wanted to say no more.

To Sister Bernadette's satisfaction, when the bell rang punctually at five o'clock, it was not the chauffeur, but Mr Rupert Murphy himself sweeping off his hat, who was standing at the door ready to escort his wife's cousin to the waiting car. The chauffeur was standing stiffly to attention with the car door held widely open and the Reverend Mother could not resist the temptation to glance over her shoulder before climbing into the back seat and, with amusement, she saw that there was a cluster of white wimples and black veils peering over Sister Bernadette's shoulders as the convent witnessed their Reverend Mother being swept away into the dark night.

'Now, Rupert, you entertain the Reverend Mother while I go and see about the dinner,' said Lucy, once her cousin was cosily ensconced in front of a fragrantly smelling wood fire. The parlour maid looked at her mistress with alarm at that announcement, but a minute later the sound of Lucy's footsteps climbing the stairs to her bedroom would reassure the cook and servants that their mistress was not going to attempt to do anything so uncharacteristic as to peer into pots or check oven temperatures.

Rupert sipped his sherry meditatively and looked across the fireplace at his guest. He was obviously waiting for a question. A highly-strung man. Success had brought wealth, well beyond what he had inherited, but no thought of retirement had crossed his mind. She felt sure of that. He was one of those people, and perhaps she was one herself, who felt that the show could not go on without them. His advice was valued throughout the city of Cork.

'I'm very glad to have the opportunity of a word with you, Rupert,' said the Reverend Mother. 'I had a visit yesterday evening from Inspector Cashman and he related to me something quite distressing.' Rupert was a busy man and she did not want to waste a minute of his time. 'He told me that he had received a visit yesterday afternoon from Eileen MacSweeney who had brought Susan Mulcahy, the daughter of the dead man, Mr Henry Mulcahy, to see him.' Patrick had put the two girls in that order and the Reverend Mother had interpreted it to mean that Eileen was the one who did most of the talking. 'The two girls had paid a visit to the solicitor, Mr O'Sullivan of Pope's Quay.' She paused there and saw his eyes flicker with interest. He put aside the sherry glass and sat up quite straight. 'This girl Susan had repeatedly asked her father to fund a university education for her; but he had always refused. She has brains. Did extremely well in her Intermediate Certificate Examination, but her father insisted on her leaving school and helping her mother to look after her young brothers.'

'And now that he is dead . . .' Rupert looked interested.

'She thinks that there is plenty of money, certainly money enough to see her through university, and I gather that Mrs Mulcahy has no objection.'

'No, poor woman. I don't suppose that she has ever had much of a mind of her own. As for the question of finance, well, not that I know anything about it, of course, except what common gossip tells, but I would have thought that man had plenty of money. I happen to know that the house here in Montenotte was paid for with cash – no bank loan, nothing. In fact, the man had a reputation of always paying cash for everything.'

'That's interesting,' said the Reverend Mother sedately. Amazing, she thought, how everyone in this city knows his fellow men's business. Rupert, despite his claim to know nothing, probably knew the extent of the Mulcahy bank account down to the last few sovereigns. She looked across at his smooth, well-shaven face and thought that it was a face that could hide secrets very effectively.

'So what's the problem with the young lady?' he asked. 'If she has brains, as you say, and she has money behind her, well, why not go ahead? She wouldn't be the first woman to qualify as a doctor from our university here.'

'She's been told that there is no money. That the house in Montenotte has to be sold to pay debts; that her mother must sell the business; send the older boys off to England to get jobs and exist for the rest of her life on what the business might fetch.'

'Told! Who told her that?' Rupert sat up very straight and pushed his sherry glass aside.

'A Mr McCarthy, executor of the will, speaking, I suppose, on behalf also of this Mr O'Sullivan, the solicitor from Pope's Quay.'

'McCarthy. McCarthy the Skins. He was in the same line of business as Mulcahy, wasn't he?'

'That's right. Susan made an appointment to see the solicitor, to see Mr O'Sullivan in his office at Pope's Quay. She asked Eileen, my former pupil, Eileen MacSweeney, to go with her for moral support.'

'And what happened?'

'Mr O'Sullivan refused to give Susan a rough figure of her father's estate and was very evasive until Mr Richard McCarthy, the executor of the will, turned up. He, apparently, was quite threatening and abusive, especially—' the Reverend Mother raised her eyes from the richly patterned Turkey rug at her feet and looked across at Rupert – '*especially*,' she repeated with emphasis, 'when the girl revealed that she had been the one who had been keeping her father's accounts during the last few years. She even, apparently, produced the accounts book from her handbag.' She sat back, then, and watched the quick expressions darting across his face.

'Didn't give it to him, did she?' Rupert's rejoinder was swift, but she could see how his rapid brain was shuttling the pieces of information and making a pattern from them.

'No, she didn't. But that was the moment when he became quite menacing. He laid his hand on Susan's handbag and attempted to take the accounts book by force.'

'But he didn't, did he?'

'No,' said the Reverend Mother, attempting to keep a note of pride from her voice. 'Eileen, my Eileen, shouted through the basement window, told him that it was assault and battery, screamed for the civic guards, hustled her friend out of the room and up the steps and made straight for the police barracks. No one followed. Of course, Pope's Quay would have been very busy at that hour and Eileen, even as a small child, was confident and uninhibited. Susan, I think, may be a different character.'

'How old is Susan?'

'She is nineteen, almost twenty, apparently. A couple of years older than Eileen, I think.'

'Under age.' He mused a little. 'I would advise that she gets her mother to brief a solicitor and that all negotiations with this Mr O'Sullivan of Pope's Quay would be carried on as between two solicitors. I could give you a few names, a good case for a promising young man. After all, Mr Mulcahy had the money to build that eyesore under my nose. The widow must be quite comfortably well off, if not rich.'

'I understand that she does not have a penny, other than the money doled out to her Monday morning, the day before her husband's death, for the housekeeping, which was greatly reduced from the usual allowance, as her daughter Sally, who has the younger boys in Montenotte, was given three-quarters of it. Patrick, apparently, had also suggested a solicitor to the girls, but Eileen had blurted out the difficult position in which Susan and her mother found themselves in.'

'Waiting for probate, I suppose. Surely the bank . . . yes, of course, the bank . . . well, I always say that everyone needs proper representation, but if the unfortunate woman doesn't have a penny to her name . . .' Rupert considered this. 'I'll fund the solicitor,' he said suddenly. 'I have my eye on a young man. He's struggling to make ends meet at the moment, but he's a clever and industrious fellow. I wouldn't like my name to be connected, wouldn't like to appear in the matter, though. You understand that, don't you, Reverend Mother?'

'Certainly,' said the Reverend Mother sedately. She tucked her hands into her sleeves and bent her eyes down upon the black serge material. Not for the world would she embarrass Rupert by allowing him to see the gleam in her eyes. It would, she thought, be quite embarrassing for him in front of his legal friends if, after months of complaining bitterly about Mr Mulcahy's purchase of land in front of his house, he was now seen to be acting for the man's wife and daughter. 'I think that I must send my bright young Eileen to see you,' she said in conversational tones. 'She has a great ambition to become a lawyer and a touching faith in the Republican movement to fund her studies. She'll give you a very clear explanation of the whole situation. And I'm sure that you will find her very quick to understand anything that you might say to her. She can act as your go-between. She would probably love to see your office and all of your law books, also.'

He laughed aloud at that and he was still laughing when Lucy came into the room. Her eyes went from one to the other and she came forward to take the chair that her husband had pulled out for her.

'I think that your cousin is trying to get me to take on as an apprentice that enterprising young lady who rescued that young fellow from the gaol, my dear. Do you remember her? The girl on the back of the motorbike? Do you remember how everyone was talking about it on the night of the law association dinner?'

'She's got her own motorbike now,' said the Reverend Mother serenely. 'And she can only become your apprentice at the establishment of a republic where education is free to all. With the optimism of the young, she thinks the new dawn is just around the corner.' The Reverend Mother thought about all the new dawns that had been just beyond the horizon during her seventy years of life and shook her head sadly. Still, that was a futile waste of time, so she returned to the problem of poor Susan, the plain but intelligent daughter of a man who, though willing to educate his clever children well above his own level, had baulked at the extra expense of a university education for them.

Had he died because of that piece of obstinacy?

Was money, indeed, the root of all evil?

How easy was it to murder someone by picking up a heavy iron bar and hitting them across the back of the neck?

Aloud she said, 'I'll ask our good Dr Scher to pass on a message to her if you will be kind enough to write down a convenient time for her to call. Eileen works just around the corner from where Dr Scher lives. He is very fond of Eileen. She's a good girl,' said the Reverend Mother judicially. 'And I think that she is an excellent friend, always very loyal. I think that Eileen will look after Susan. She has a very strong sense of justice and she would sympathize very much with Susan's aspirations.'

'And what about the brother? Fred, is that the name? The oldest of the family?' asked Lucy. 'Is he still in gaol? Has he been charged with the murder of his father?'

'As far as I know, he has not been charged with murder. There was some sort of Free State/Republican trouble out in Douglas Passageway and I understand that he was arrested because of that.' The news about Fred Mulcahy's confession had somehow reached the newspapers. Hinted at carefully by the *Cork Examiner*, it had, she understood, been blazoned forth by some of the cheaper English papers where 'The Body in the Trunk' had been headlines a week ago. There had been trouble at the barracks about the leaking of information, Patrick had told her. Everyone guessed who it was, but nobody had been formally accused. *All this Catholic/Protestant business – like treading on eggshells*, had said Dr Scher who was taking a huge and very vocal enjoyment in the publicity and had joyfully informed her that one of the English newspapers had declared that the naked body of a man had been delivered in a trunk to an order of walled-in nuns who had not seen even the face of a man for forty years.

'One has to take into account that the man was intensely focussed on business and the making of money,' she remarked and that caused a diversion.

'Great businessman,' said Rupert enthusiastically. 'Couldn't put a foot wrong when it came to investing his money. Someone told me that.'

Probably the local bank manager. Men, within the safety of their closed circles, were incurable gossips. The Reverend Mother turned a placid face towards her host and waited for more details.

'I thought you didn't like him,' said Lucy. 'And that,' she said behind her hand to the Reverend Mother, 'is the exaggeration of the year. You should just have heard him! The air was blue on occasion.'

'Oh, he was all right. All right in his place.' Rupert waved a careless hand. 'Nothing wrong with Shandon. He should have stayed there. He had two fine houses there, could easily have bought the third, turned them into one, got an architect, made a proper job of it, not just a hole in the attic; thrown the whole thing open, made bigger rooms downstairs. Moved the tanning yard. Of course he had done that already, but, if you think of it, that left him a large space to expand into at the back. Should have done that. I'd have recommended a good architect if he had asked me.' Rupert drained his sherry glass, tilting his head and swallowing the last drop.

'Anything rather than have him in our back yard,' said Lucy.

'Dinner is ready to be served, madam.' The parlour maid had knocked twice and now came in.

'Hope you have a good appetite, Reverend Mother, Lucy has been slaving over a hot stove all the afternoon.' Rupert was now in a good mood.

The Reverend Mother smiled. Men always expected a tribute to their feeble jokes, but her mind was very busy with ideas.

Food for thought was the phrase in her mind as she moved down the hallway towards the elaborate dining room.

EIGHTEEN

W. B. Yeats
'Life is a journey up a spiral staircase.'

D r Scher was waiting at the top of the lane when Eileen came out of work on Friday evening. She waved happily at him. She was in a very good mood. It had been such an exciting day. She had told the whole story to the owner of the printing works and he had, to her surprise, given her permission to take the afternoon off work. The name of 'Rupert Murphy and Partners, Solicitors,' was a very well-known one in the city and if they were to throw any business in the way of a struggling printing business, then that would be of the greatest assistance. Where Rupert Murphy led, other solicitors would follow. And the entire city knew that solicitors had money to burn.

And so, with everyone's blessing, she had met the great man, had been taken into his book-lined office and had accepted a glass of sherry, while promising not to tell the Reverend Mother. And she had told him everything that she knew about the affairs of Henry Mulcahy, deceased. Once she had got the message from Dr Scher, she had rehearsed everything in her mind and, despite the heady effects of the sherry, Mr Murphy had congratulated her on the clarity of her explanation, enquired about her ambitions, had presented her with a copy of a law book for beginners and then had sent an underling to fetch another solicitor, from further down the South Mall, by the name of Binsy. Once again she had gone through everything with this young man and Mr Murphy had not interrupted even once, just occasionally looking down at his notes, nodding and smiling. And then Mr Binsy had used Mr Murphy's telephone to contact Mr O'Sullivan. He had made an immediate appointment for the following morning. And when Mr Binsy had departed, after effusive thanks to

Mr Murphy, Eileen had another sherry and had opened her
heart and her ambitions to the great man.

'Oh, Dr Scher, you'll never guess where I've been today,'
she began eagerly once she saw him. Dr Scher was always
sympathetic, always interested in Eileen, ever since that time
when he had dug a bullet out of her; she had expected him
to be an appreciative audience, but, this time, he did not
respond. And he did not say any of the things that Dr Scher
normally said. She had not been surprised to see him, he
lived on South Terrace, a stone's throw away from her place
of work, but she was surprised that he did not tease her
about the absence of her motorbike – *'couldn't start that
gadget again!'* he would say. *'Ah, it knows that women
shouldn't have motorbikes.'* He didn't even admire her
dashing new scarf which she had wound around head and
shoulders in a very fashionable style. He looked very tired,
she thought, tired and dispirited. Dr Scher was always full
of smiles when he met her, trying out silly jokes on her and
paying her compliments on the most daring of her outfits.
But now his face was drawn and he had a tired, defeated
look on his face.

'You've left your car running, Dr Scher,' she pointed out
and then felt a throb of apprehension when he did not respond.
They had a running joke about his absent-mindedness.

'Sit in it,' he invited and she followed him to the car. He
was going to drive her home, perhaps. But possibly there was
something more to his invitation. He said no more, just held
the door open, waited while she swung her legs in and then
closed it, went around to the other side, got in and looked at
her. The light was dim and the car slightly steamy, but she
could see the expression on the elderly face that looked down
at her and she felt a throb of apprehension.

'Eileen, Mrs Mulcahy died in the hospital this morning,'
he said.

Eileen's eyes widened. 'Mrs Mulcahy. Susan's mother.'

'That's right,' he said sombrely.

'Oh, poor Susan! First Bridie and then Mrs Mulcahy. Poor
Susan,' she said, again. 'And her father, too! Poor, poor Susan
and them all. Fred will be broken-hearted. He loved his mother.

Has anyone told him?' When he did not respond, she asked, almost fearfully, 'What happened to her, Dr Scher?'

He took a long breath, and paused for a while before answering her. And when he spoke it was almost as though he forced himself to utter the words.

'They received a box of chocolates through the post, that's what Susan told me. Nothing unusual in that. Cork people are a generous lot.'

'A box of chocolates? For both of them?'

'No, actually, it was addressed to Susan. It so happens that she, odd girl, doesn't like chocolates and so she handed it over to her mother. Her mother, a "sweet tooth", according to Susan, was very pleased and she took it off to bed with her. She and Susan sleep in one of the bedrooms that are still furnished, but Susan stayed up late, so late that she decided not to disturb her mother and dozed in front of the kitchen fire when she had finished what she was doing.'

'Poor, poor Susan.' Eileen's mind shied away from the horror of discovering a mother lying cold and dead. And so soon after the other tragedies in her family. 'Is anyone with her?'

'The poor girl was adamant that she did not want to stay in Montenotte with the rest of them. I drove her across to there. She told the news to her sister and the brothers, but then she insisted on going back. She said that she had a job to do in Shandon Street. She said that she had to clear out the office and that no one but she could do that. She wanted to go through all the account books and the bills and, well, all sorts of things. She was absolutely determined that nobody but she could do that. Though, I would suppose that, from what I know about the law, all of these things should be handled by her father's executor, should have been handed over to him.'

'I don't blame her for not handing them over to Mr Richard McCarthy. I didn't like the look of him, much. Looks like a crook to me.' Eileen was sorry that she had said this. Dr Scher, in simultaneously negotiating a loading crane on George's Quay and turning to look at her, almost went into the back of a lorry. Eileen decided to say no more. Susan, she had little doubt, would be able to talk about the young man and why she so frantically wanted to go through her father's papers before they were handed over to her father's solicitor and his executor. What about Fred, she wondered. Surely this third murder, two of which happened while he was in prison, surely that would mean he should be freed now.

But she said nothing until the Humber had struggled its way up the steep incline and stopped in front of the house in Shandon Street. The dark, navy-blue blinds were all drawn and Eileen thought with pity of the poor girl, all alone, inside the dark rooms. She didn't get out immediately, though. It would be better for Susan if she knew all the facts before going in and so she turned to the doctor.

'What happened to Mrs Mulcahy, Dr Scher?'

'She was poisoned. I'm fairly sure,' he said, spreading his hands in a gesture of defeat.

'Poisoned!'

He nodded. 'In all probability by the chocolates. Otherwise Susan would be ill, also. They both ate the same supper. Those chocolates that someone sent to Susan.'

'Someone?'

'It has a card with it. Scribbly handwriting, Susan told me. I didn't see it myself. Inspector Cashman has it now.'

'What did it say?' Eileen had no great opinion of Patrick Cashman. He might have achieved a Leaving Certificate with the Christian Brothers in the North Monastery, but she had never heard that he had gained any prizes or any 'first in all of Ireland' as she had done in the English Literature paper. 'It wasn't signed, was it?' she asked.

'No, not signed. Said: "Thought I'd send you these" and then just initials. T.B. That's what Susan told me.'

Eileen thought about that. It was a Cork custom to give small gifts: sweets, a cake, a bottle of whiskey, something like that to the bereaved in the week or so after a funeral. A week was considered the appropriate time – still a house of mourning, but recovery slowly beginning to arrive.

'Did Susan or Mrs Mulcahy know anyone with the initials T.B.?'

'Don't know. You can ask her, yourself. Get her to talk. That will do her good. It's those people who go around tight-lipped and wordless, those are the ones that have break-downs a month or so later. It's natural to cry and to talk about the person who has died. Encourage her to do that.'

'And encourage her to nail the bastard that did that to her mother and to poor Bridie,' said Eileen with determination.

'Good girl,' said Dr Scher. 'Now out you get and I'll find a youngster to mind my car. I'm well provided with sweets.'

There was no answer to several tentative knocks from Eileen. Perhaps Susan was out. That seemed unlikely. Had anything happened to her? For a moment she got a fright and turned back to where Dr Scher was dangling a bag of sweets in front of a couple of barefooted boys. He left them immediately he saw her face and joined her on the doorstep. She knocked again and then the knocker was taken from her and a thunder of knocks from Dr Scher caused various heads to pop out from doors and windows. He was worried, thought Eileen, going back onto the pavement and looking up at the windows. There was a movement of one of the blinds in the second storey of the house and she was reassured.

'Give her a minute,' she murmured when she re-joined him. Susan had probably been crying and would want to wash her face and pat cold water on her eyes before meeting people. But when Susan opened the door a few minutes later, her face wore its usual pallor and her grey eyes were clear and resolute. Rigid and stiff, taking a step backwards imme-diately as soon as she saw Eileen, stepping right back, right against the wall, almost as though determined to avoid the hug that Eileen was about to give her. Her voice was steady and controlled – too controlled. After all, she had lost her mother that day. An odd girl. Still she might be afraid of breaking down if she allowed herself to be comforted. Eileen wished that her own mother was here. Maureen MacSweeney hugged almost everyone in a completely unselfconscious way. Eileen felt tears prick her eyes at the thought of her mother, but Susan was utterly tearless. White-faced, but dry-eyed. She held out her hand to Dr Scher and then to Eileen, sticking it straight out as though resolutely keeping a distance between them. There was a frozen look about her and she

moved in a strange way, almost as though she was a large
doll, or something like that. My mother would probably hug
her anyway; would pat Susan's back, would pour out a torrent
of talk; this was Eileen's thought, but somehow she could
not bring herself to do that. She wondered whether Dr Scher
was disappointed in her. She could see him look from her
to Susan and then back to her again. Her face grew warm
with embarrassment.

'I brought you a friend to stay overnight, Susan,' said Dr
Scher. 'I'll let your mother know, Eileen. Don't worry about
that. And I'll pick you up in the morning for work. Susan,
too. You'll come with me, Susan. My housekeeper . . .' He
looked dubiously, from one to the other, and then seemed to
decide to say no more to them. He turned the knob on the
front door and looked back at them.

'Better get back to my car or those little hooligans will be
climbing all over it,' he said hastily. Even after the hall door
slammed behind him, Eileen could hear his booming voice
and the delighted giggles and hoarse shouts as he embarked
on his favourite game of 'catch the sweet'. And then there
was a roar of the engine as he cranked up his car, more shouts
and after that the street outside grew quiet again. Eileen forced
herself to speak.

'You wouldn't have a cup of tea, would you?' she said with
a memory of her mother visiting a grumpy old lady. 'My throat
is dry. I've been pounding away at that typewriter all the
afternoon.'

'Yes, of course.' That had been the right thing to say. As
her mother always said: tea costs nothing much and it's a great
way of getting people to talk while it gets made and poured
out. Susan led the way to the kitchen and somehow things
became more normal as Eileen found a couple of mugs and
the teapot which she put to warm on the range.

'Your range looks as clean as a whistle; is it going to be
sold with the house?' she asked. The question had just popped
into her head but it had been a good one. The stove and its
pipe had been black-leaded and it shone with a dull lustre.
Even the kettle had been scoured clean of soot.

'The whole house has been scrubbed from top to bottom,'

said Susan in a more animated tone. 'And every room in the place has been painted. The auctioneer was supposed to call yesterday to value it. We had everything ready. Never turned up! I suppose that Richard McCarthy took it upon himself to cancel that. He had been telling my . . . he had been saying that we shouldn't sell, but should bring Sally and the boys back here – they'd easily fit, according to him, all thirteen of us! He had some plan to ship the older boys off to England,' she said that in a steady voice and then stopped. She had the look of someone who is thinking hard and Eileen felt less embarrassed, less at a loss. Susan was putting her brain to think about the finances and that would help to screen the terrible event of Mrs Mulcahy's death. Everyone has a different way of dealing with grief. Her mother had said that and she decided to ignore Dr Scher's words. Keep Susan's mind busy with the affairs of her father's business and just be there as a friend if she needed to talk.

And so Eileen sat down at the well-scrubbed kitchen table and poured out the whole account of her meeting with the prestigious Mr Rupert Murphy and about the young solicitor that he said would look into the affair as a piece of experience for him at the beginning of his career. The more she talked and the more she explained, waving her hands and reliving the scene, the better that Susan began to look. There was even a tinge of colour in her cheeks and she made the tea in a very competent manner, going out to the scullery, fetching a jug of milk while still talking.

But then she stopped, looked at the jug in her hand, covered with a bead bordered circular piece of linen. Took off the linen and then without sniffing it or inspecting it under the light from the oil lamp above the table she crossed the room and suddenly poured it down the sink. Eileen's eyes met hers and knew that the same thought had occurred to both.

Poison could be added to milk more easily than inserted into chocolates.

'Give me a clean jug and I'll fetch a pint from the shop across the road,' she said. Susan would not like to have to meet people who would ask about her mother. She accepted the shilling from the table drawer, though, and decided that,

without saying anything about it, she would get a fresh loaf
of bread and a fresh half pound of butter for their breakfast.

'All the doors and windows are locked, now,' said Susan.
She made the remark while vigorously stirring the tea in the
chipped brown pot.

'I'll knock three times when I come back,' said Eileen. She
knew what Susan meant, though. Susan was clever. Dr Scher
would have broken the news to her that her mother might
have died of poison, a poison that had been meant for Susan
as the chocolates had been directed to her. Eileen eyed the
piles of accounts books on the kitchen table and the sheaves
of neatly clipped bills and saw that Susan, too, was looking
over at them.

'You're going to prove that there is plenty of money to keep
the house in Montenotte and to keep the business going for
any of your brothers who want to work on it, aren't you,
Susan?' Now she did venture to give the girl a quick hug and
she was not repulsed. There was a faint flush on the white
cheeks and she nodded when Eileen said impulsively, 'Let me
help you. We'll work on it together tonight. I'm not like you;
I'm not great at arithmetic, but I've done accounts in the
printing works. If you write it out tonight, then I can easily
type it up tomorrow – a balance sheet, that's what it will be
– it'll look very professional if it's all typed up.' Impulsively
she gave Susan another hug and then dashed off, through the
door, hearing the click of the chain once she was out on
the pavement.

It was quite dark by now, but the shops were all still lit up
with oil lamps dangling over counters. She pushed open the
door of the shop directly across the road. First of all, it was
just a young girl behind the counter, but she was rapidly pushed
aside by her mother, dying to know all the details about the
latest death in the ill-fated house across the road.

'What a terrible, terrible thing. There's been no luck in that
house ever since that man, God have mercy on his soul, went
and built his tanning yard on top of our *cillín*. That was a
terrible sin and disgrace. I was saying that only the other day
to Mr Sweetman, when he was tending the graves. Decent
man that he is. Wouldn't say a word against anyone, but he

shook his head and I knew what he was thinking,' said the woman as she scooped out a generous half pound of butter from a wooden cask.

It was a good ten minutes before Eileen managed to get away from the loquacious owner of the shop and when she returned to the house and gave her promised three loud knocks, there was no answer.

NINETEEN

W. B. Yeats
'But they mistook the brightness of the moon,
For the prosaic light of the day.'

E ileen had knocked on the door so often without reply that now she put all of her energies into pounding metal upon metal, alarming quite a few passers-by and bringing a reproach down on her head by a woman carrying a baby beneath her shawl.

'That's a house of mourning, girleen,' she said accusingly and Eileen forced herself to wait until the woman had turned the corner into Cattle Lane before beginning again.

And then, at last, just as she was beginning to get thoroughly frightened, the door opened a crack and then a little wider.

'Thank goodness you are all right.' Eileen slipped inside and pushed the door shut. 'Didn't you hear me? God, I thought something had happened to you, now, Susan. You gave me a fright.' And then she stopped. There was not much light in the hallway, but in the shadows beyond the stairway, she saw another figure. And then, when her eyes began to get used to the dimness, she saw a thatch of red hair.

'Fred,' she said. She was none too pleased to see him and she knew that there was a flat note in her voice. 'What happened? I thought that you were in gaol.'

He gave a harsh laugh. 'Oh, so you knew that, did you? Knew that I was in gaol. You didn't do much visiting, did you? Not too Christian, are you? What is it the Bible says? "I was in prison and you visited me." That's it, isn't it? Not Eileen MacSweeney, though! Much too busy with other matters.'

'Oh, shut up, Fred,' said Eileen. And then, partly for Susan's sake and partly because the boy's face was very white, she said, 'Come and have a cup of tea, and then you'll feel better.

Let's make some fresh stuff, Susan. That stuff we made earlier must be stone cold by now. Where on earth were you? I was knocking on that door for hours.'

'We were looking for something, something that Fred gave my mother. He searched the attics, but there is nothing there. They've all been cleared out, clean as a whistle and so we went out to have a look in the sheds.' Susan stopped abruptly and Eileen was conscious that Fred had turned and looked hard at her sister. She shrugged. She didn't care, really. Fred always had to have some sort of secret. Nothing to do with me, she thought, as she turned away from the brother and sister and picked up the teapot. Susan was ill-at-ease, uncomfortable, worried. Best to give her a chance to recover.

Eileen tipped the contents of the teapot down the sink and ran the tap to wash the tea grounds away. Nice house, she thought. Water on tap. No going to a standpipe for it. Mr Mulcahy must have had his own well dug, or did it himself. *Running water* – that was one of her own mother's dreams.

There was no further word from either of the Mulcahy pair. When she turned back to put the teapot on the range, they were both standing there, rather stiffly, not looking at each other. Both looking at her. She busied herself for a few moments at the range, ladled fresh tea into the teapot, moved the kettle over the hotplate and waited for the steam to puff from the spout, glancing over her shoulder at the brother and sister. Susan, she thought, was still looking very worried. Perhaps it would be best to have it out in the open whatever it was. *No secrets from each other*; that had been one of the rules that they had made, the eight of them when they were hiding out in the safe house in Ballinhassig. One of the things that had made everything so comfortable and easy-going, such fun, despite the danger.

'What were you looking for, Fred?' she asked, doing her best to make her voice sound casual and incurious as she poured water from the bubbling kettle on top of the leaves.

He didn't answer and she turned around, slightly irritated. Trust Fred to make a mystery out of nothing.

And then she saw his face. Slightly smug. His hand went quickly to his pocket, touched it as though to reassure himself and then he took it away hastily. It had been enough, though. Eileen had lived for almost a year in a house full of young Republicans, all of whom were thrilled and excited to have a gun in their trouser pockets and who continually reassured themselves that it was still there. She had done it herself in the days when she carried a gun.

'Jesus, Fred, that's a gun you've got there,' she said. She was sure of it now. She could see the shape of the bulge in his pocket. Fred was newly released from prison. Every item of clothing would have been thoroughly searched there. Where had he got that gun? Her mind made a leap.

'Don't tell me that you gave your mother a gun!' she said, her eyes going from his face to Susan, who had flushed and looked panic-stricken. Neither spoke, but their faces told her that her guess had been correct. What a crazy thing to do. To give an elderly woman a gun! Trust Fred!

'You did, didn't you?' It would have been easy enough. One by one, people had been deserting the Republican cause, in most cases leaving their guns behind. Eamonn had recently told her that Danny, another one of the crowd in the safe house at Ballinhassig, had now gone back to his parents and had re-joined his class at the university with some story of having had a dose of TB in order to explain his absence to the university authorities. Those small pistols were, she guessed, now easily available to the few who still served the Republic and lived in safe houses around the countryside. Fred, who talked forever about his hatred of his father, had given his mother a gun. His face was enough for her to know that her guess had found its mark. He had crimsoned with anger and Susan had gone very pale, even paler than before. Eileen thought quickly.

'None of my business,' she said. She supposed that Fred, who always had a lot to say about Mr Mulcahy's brutality, and continually embarrassed everyone with outbursts of hate against his father, might have thought that his mother needed protection. 'But, I'll just say this one thing, Fred; that if you've been freed from gaol, it would be because they can't find any real evidence against you, except your stupid confession, but that doesn't mean that they won't be keeping a good eye on you. It's against the law, nowadays, to carry a gun, you know. I'd get rid of that, if I were you, and that's all I'm going to say. Would you like a slice of bread, Susan?' Deliberately she turned away from him. She was not his keeper and he could do as he pleased.

'I can see that I'm not welcome here.' He took a step forward so that he was between her and Susan. He had an aggressive look on his face. Never liked to be told what to do. That was Fred. 'I'll be off to Montenotte, then,' he said after a moment when both girls looked at each other and then looked away. 'Never liked this place, anyway. If I had my way, the house would be burned down. Did you hear me, Susan? I'm off. Sally will give me a bed for the night.'

He was expecting to be begged to stay; Eileen could tell that by the tone of his voice. She said nothing, though, but kept her head down. The bread had been meant for the morning, but now it filled a moment to be hacking a couple of slices off it and slathering some butter over them. The quick, angry strokes of the knife relieved her feelings. I suppose Susan will beg him to stay, she thought, as she chopped up some more butter, icy cold it was. Kept by an open window covered with an iron mesh screen. She had seen the woman take it from there. Butter was a luxury and nothing would be allowed to happen to it. Eileen thought about how good it was going to taste and curbed her impatience with that stupid Fred.

Susan, however, said nothing. There had been a silence after Fred's outburst and that silence would leave the boy no room to go back on his words. For the want of something to do, she cut the slices into halves, keeping her eyes fixed on her task and then she heard, rather than saw, him go to the door and open it, but when she looked up then, she saw him take the revolver from his pocket, pretend to examine it, carelessly moving the barrel around the room, as though taking aim and then replacing it. She couldn't help it. A smile curved her mouth and although she immediately sucked her lips between her teeth, she knew that he had seen it.

'Bitch!' he said and a second later the front door slammed behind him. The two girls looked at each other.

'Sorry,' said Eileen to Susan. A lie, she thought. She wasn't really sorry. Fred was a nuisance. She was glad that he was gone.

Susan shrugged her shoulders. 'Don't worry. I'm not sorry that he's taken himself off. He'd have been a pest this evening when we are going over the accounts. He's very good at mathematics, much better than I would be, but he would, forever, be trying to find cleverer and shorter ways of doing things and muddling everything up. And he would want to be in charge.' She drank her tea, ignored the bread and then stood up in a determined fashion. 'I'll go and light a fire in the front room, now,' she said, 'and then we'll get down to work. We'll have everything ready for tomorrow morning. I'm not going to let Richard McCarthy or that crooked solicitor, that Mr O'Sullivan, bamboozle me out of my rights. I know that the money should be there and I am going to prove it.'

It was almost eleven o'clock by the time that the two girls got to bed. Susan had been cheerful and determined, copying out rows of figures in neat, careful handwriting and Eileen had been bored stiff, driven to counting the drawers on the oak filing cabinet. Ninety-one, she made it. Thirteen rows of them. A great piece of carpentry. A little rough in places, but solid oak. She passed some time sliding them in and out and thinking how much she would like to have it.

But she had been most impressed by the sum that Susan came up with after hours of work. There had been more money in the turning of those hides and skins into leather than she could ever have realized. She was conscious of a slight feeling of envy. Susan could easily afford to go to university; now that both her father and her mother were dead, there would be no one to stop her.

'Could Richard McCarthy stop me?' It seemed almost as though Susan had read her thoughts.

'I don't see how. There's pots of money there if your figures are right.'

'Oh, my figures are right,' said Susan. Her voice was confident, but her face was worried, every spot and blemish standing out against the pallor. She should do something about her skin, thought Eileen. Perhaps Ponds Vanishing Cream. She had seen that for sale in a Medical Hall in South Main Street and had studied the label for a while as she wondered whether her mother would like some for her birthday. She had ended up with a bottle of eau de cologne which had looked more exciting, but something like that might be what Susan needed. Still, that wasn't the worst of Susan's worries now. She would, she thought, keep that suggestion for later on when all was settled.

'Can't see how Richard McCarthy can stop you.'

'Oh, can't you,' said Susan grimly. 'I can. He could make a very good case. Nine or ten good cases. He could say that the money should be reserved for educating the younger boys, or even Fred, who knows? He has his eye on me for a wife. Probably thinks that I would be a good bargain, hard-working and economical. He wouldn't want a university student for wife.'

'You'll have to fight, fight for your rights. After all, it's a good job, being a doctor. You will be able to earn good money. Think about Dr Scher; he has pots of money; spends thousands of pounds in buying old battered pieces of silver and putting them into a cupboard, not even using them. He must be rolling. You could always help out with the little boys once you qualified. If you want to be a doctor, then you go ahead. I'd fight, if I were you.'

'I intend to,' said Susan. 'Nothing is going to stop me, now.' She sat very still for a moment, staring ahead, her eyes fixed and intent, not looking at anything, but Eileen had a feeling that the needle-sharp brain was devising a plan. Susan, she thought, was not thinking of earning money, she was not thinking of buying a short skirt and silk stockings, of having her hair cut short in a 1920s style, as Eileen would have been planning. No, Susan had a fanatical look in her eye, a look of steely resolve.

'Richard McCarthy won't get in my way, if I can help it,' was all that she said, but her eyes showed that her brain was still active.

Eileen smothered a yawn. These figures had been exhausting. Susan turned to her instantly. 'Let's find you somewhere to sleep. Not much choice, I'm afraid. It was just Bridie, and my mother and myself living here for the last couple of weeks. Sally has all the boys over in the new house. Well, the fire is out, anyway. I forgot to put more wood on it. Sorry, you must have been cold.'

Susan seemed almost absent-minded as she led the way up the stairs. A big house. Eileen peeped through open doors, immensely impressed by the four flights of stairs, by the large drawing room with its tall ceiling and by the small room, now empty, but which had been fitted, on its four walls, with twenty coat hooks and a shelf below, at knee height, where school bags and outdoor shoes could be placed. And in one corner, a large copper cylinder for hot water with a clothes horse above it where wet coats could be dried. A cloakroom, Susan called it, just like they had in the convent school. But above all, she loved the bathroom with an immense wooden bath, painted white and large copper taps attached to another hot water tank.

'My father built on all of these small rooms at the back,' said Susan when she saw Eileen's interest. 'He built a new block with the washhouse on the ground floor, the cloakroom on the next and then this bathroom and on the top floor is Bridie's little bedroom.'

It had not been great, Bridie's room, Eileen thought, as she looked around the small, bare room. Only a bed and a row of hooks on the wall there now, but there was a lighter patch against the other wall as though a child's bed or cot had been there. Eileen wondered for a few minutes whether Fred had slept there once when he was a small boy. She didn't ask Susan, though. The less said about Fred the better, but he was in her mind. There had been something rather menacing about him, something different to the usual 'spoiled boy' attitude and she wondered whether he was frightened.

And yet, he shouldn't be. It was not surprising, really, that he had been released from prison. After all, he could have had no part in the deaths of Bridie and of his mother and it would be strange if these last two deaths had not been connected with the death of Mr Mulcahy, whatever the talk about suicide. What Fred needed to do now, was to keep himself inconspicuous, just inconspicuous. Not go around waving guns. Eileen yawned widely. Those figures had been exhausting.

'Shall I sleep here, Susan?' she asked. She looked dubiously at a small narrow bed in the attic. She didn't like to feel the bedclothes, but they would be very damp, she thought and decided to sleep in her own clothes. She would be fine. In any case, she was dead on her feet, exhausted with the efforts of adding up farthings, halfpennies, pence, shillings and pounds or at least endeavouring to check Susan's rapid calculations.

'No, no, you sleep downstairs, in my mother's room. That's more comfortable. I'll sleep here. I'll be fine.'

Suddenly Susan sounded decisive, almost as though she had come to some decision, or at least banished her worries. 'Let's go downstairs, and I'll find a nightdress for you from the hot press in the kitchen. Be careful on that corner. That stair needs to be screwed down. People get a fright when it squeaks and then they knock against that sharp corner.'

'Squeals more than squeaks, sounds like a banshee,' said Eileen with a giggle as she bounced on the step, drawing a groaning protest from the wood. And then she thought that had not been a very tactful thing to say. After all a banshee was supposed to give notice of a death in the house.

And this house had too many deaths, three of them; one occurring after another.

She bit her lip, rounded the awkward corner carefully and followed Susan down to the second storey of the house.

There was only one bed in the room, a very large room with a high ceiling, blinds pulled down over the window and a double bed, standing isolated in the middle of the floor, walls painted, wooden floor shining with polish, even so it had a strangely creepy atmosphere and Eileen wished that she could sleep somewhere else, perhaps in that nice warm kitchen, but not this room. Susan and her mother must have slept there together while Bridie slept in the little attic bed. Eileen could hardly blame the girl for not wishing to sleep there on the night after her mother's death, but she didn't very much like the thought of sleeping in a bed where someone had died less than twenty-four hours ago, although everything was scrubbed clean and fresh sheets and blankets put on the bed.

Nevertheless, she was dead tired. She couldn't bring herself to wear the nightgown. Once Susan had gone upstairs, she stretched herself, still wearing her clothes, even her leather coat, on the bed and wrapped the blankets around her, burrowing her head into the feather-stuffed pillow that smelled of starch. She fell asleep almost immediately. Her dreams were confused. Someone was going to kill her. She knew that perfectly well, but, with that strange logic of dreams, it did not bother her as much as the feeling that she just could not see the face of her assailant, although it was continually turning, just for a second, towards her. Eventually, with a strong effort she managed to wake herself. Or was it something else that roused her. Something, someone, some sound, something wrong.

She sat up in the bed, shivering slightly and wishing that she was at home with her mother. The sound had come from upstairs, from the ceiling above her. Footsteps. Stealthy footsteps, walking across the room above. Rapidly she identified which room it must be. It must have been part of what Susan had called the boys' room. It had been a big room, a huge room, spanning the whole top storey before the two houses had been separated, once again. It had been like a dormitory for the boys, Susan had told her, ten iron beds, five against each of the two walls, a small bedside cabinet for each boy and then an enormous wooden clothes press that had taken up most of the third wall, the one facing the windows. There had been a huge table for homework and a cupboard for school books. All that furniture had gone to the auction, leaving the rooms bare and echo-filled.

And now someone was up in that empty room. Not Susan. She had been wearing slippers. Eileen had noticed that. Old-fashioned slippers, looked as though they had belonged to her mother. Old-fashioned, soft-soled slippers that made no noise on the bare wooden floors. Definitely not Susan. These footsteps were cautious, but heavy. Someone wearing boots, but trying to walk quietly. And then a silence. An ominous silence, just as if some intruder was standing just above her head and listening intently to the faint sleepy noises from the room below.

And then they started again. By now Eileen was completely awake and she knew that she had not imagined those footsteps. Heavy footsteps. A man's footsteps. A creaking board on the floor just above the door of her room.

Could Fred have come back?

And yet it did not sound like Fred.

Fred was lightly built and like the other boys in the house in Ballinhassig, he walked with a spring in his step. She and Aoife used to hear the six of them running up and down the stairs, shouting and laughing.

And why should Fred be in the attic? It was a good four hours since he had left the house and gone across to the house in Montenotte.

Why should he steal so quietly through his parents' house? It wouldn't be like Fred, in the mood he had been, to show any consideration for the two sleeping girls. If he had come back, then he would have hammered on the front door until he woke his sister. He was unlikely to have a key. He had left his father's house a good two years ago.

And the footfall had been that of a heavy man, a heavy man, wearing boots, treading cautiously. He was coming down the stairs now. Eileen listened intently, listened for the squeak on that step that Susan had warned her about. Surely the man, whoever he was, should have reached that point.

Cautiously, Eileen sat up and swung her legs over the side of the bed. She sat very still for a moment, listening intently and then slowly and cautiously, she moved on stockinged feet to the door. If only she had her revolver! She had hidden it under the roof of her mother's little two-roomed shanty on Barrack Street. Carefully she turned the knob of the door. Another creak and then a stumble. Someone, going down quietly and cautiously, had almost tripped on the steep and unexpectedly sharp corner of the stairs. But oddly, the creaking stair had been avoided. As if the intruder had known that it was there, had taken precautions to avoid stepping on it, but then had stumbled.

He had recovered himself instantly, though. And the footsteps came on down.

Eileen stood very still, pressed in against the door, shivering, listening, waiting, wondering what to do. The cautious and stealthy footsteps had passed the room where Susan slept; had not even hesitated. That was not the goal of the intruder. And then they passed her door and she breathed a sigh of relief. But still she held her breath, still she stayed very still. The footsteps had passed the small cloakroom now, crossed the landing and went down the last flight of stairs, more confidently now, stepping down the bare steps quite quickly. Eileen opened her door and looked out. She began to creep slowly forward towards the head of the stairs. It was dark, midnight dark. The man, whoever he was, must have had some sort of light, a torch, or an old-fashioned candle lantern. The latter, she thought. There was a slight whiff in the air, that slightly soapy smell of candle grease, almost a faint trace of smoke in the damp air.

And then she heard a click. It seemed almost shockingly loud in the silent house. She knew what it was instantly. The front door. He had left, left by the house door. Eileen tried to get back into her room quickly, but she was too late. By the time that she felt her way to the window, there was no sign of anyone in the street outside. She opened the window and leaned out. Quite a foggy evening. The rain had stopped, but trails of fog wreathed around the gas lamps. The bells of Shandon rang out. Midnight. Did she dream it? Or did someone really walk past the attic room where Susan lay sleeping and creep surreptitiously down the stairs, past the room where she herself had spent the night and then let themselves out through the front door.

There was an oil lamp in this bedroom, hanging from the centre of the ceiling, but she was not sure how to light it so Eileen fumbled her way to her bedside, struck a match and lit a candle. She sniffed at it. Did candles smell? Yes, she had been right. That smell on the stairs had been that of a candle. She bent down, pulled out her shoes from under the bed and buckled them on. At least she would make sure that the front door was properly closed and that the chain was fastened on it. She wouldn't alarm Susan, but would creep quietly down. For a moment she half-hesitated. What if the heavy-footed stranger was still in the house, but she told herself that that was stupid. She had definitely heard the front door click. In any case, no harm had been meant to either girl. There was no lock on her door. She had noticed that last night, no key, no keyhole, even, just a door knob. And yet, she was certain of this, the mysterious night wanderer had not tried the handle.

She stood for a moment on the landing, looking up at the set of stairs that led to the bathroom and from there up to the attics. She was half-tempted to go up there, to turn that corner by the creaking step and to rouse Susan. Best not, though. Perhaps it was all her imagination. There was no sound from Susan's room. She wouldn't wake her up. The girl had an important meeting tomorrow with the solicitor and needed to be clear-minded and fresh. It would be up to Susan to convince Mr Binsy that Richard McCarthy was fraudulent, and that his figures could not agree with the figures in Susan's account book. No, she thought, she would allow Susan to have a good night's sleep. If she found the chain on the door, then she would know that no one had left through it as she had watched Susan fasten it before they both went up to bed. So she went down the main stairway, holding her candle up to see her way safely on the steep steps.

She would have a good look around, she told herself. It was puzzling, though. What could anyone want in the attics of the house? Nothing was left there, except that one bed where poor Bridie had slept. And Susan had been undisturbed. Certainly nothing of value. And Fred had definitely had a gun in his pocket so he had found that. Why should he or anyone else be searching there in the middle of the night?

And then she heard something. An odd sound. A crackle. And then a smell of smoke. Not from the kitchen. In any case, Susan had carefully turned the stove right down and shut it up for the night. She had watched her do that, thinking at the time how much her own mother would love to have one of those ranges instead of having to cook on an open fire.

No, the smell and the sounds were coming from the front room of the house. She dashed to it, pulled open the door, and then screamed, 'Susan! Susan!'

It had been the wrong thing to do; opening that door had been stupid. She realized that instantly. There had been a roar from the room, almost as she imagined a tiger would roar. Even from behind the heavy wooden door, she could hear how the flames crackled from the room. Still some furniture in there, of course, some wooden chairs, and a table.

But she had seen enough before she had hastily closed the door against the leaping flames. The big oaken cupboard, with the ninety-one small drawers, where all of the neatly arranged and docketed receipts, bills of sales, books of orders, accounts books and deeds had been carefully arranged and patted into place before Susan had closed the door on all of the hard work and they had gone up the stairs to find their beds; she had just seen that.

And the whole cabinet was now a blazing inferno.

'Susan!! Susan!!' screamed Eileen, hastily shutting the door. By now the smoke was eddying out through the cracks of Mr Mulcahy's office door. The worst thing, though, was the sound of crackling. The fire was devouring everything in there. She went to the front door, but once again the sudden draught sucked at the fire and tongues of flame licked at the new paint around the door of the front room.

And at that moment, Susan came flying down the stairs, in her bare feet, with her long old-fashioned nightdress flying behind her.

'Oh, my God! Fred! I'll kill him! I swear I'll kill him!' she screamed. Without hesitation, she wrenched the door of the office open and plunged in, only to back out when the heat of the flames met her. 'Get out of my way! Don't just stand there. Get water, get a bucket from the back kitchen. Go on. We must put that fire out. I must save the papers! I'll kill Fred. I'll kill him; I swear I'll kill him. After all that I have done. I'm not going to be stopped, now.'

And before Eileen could stop her, she had wrenched the door open and then screamed.

Eileen screamed too. The buttons on her leather coat had never before seemed so stiff, so awkward, so seemingly-impossible to open, but in the end she managed to tear it from her back and swathe Susan in its folds, dragging her away from the flames and into the kitchen. Resolutely she kicked the door shut behind them and pulled Susan into the washhouse. Then she began pumping water over the terribly burned girl.

TWENTY

St Thomas Aquinas
'Misericordia sine iustitia est mater diffluat; iudicium
enim sine misericordia saevitiam.'
(Mercy without justice is the mother of dissolution;
justice without mercy is cruelty.)

'It's that Fred Mulcahy to see you,' said Sister Bernadette in a hoarse whisper. 'Shall I tell him to go away?'

Sister Bernadette was looking at her in a troubled way and the Reverend Mother realized that, of course, gossip had spread through the city and wild rumours about Fred had been part of common gossip on doorsteps and in muttered conversations across shop counters.

The Reverend Mother had been closeted with Mr Hayes, the auctioneer, when Sister Bernadette came to announce that Fred Mulcahy wanted to see her. There were marks of a dilemma on Sister Bernadette's open and honest countenance. On the one hand, someone who had once been a small boy who stole sugar from the convent kitchen had no right to come demanding to see the Reverend Mother and causing her to break off her conversation with a charitable gentleman. On the other hand, she sensed that the Reverend Mother was getting slightly tired of Mr Hayes. During the few weeks since the macabre discovery of the body in the trunk, Mr Hayes had called on numerous occasions. The un-Christian thought had crossed the Reverend Mother's mind that he had found a convenient charitable outlet for his leftovers, as well, of course, as having the opportunity to spill over some of his exuberant store of talk into her ears. Nevertheless, she had to admit that the books and clothes that he brought were all of good quality and today he had something special, or so he said, guarding a large box, like a magician about to stun his audience.

'Educational! Pure educational!' he was saying as Sister

Bernadette crept into the room after a polite knock. 'Wouldn't bring you anything that wasn't educational, Reverend Mother. None of your ordinary toys, this. Just you look at this, sister!' He kept his hand on the box for an extra second and allowed them to peep at the brown luggage label tied to the box. It said in an ornamental hand 'Children's Toys' and then he snipped the string, pushed back the flaps, dumped a wodge of tissue paper on top of the highly polished floor and stood back with the air of one who is about to exclaim: *'Abracadabra!'*

'Well!' said the Reverend Mother and her one word released an avalanche from Mr Hayes.

'That's right, Reverend Mother. A little toy post office! Would you ever! Just look at the lovely little cash register, and those little stamps and the weeshy little scales for weighing the letters and the ducky little parcels! Look at the tiny little weights, all in ounces! The reverend sisters could get the children to write little letters to each other, weigh them, stamp them, pop them in the post box, get a little boy to be the postman, look at that dotey little cap, Reverend Mother! Wouldn't a little boy just love to be wearing that . . .' Mr Hayes raised his hand, fingers splayed in rigid ecstasy while Sister Bernadette peered into the box with an enthusiasm which matched his own. The Reverend Mother looked down at the little post office, from the era of King Edward, she guessed, and tried to banish a thought that the original owner of this enchanting toy might now be mouldering in a grave in Flanders.

'And look at these!' Mr Hayes opened a small box and displayed its contents. Had he heard Sister Bernadette's penetrating whisper about Fred Mulcahy? From time to time, he cast looks over his shoulder, but then went back to praising his gift. The miniature envelopes and sheets of writing paper were yellowed with age, but stiff with quality and there were even a couple of quarter-size pens and minute ink pots to be placed on a counter.

'You must bring that post office down to the infant classroom and show it to them, Mr Hayes; we'll go straight away,' said the Reverend Mother with admirable quickness of mind. She would introduce him, organize a chorus of gratitude, a great clapping of hands, something that the infants loved to do, and then leave him to Sister Perpetua and her lively class. Sister Bernadette could be trusted to show him straight out of the front door once he got tired of the little recipients of his charitable donations. In any case, it would be good for the children. The man's enthusiasm would be catching; enthusiasm was always infectious and it was something that she wished, sometimes, that her teachers would show more of. He would get them all excited about the prospect of playing post offices, writing little letters and practising their handwriting.

And, hopefully, no one would try to steal anything while he was actually on the premises.

In the meantime, she would see Fred Mulcahy in the quiet privacy of her room.

The story of the fire at Shandon Street had been in the *Cork Examiner* and everyone knew that Susan had been in the Mercy Hospital for the past week. Her flimsy nightwear had blazed up and she had suffered multiple burns. Eileen, wearing a leather coat, had escaped with only a few blisters on her hands, but Susan, wearing nothing but a linen nightgown had been almost at death's door for a day or two.

And it was of Susan that Fred spoke when she released him from the sombre waiting room where Sister Bernadette put unwelcome visitors in preference to one of the highly polished parlours, decorated with useless pieces of heavy old-fashioned silver, donated by the pious. Fred had followed her in silence up the corridor and through the door of her room, holding it open politely for her. She had expected him to be embarrassed. After all, on the last occasion when they met, he had pointed a loaded gun at her and advised her to keep out of his way. However, he seemed to have forgotten this. A few weeks are a long time for the young, nevertheless, she would have expected him to say something, to stammer out some sort of apology. Fred was always someone to rush into speech. Now, however, he seemed suddenly older, more mature, perhaps more self-assured. Had it taken the death of two parents to give him confidence in himself? The thought gave her a pang. Two very hard-working parents, with faults no doubt, but, on the whole, they had done very well for their enormous family. Still it was for God to judge.

'Sit down, Fred,' she said gently. She would not insult him with offers of tea and cake.

'I've been to see Susan,' he said abruptly, though he did not sit down, but stood facing her. 'She is much better now. A bit dopey. Dr Scher has been giving her morphine for the pain. She asked me to go and see you. She said that you would not refuse to see me, she thought.' And then, almost not drawing a breath after his last sentence, he said hurriedly, 'Today is my birthday, Reverend Mother. I'm—'

'Of course,' she said cordially extending her hand. 'Yes, of course, you are twenty-one today, that is right, isn't it, Fred?' Well, at least that was one problem solved. There would be a guardian for that large family. Was he now the inheritor of the large amount of property and cash left by his father? She didn't really know the answer to that question and was rather annoyed with herself. Really she should study the laws of her country. In the meantime, she would have to ask her cousin's husband about the position and hope that he wouldn't go into too many complications.

She sank down onto a chair, feeling exhausted after her session with Mr Hayes. He, also, took a seat, but said nothing. The phrase, *'What can I do for you?'* trembled on her lips, but she bit it back. Let the boy tell what brought him to her.

'I wanted to apologize for my behaviour on the night when my father's body was discovered,' he said. 'You must have thought me very rude.'

She swallowed a smile, though she felt the corners of her mouth twitch. 'Rude' was a slight understatement, she thought, remembering that gun pointed at her heart and hearing the sound of the shot in her ears.

'I must have been mad!' These words sounded more genuine. 'It had been such . . . such a nightmare . . . I'd been like a criminal in my own father's house, ducking away when I heard his voice on that last day, keeping out of sight of that oily auctioneer, slipping away, ashamed to be discovered lurking there up in the attic, until I could get out of the place . . . and then everything else going wrong. Being thrown into prison probably served me right.'

She gave him a smile. After all, he was still very young and perhaps now he would grow up a bit.

'I'm sure that you will never do such a thing again,' she said encouragingly. It did sound a little like the usual post-script to a scolding of a badly-behaved pupil, but she could not help that.

'What should I do now?' he said, sounding, indeed, so like a small boy, that she felt her impatience returning. 'I want to do my best for them all,' he said quickly, almost as though he had sensed her thought. He hesitated a little and then said, 'Susan is just thinking about getting the money to go to university, but I have to think of them all. Little Frankie is only six, after all, poor little fellow.'

'And yourself, you wanted to go to university, too, didn't you?' It had been, according to Eileen, one of his bitter complaints against his father.

To her surprise, he shook his head. 'No, I'm going to give that up. We'll have to keep the business going, that's impor-tant. There's all those children to see to. They'll all have to have a decent education, clothes, books and toys. I never had toys. I used to envy boys in school who had toy trains. It's just a matter of getting my hands on the money to look after them all.'

'You could, perhaps, go to see the solicitor that Susan was going to visit before this fire, before she was burned so badly.' Eileen had told her all about this solicitor, and Lucy had dropped in to see her with a message from Rupert.

Fred's face darkened. 'Someone that Eileen MacSweeney found. I'll hire my own solicitor,' he said. 'I'm accepting no charity. I was thinking that we might sell the house in Montenotte, Reverend Mother. The older boys can be weekly boarders in Farranferris. Susan agrees with me, but Sally doesn't.' His face softened at the mention of his second sister. 'Poor old Sal,' he said. 'Everything has been messed up for her. She was going to have a big party in the new house, she had everything planned. She's not a bit like Susan, you know, Reverend Mother, she is very easy to get along with, not always trying to prove that she is better than you, she just wants to have fun, new clothes, dances, all that sort of thing.

She's great with the little ones. She's been like a mother to little Frankie and Jamie, too.'

'I don't think that I've ever met Frankie,' said the Reverend Mother. She remembered Jamie, she thought. That's if he was the one who tried to flood the back yard by blocking the drain with an old coal sack and then pumping violently until he was discovered. A bright boy, she thought, remembering his angelic expression as he had insisted to Sister Bernadette that he just wanted to be kind and to make a swimming pool for the wild swans who had flown overhead. 'I remember Jamie,' she said. 'A clever little fellow, but I don't remember Frankie.'

His face broke into a boyish grin, which she thought looked very attractive.

'You're just as well off not knowing Frankie. You wouldn't want to have him here in your school, Reverend Mother, I can tell you that. Real little monkey. Got a will of iron. He's a chip off the old block; that's a sure thing. Even yells like my old man did, if something doesn't suit him.' He was silent for a moment, staring towards the portrait of the sainted foundress of the order, not seeing it, probably, but visualizing a picture within his own mind. 'Oh, well,' he said with a half sigh, his face suddenly serious again, 'I don't suppose that he had too easy a life of it.'

He was speaking, she knew, not of his six-year-old brother, but of the father that he had resented so bitterly. Perhaps Fred Mulcahy was beginning to grow up, beginning to see things from others' viewpoint. She watched him turn matters over in his mind and waited while his eyes remained fixed on the ornate portrait of Mother Catherine McAuley. It was only when he turned back towards her that she asked the question that had been burning on her tongue since the moment when he had entered her room.

'Why did you give your mother that gun, Fred?' she asked.

He looked at her with startled eyes for a moment and then nodded.

'Eileen MacSweeney told you that, I suppose. She and Susan are great friends all of a sudden. Don't know what she was doing in my house.'

She looked at him sharply. Her mind was unclear about the

laws of inheritance. Would it be Fred's house? Fred Mulcahy was no heir to a baronetcy; would the house and all of his father's possessions and wealth not be divided equally among his children, or did it all go to the eldest son? She wasn't sure.

Unless, of course, that Mrs Mulcahy had made a will. Unlikely, she thought. The woman had only been a widow for a week. During most of that time Fred had been in prison and would have been unlikely to be able to influence his mother into any rushed decisions. She decided to ignore this, though. She had a more important question to be answered.

'Why did you give your mother a gun, Fred?' she repeated and this time he answered readily.

'She was scared; she wasn't used to being in the house without him there – and, of course, he was off, playing the lord over in Montenotte, and she was left in Shandon Street with only Susan and Bridie for company. She told me she was worried about a break-in; that she was sleeping badly. She relied on me; that's why she told me about her worries.' The boy's face softened.

'But she relied on your father to keep her feeling safe,' pointed out the Reverend Mother.

'That was the way that he wanted it. She relied on him for everything, to do her thinking for her and to keep her safe. She was lost without him and so I gave her a gun and told her that would scare off any intruder,' he said.

'And then when you saw your father's body, you were afraid that for some reason your mother had shot him, and so you emptied your gun into the dead body and later confessed to the murder.' It seemed a senseless, ridiculously imprudent act, but then he was an odd boy, emotional, over-charged and impulsive. She had got a good picture of him from Eileen's words when she had popped into the convent yesterday evening and they had enjoyed a chat together in the dim privacy of the empty chapel after the evening services.

'You wanted to protect your mother, was that it?'

'Or someone else,' he said and lowered his eyes to study the polished oaken boards of her floor.

She was immediately alert. 'Bridie?' she queried.

He shook his head. 'No, I didn't think that Bridie had

killed him, no more than I really thought that my mother had killed him once I had time to think, once I was in prison and I tried to imagine what might have happened.' He hesitated for a moment and then leaned slightly forward. 'I told you a lie, Reverend Mother, when I said that Susan suggested that I come to see you. It was my own idea. I was the one who wanted to ask your advice. To ask you about Susan.' He stopped then and left a long pause, rubbing his hands together and looking at the ceiling as though for inspiration. But the Reverend Mother did not offer him any help. She tucked her hands into her sleeves and waited for what was to come.

And then as the clock suddenly struck the quarter hour and she looked towards it with the automatic reaction of a very busy woman, he was spurred into action.

'I'm very worried about Susan, Reverend Mother. She's an odd girl. Very hard, very tough, very determined to get her own way. I'm worried about what that might have led to . . .'

She bowed her head, that neutral gesture by which she signified that she was listening and he hurried on rapidly. 'She's always been like that. Once when she was ten years old they were having a test in school and she stayed up all night studying. She knew that she'd pass. She was always clever. But she wanted, not just to have the top mark in the class, but to have the highest mark possible. She was never content from that day on with less than a hundred per cent. Sally told me that. She used to get fed up with Susan keeping the light on for half the night.'

'I see,' said the Reverend Mother. It was one of those small remarks that she inserted to keep a conversation flowing, to move the speaker onto the next point and he reacted instantly.

'She wanted to go to university, but my father wouldn't agree. And so, it's a terrible thing for a brother to say, but I think that Susan may have been the one who killed my father.' He rushed at his second sentence rather like a man determined to plunge into the icy waters of the Atlantic Ocean.

'Using your gun?' she queried.

He bowed his head.

'Let me get this straight. You think that Susan shot your father in the heart and then placed his body in the trunk that was to be taken away by the auctioneer's men that evening.'

'I wish that I didn't believe it,' he said impatiently, 'but if it's true, Reverend Mother, would she, would she hang? Is there anything that I can do or say to help her?'

The Reverend Mother thought about the laws of the land. 'If Susan is found guilty of the murder of your father, then she would probably be hanged, unless she were to be found to be insane.'

'That's it,' he said, suddenly as elated as though she had solved all of his problems. 'Thank you, Reverend Mother, you've been a huge help to me.' He got to his feet and picked up his hat. 'That's it,' he said. 'Insanity. She's always been a little odd. I could bear witness to that. And Sally, too. I'll tell her what to say.' He made for the door. She stopped him before he reached it.

'Susan shot your father in the heart. Is that what you truly believe, Fred?'

'That's what I truly think happened, Reverend Mother. She had a terrible temper, even as a small child, poor Susan. Always terribly jealous of Sally who is so pretty and who was always my father's favourite. And knowing my mother, she might well have handed my gun over to Susan to take care of for her. My mother would have been frightened that the gun might go off.'

'And the murders of your mother and of Bridie. Was she also responsible for these?'

He bowed his head. '"That way madness lies", doesn't it, Reverend Mother?' And then he left, shutting the door quietly behind him.

A well-educated young man. That quotation from King Lear came readily to his lips. Not very well informed, though.

Fred Mulcahy did not appear to know that his father had been killed, not by a bullet through the heart, but by a blow to the back of the head. The smear of blood over the breast of the coat and shirt had been caused when the murderer wiped clean the instrument of death, or so Dr Scher believed. Patrick had kept that information to himself for the moment

and the coroner, under instructions from the superintendent
of the Civic Guards, had merely given a verdict of 'murder
by person or persons unknown'. Fastest coroner's court in the
history of the city, had been Dr Scher's verdict.

Thinking of Dr Scher, she jerked the ornamental tassel on
the end of the bell pull. By the time that Sister Bernadette
arrived, she was sitting at her desk and writing a note.

'Oh, sister, is Dr Scher still with Sister Assumpta?' she asked.

'Yes, he is, Reverend Mother. He says that it will be a long
quiet farewell,' said Sister Bernadette, crossing herself respectfully at the thought of the ancient sister's ultimate demise.

'Perhaps you could ask him to come and have a word with
me on his way out,' said the Reverend Mother. She picked up
the envelope from her desk and handed it across to the lay
sister. 'And ask Sister Imelda if she would be kind enough to
deliver this note to Inspector Cashman at the barracks. Tell
her to be as quick as she can.' Fifteen-year-old Sister Imelda
found walking slowly with eyes on the ground to be one of
the hardest aspects of life in the convent. She would be
delighted to have official sanction to trot quickly down the
street and perhaps even to break into a run if there were not
too many people around.

In any case, she really did want to see Patrick as soon as
possible. These murders had to be stopped.

She hardened her heart with a memory of the three dead
people, a hard-working ambitious man; his wife who had borne
so many children and had loved and cared for them all, and
Bridie, poor Bridie who should, perhaps, have been better
cared for by the convent at a most vulnerable time of her life.

The sooner this murderer in their midst was behind bars,
the safer life would be for the Mulcahy family and their friends.

TWENTY-ONE

St Thomas Aquinas
'Inter omnia vero hominum studia sapientiae studium
est perfectius, sublimius, utilius et iucundius.'
(Truly, of all human pursuits, the pursuit of wisdom is
more perfect, more sublime, more useful, and more
full of joy.)

Patrick arrived with a promptitude which paid tribute to the speed of Sister Imelda's young legs. She had then the fun of coming back to the convent seated demurely in the back of the police car, like a lady, according to Sister Bernadette's surreptitious whisper. Dr Scher hospitably offered him some tea on her behalf, but he declined it with a shake of his head. He looked taut and had dark shadows under his eyes. There had been an article in the *Cork Examiner* this morning with a lot of criticism at the lack of progress on what they melodramatically called 'The Shandon Street Killer'. Patrick, like all deeply insecure people, was a harsh critic of himself and this article would only reinforce his anxieties. He was, she thought, on edge in case yet another murder would occur. She had already spoken with Dr Scher and they had both agreed that Susan should remain in hospital under the care of a battalion of nuns until this case was unravelled.

'I read your note, Reverend Mother,' he said. 'I've gone through everything and I've got them all here, all in envelopes. May I use this table, Reverend Mother?'

Unceremoniously he took Dr Scher's tea tray and dumped it onto the broad windowsill before returning and opening up his attaché case. He removed a folder from the inside and then carefully took envelope after envelope from it and spread them over the table. Each envelope, she saw, was labelled in Patrick's neat handwriting.

'This was the first label,' he said. 'This was the label on the

trunk that held the body. You remember it, Reverend Mother.'
He opened one envelope and held it up. It said 'OLD SCHOOL
BOOKS'.

'Yes, I remember it,' said the Reverend Mother. She peered
at it and then took her glasses from the drawer of the desk.
'Yes, I thought that I remembered that very distinctive full
stop. Rather an old-fashioned way of making a full stop. I
had a distant cousin who always made full stops like that.
Whoever wrote that hand, I would say that they learned it
from an old-fashioned governess.' She looked from one to the
other and for a moment, to her shame, slightly enjoyed their
puzzled expressions. She could see them mentally going
through all of the inhabitants of the house in Shandon on
that fateful day when the auctioneer's men removed the trunk
and its gruesome contents. An old-fashioned governess did
not seem to fit into that picture.

'And the handwriting samples, Patrick?'

'I'm afraid that I have had no luck with these,' said
Patrick regretfully. 'These were the people in the house on
that Tuesday afternoon and evening before the trunk was
removed to the auctioneer's rooms. I asked each person to
print those three words on a similar label. In fact, I got them
to do it twice, one on each side of the label.'

'That was clever,' said Dr Scher admiringly. 'Didn't give them
a chance to match their first version.'

'That was Joe's idea. Didn't work, though,' said Patrick
ruefully. One by one, he ranged the neatly labelled envelopes
on the table reading them aloud as he pulled the label out.
'Mrs Mulcahy, Susan Mulcahy, their servant, Bridie, Mr
Hayes, the auctioneer, Mr O'Sullivan the solicitor, Mr Richard
McCarthy business colleague and executor of the will. And
this is Fred Mulcahy's handwriting, just in case he was still
in the house after his father arrived. You can compare them
for yourself. I've been over and over them with a magnifying
glass. Not one shows any resemblance and certainly none of
them make a full stop like that.'

The Reverend Mother allowed Dr Scher to do the checking.
Patrick, she knew, was utterly meticulous and his eyes were
fifty years younger than hers.

'And the card sent with the chocolates to Eileen, what about that?'

Patrick picked it up. '"Thought you might like to have these", that's all it says, but the parcel was addressed to Susan Mulcahy. This is the card, nice card, isn't it? Little fancy border on it.'

The Reverend Mother looked at it. Yes, a good quality card. Lucy used cards like that – it suited her cousin's impetuous nature to dash off a card rather than to write a formal letter. And yes, the handwriting was an elaborate copperplate, seldom seen these days.

'And you checked this also with the handwriting of these people who were in the house at or near to the time when Mr Mulcahy was murdered.' It was an assertion rather than a question. Patrick would have done that.

'Not a single one resembles it. And you can see for yourself, Reverend Mother. The handwriting here is quite different to the one on the "School Books" card. You can see that, Dr Scher, can't you?'

'How was the box of chocolates wrapped?' The Reverend Mother withdrew her attention from the card.

'Just in brown paper,' said Patrick. He delved once more into the folder and this time brought out a large envelope. Carefully he extracted a piece of brown paper, slightly stained and very much crumpled, though it had been carefully smoothed out before being put into the envelope. Stuck to the centre of it was yet another luggage label. And on the label was written 'Miss Susan Mulcahy, Shandon Street.'

'Not a full address, of course, but posted in Cork city, that was enough. Everyone knows Shandon Street and everyone knows about the Mulcahy family in Shandon Street.' Patrick hesitated for a moment and then said, 'I found this in the rubbish bin, that's why it looks so crumpled.'

'You are very thorough, Patrick,' said the Reverend Mother.

'Not thorough enough,' he said with a grimace. 'I'm afraid that it was only yesterday that I thought of sending a man up to search the rubbish bin. Susan Mulcahy had told me that she couldn't remember what had happened to the wrapping paper. She thought her mother had probably burned it. But here it is now.'

'And you can't find any match for that, either, I suppose,' said Dr Scher coming over to join them.

'On the contrary,' said Patrick. 'I'm afraid that I have. The writing on the card is unknown, fits nobody's handwriting as far as I can judge from the samples, but the handwriting on the parcel label is almost certainly the handwriting of Miss Susan Mulcahy herself. Look for yourself.'

The Reverend Mother donned her reading glasses again and bent over the table, looking from the label stuck onto the piece of brown paper to the label written by Susan. Careful, good handwriting, well-formed and perfectly mature. Yes, there was no room for doubt. The handwriting was the same.

'But, what on earth? Why should the girl send chocolates to herself? Poisoned chocolates, too. It doesn't make sense.'

'You forget, Dr Scher, Susan Mulcahy disliked chocolates.'

'So, of course, someone else sent them to her. Picked up a label in her handwriting.' There was a note of great relief in Dr Scher's voice. He had, of course, worked tirelessly over the burned body of the girl, anointing wounds, administering pain-deadening draughts, dragging her back from the gates of death. It must be, she thought, a process akin to creation. To lose Susan now would be a pain akin to a mother's loss of her child; she understood that.

And then she dismissed Susan from her mind. This murder had to be solved, but she had to be certain before making an accusation. She stared down, meditatively, at the label on her desk which she had taken from the bin, the label from the toy post office. Handwriting, like fashions in clothing, changed over the years. The Victorians would be shocked to the core to see the short dresses and form-fitting clothes worn by Eileen's generation. And Victorian governesses would be horrified to see the plain, unadorned style of handwriting practised nowadays by the grandchildren of their charges who had spent weeks and months practising swooping, intricately curved letters. Handwriting for them was an art form. It would have been practised by all of her generation. The young people of the 1920s would soon be bashing out letters and essays on typewriters. Parchment, except for lawyers' documents, had now dropped out of use. She shrugged her shoulders. The world had to move on. Her generation were busy dying or were already dead and buried. A husband, or a wife gone. A house sold and its contents sent to an auction. Progress, she thought, was, on the whole, a good thing. Why spend so long drawing letters when it was the meaning of the words that counted.

TWENTY-TWO

St Thomas Aquinas
'. . . *nihil factum, id est nullum praeteritum est eligibile.*'
(. . . nothing over and done with, that is nothing past,
is an object of choice)

'Come in, Mr Hayes, how very kind of you to come. I just wanted to ask your advice, to have a little talk with you, to decide on the best thing to do.'

'I wouldn't be one to be giving you advice, Reverend Mother. You'd run rings around me.' Mr Hayes looked a little embarrassed.

Probably very little education and a hard childhood. His father had been a rag and bone man and then a door-to-door seller of old furniture in the narrow back lanes behind the old cathedral. But the son had been born with a silver tongue, or *full of the oul blarney*, as Cork people put it. And so Mr Hayes had graduated from a small shop in South Main Street to his present palatial auctioneering premises beside the South Mall, buying and selling to the rich citizens of his native city.

One of the few who had managed to rise from poverty to prosperity. Good suit, good house, she had heard, brand new car . . .

'I see that you have your starting handle with you, Mr Hayes,' she said.

He smiled and his puzzled air vanished. Now he was on home ground and he launched into his usual explanation. 'Better be sure than sorry, Reverend Mother. I'm never one to leave temptation in the way of anyone. Cost a raft of money that Ford car of mine. Wouldn't want to lose it. Not saying a word about the people around here . . .' And then, uncharacteristically, he ran down fast and cast a puzzled glance around the small chapel into which she had escorted him.

'Let me put it over here, Mr Hayes.' Politely, but firmly,

she held out her hand and took the heavy starting handle from him and laid it on the high ledge of the stained glass window.

'You were talking about a wooden chest, Reverend Mother,' he prompted, placing his respectable black bowler hat on top of the starting handle, with, no doubt, an obscure feeling that hands had to be empty in a convent chapel.

'Yes, of course, Mr Hayes.' She led the way to the other side of the altar and indicated a space to the side of the marble steps, close to the altar boys' seats. 'Something that would fit here. Something that would hold about fifty small prayer books. You can see that we leave them on the window sill at the moment, but they get very damp.'

'That would be the way of it, Reverend Mother. You're near the river here, aren't you? Terrible place for damp, here, I'd say, Reverend Mother. Not that the good Lord would mind; he'd be at home anywhere.' Mr Hayes had taken out a professional looking tape measure and was busy jotting figures into his notebook. 'Or you could have it over there by the stove,' he said with a quick glance around the chapel. 'Yes,' he said enthusiastically. 'That would be the very place for it. If I've said it once, Reverend Mother, I've said it a thousand times, Cork is a very damp city. And damp is a terrible thing. Does harm to everything, harm to houses, harm to furniture, harm to books—'

'But not as bad as fire,' interrupted the Reverend Mother.

And he stopped abruptly. Very intelligent eyes, she noted. Even by the dim light of the overhead gas lamp she could see them. Intelligent, calculating eyes. She had gone too far now to take a step backwards and so she plunged on.

'Dreadful that fire in the Mulcahy household, wasn't it? I suppose,' she said, hearing with surprise how detached and dispassionate her voice sounded, 'I suppose that the fire was meant to destroy all evidence of Mr Mulcahy's accounts, including, of course, the money that was owed to him for the sale of the house on Shandon Street. It was sold by auction, wasn't it?' She did not wait for a reply. Eileen had told her everything yesterday evening as they had both sat by the hospital bedside of an unconscious Susan. 'Of course,' she went on, 'he might have been able to be put off for a while with tales of a non-payment by the buyer of the house, but Mr Mulcahy was a shrewd businessman. He knew that something was wrong. That was the reason for the meeting in Shandon Street, wasn't it, nothing to do with a will, was it?' The signature on that will had definitely been forged. Patrick had been sure of that once he had compared the signature on Mr Mulcahy's bank account. Whether there had been another will, making provision for the children; that was yet to be established, but there was no doubt that the will held by Mr O'Sullivan had been forged. Mr Mulcahy, a courageous man, had wanted to have it out with those whom he suspected of swindling him.

Mr Hayes had recovered and, as usual, took refuge from embarrassment in a flow of words. 'Yes, yes, Reverend Mother, it's all very upsetting, isn't it? That terrible fire in the house, and that poor fatherless girl at death's door. You'd be dead with worry about her, that's it. You have a great heart, Reverend Mother, I've said that time after time again. "You can search the length and breadth of the city and you won't find anyone with a better heart than Reverend Mother Aquinas". You can ask anyone, Reverend Mother and they'll tell you that's what I say about you,' he said in the tones that he probably reserved for elderly senile customers. He was edging slightly away from her, slightly towards the window where his hat reposed like bird of ill-omen on top of the deadly starting handle. She schooled herself to stay very still.

'It's interesting about those labels,' she said. And had the satisfaction of seeing how he stopped abruptly.

'You see, Mr Hayes,' she said, 'the "Old School Books" label and the card sent with the poisoned chocolates, both with a very outmoded style of handwriting, were a bit of a puzzle. But then I wondered if they could possibly be cards left over after the sale of goods. An auctioneer might well have a drawer full of such labels and cards – perhaps a card sending some extra goods to the auction. And that label, that card, well, they did make everything rather confusing. As for the box of poisoned chocolate with a label saying "Susan Mulcahy, Shandon Street" just stuck on to the wrapping paper . . . I suppose Susan had probably labelled some of her personal possessions that she had not wanted to be taken to the auction.'

'Old labels, always throw them out. I suppose anyone could pick them from the rubbish,' he said, but his heart was not in it. He was moving again, now, one foot on the altar step.

'Please do not step on the altar stone, Mr Hayes,' she said abruptly and, with that automatic respect that Cork people have for the voice of nuns who had scolded them when they were tiny children in the infant school, he stepped back obediently and looked at her abashed.

'Bridie's death was just so unnecessary,' she said and heard a note of deep sadness in her voice.

He heard it also and she saw his head swing around. The glowing red light on the altar brought a touch of colour to his cheeks and lit those keen eyes.

'Poor old Bridie, nice woman. No wonder you're upset, Reverend Mother. Devoted she was, absolutely devoted. She'd let those children run rings about her. So the neighbours said. A slave to them all, she was, and that's the truth, Reverend Mother. I was talking to a woman, very nice woman, a raft of children, she had and that's what she said. "I wouldn't tell you a word of a lie, Mr Hayes, but that poor Bridie, she's a slave to the family, and as for that young Fred; well, Bridie would lie down and let him walk over her." Those are her very words, poor woman, lives in one room in Chapel Lane. Dreadful place.' Suddenly he had cheered up and the fluency had returned. A man who believes too strongly in his ability to talk himself out of anything, she thought, as the words poured out from him.

'Poor old Bridie. That's right. A slave to them all. I saw it myself anytime that I was in the house. Running around after them all, poor woman. And I suppose that was her downfall, poor woman.'

'Inclined to gossip,' put in the Reverend Mother and he responded eagerly.

'Well, there you are, Reverend Mother, I wouldn't deny that. Henry Mulcahy himself said the very same thing to me. "Sees everything, that woman", that's what he said to me. Used to wear those slippers, and you'd suddenly find her behind you, pretending that she was just going up to her little bedroom at the top of the house. But there you are, Reverend Mother, I always say that if the heart's in the right place, then you can forgive a lot, isn't that right, Reverend Mother?'

'It was so very kind of you to give her a lift when she told you that she was going up to the barracks,' murmured the Reverend Mother, bending down to pick up a hat pin from beneath the kneeler of the front seat.

'Well, she suffered from rheumatism, Reverend Mother, I knew that, of course, always one to tell everyone everything, that was Bridie for you, Reverend Mother . . .' Suddenly Mr Hayes stopped and the little chapel became very quiet. He had made a mistake. Had betrayed his knowledge of where Bridie had been going on that fatal morning. Her mention of her destination would have frightened him. He might have been nervous, all the time, that Bridie knew, that she had seen him. After all, she slept right up in the attic, and may have slipped up to her bedroom. She was on her way to the barracks when he picked her up in the car. She told him where she was going, poor thing. Bridie always poured everything out to everyone, or almost everything. He didn't know why she was going to the barracks, of course. He didn't know that she had been induced by Mrs Mulcahy and Susan, egged on by Mr McCarthy, to confess to the murder, in an effort to save Fred. But Mr Hayes, of course, feared that she might have seen him. He would have known she had been around the house cleaning and might have been in the attics at the time of the murder; had thought that she might have seen him come back into the house.

'You were very useful to the family, Mr Hayes,' she said aloud. 'I suppose that you arranged for the sealing up of the partition between the two attics. It was kind of you to do that.'

'Not at all!' Now the man had relaxed. Perhaps she had misunderstood his step towards the deadly weapon on the opposite window sill. 'All part of the service, Reverend Mother, all part of the service. No good showing people over a house and telling them that it's going to be partitioned. Empty the furniture, get the place painted and build that partition in

the attic. That's what I told Mr Mulcahy, God have mercy on
him! Found a good little carpenter for him, too.'

'And I'm sure that you went up yourself to make sure that
the job was carefully done,' said the Reverend Mother cordially.
Susan had heard the man leave, had heard the door slam; had
heard him cranking up his car. But, of course, the auctioneer
would have made copies of the keys, would have known that
the two houses were joined at the attics. He had driven away,
parked in a back street, came back, perhaps through the yard,
went into the empty house, up the stairs, unscrewed a panel,
came back into the first house, murdered Mr Mulcahy, tipped
his body into the trunk and then went back by the same way.
And, of course, if for some reason Bridie had slipped up to
her room, then she may well have seen him come back in. In
any case, he could not run the risk once he had heard from
the woman that she was on her way to the barracks.

'I suppose that the carpenter had to make a panel above the
water tank in the roof,' she said, taking his tape measure from
him and once again checking the space beside the altar. That
water tank, she thought, had probably been the pride and joy
of the late Mr Mulcahy. When he became prosperous enough
to have running water in both houses, he had built a huge tank
in the roof which rested on the party wall of both houses.
She had suspected something like that as soon as Eileen had
told her about the running water and the upstairs bathroom
and had got Patrick to check on this.

Susan, of course, with her emphasis on gathering the financial facts together, had been the intended recipient of the
poisoned chocolates. Mr Hayes, a man who knew everything
about what was going on in the city, may have seen Eileen
go into Rupert's law office, just around the corner from his
auctioneering rooms, and then panicked when he saw the
two girls together delivering the leaflets to his rooms, may
have followed them, overheard their conversation. Once his
embezzlement came to light, then he would be looked upon
as a possible suspect. It was ironic that Mrs Mulcahy, not
Susan, had been the victim of the poisoned chocolates. The
auctioneer and his accomplice had, relying on the woman's
nervous, unsuspicious nature, counted on her asking no

awkward questions. The solicitor, Mr O'Sullivan, was probably an accomplice. Much better for Mr Mulcahy to will the money to his wife, than to allow Fred with his sharp mathematical brain to start looking into financial matters. Or Susan, of course. It had become important for Mr Hayes to eliminate Susan once he realized that Eileen was taking her to see a solicitor. The chocolates had not worked and so he had slipped into the house, using the same method as before, and set fire to the cupboard which held the accounts. Whether he had meant to burn the two girls to death was something that was unsure and would have to be left to the judgement of God. What an unfortunate coincidence it was that Susan had been with Eileen when she delivered the bundle of leaflets to the auctioneer's office.

He had not replied to her last words and she knew that she had made a mistake. In her desire to elicit all of the facts in an easy-going fashion, she had turned her back on him and he had slipped quietly across the chapel floor. Moved quietly on those rubber-soled shoes of his.

When she turned around, he was standing beside her and in his hand he held his starting handle. The ideal weapon, of course, short, heavy, made from iron. Odd that it had not occurred to either Patrick or Dr Scher, both of whom regularly used a similar instrument, to name it as a possible murder weapon.

'God above sees you, Mr Hayes, and you will not escape punishment for your murder of three innocent people,' she said. And with a strong effort of will, she kept her voice so low that it was barely audible to him. Would he answer? The thought flitted through her mind that she was relying rather heavily on the man's almost compulsive loquacity.

'Well, I'm sorry about poor Bridie and the woman, but Henry Mulcahy deserved it. Wouldn't give me a couple of months to pay up; that was all I asked for. And I'm sorry about this too, Reverend Mother. Had a great respect . . .'

But before the next word left his lips, the Reverend Mother had reached behind the altar boys' seats and snatched at the church bell and hauled on it more enthusiastically than any altar boy was ever allowed to do.

*   *   *

'What made you first think of the auctioneer?' asked Dr Scher when they were both seated in her room. Once Patrick and his sergeant had removed Mr Hayes and explanations had been given to the convent for the ringing of the chapel bell, Dr Scher had taken her pulse, fed her hot sugared tea and made up the fire to an extent which made her fear for the chimney. And then, to her slight amusement, he had gone out to his car, fetched his starting handle and examined it carefully, testing the weight and balance of it with one hand and then with two. She gave a glance over her shoulder at the object, now lying behind them on the windowsill before she answered his question.

'Perhaps, subconsciously, it was that starting handle always in his hand when he came into the convent,' she said soberly. 'Somehow, perhaps, the image of that stayed in my mind and then, one day, I suddenly thought what an ideal weapon it would make, and yet would arouse no suspicion in the victim's mind. It was, after all, the act of a careful man to separate his starting handle from the vehicle itself, and that was what Mr Hayes was in the habit of doing. No one would remark on it. However, I think, consciously, it was the handwriting on the label on that trunk, and on the other labels that came to light, which made me concentrate on the auctioneer,' said the Reverend Mother. 'The handwriting, though all different, was mostly that of my generation, or perhaps the generation after mine who had been taught by old-fashioned governesses. These people are busy emigrating, or at least selling houses too big for them and contents which will not fit or be suitable for the smaller residences to which they are reduced and so they had recourse to an auctioneer. Mr Hayes probably had a drawer full of these labels: "Old School Books" may well have been an item for sale at one of these auctions, and the card saying: "I thought I'd send you these" – that could have been some last-minute additions to a sale, perhaps some small objects like toys,' said the Reverend Mother, thinking of that wonderful post office with the ornate copperplate style of handwriting on the label.

'Eileen told me that she dropped off some printed leaflets to him when she was with Susan,' she said aloud. 'The sight of them together may well have alarmed Mr Hayes. He probably knew how sharp and clever Susan was reputed to be and he didn't want her confiding suspicions in anyone. He could well have followed them and overheard them talk. Eileen might not have been able to keep to herself her conversation with Mr Rupert Murphy. She might have been pouring out the whole story to Susan and I know from past experience how carrying Eileen's voice is. And that would have alarmed him. And so the poisoned chocolates.'

'For a while I was afraid that Patrick might be thinking of Susan,' said Dr Scher. 'I was worried about that. I don't mind much about Hayes; he's better out of this world. Once someone starts on the slippery path of crime and then murders, not once, but twice more to cover up his first murder . . . Three people dead, well, there is no end to what they will do next!' He looked at her sharply and poured out another cup of tea and handed it to her.

'Don't feel bad about him, Reverend Mother,' he said soberly. 'A man who has murdered three people already won't hesitate over a fourth. It could have been you, or it might have been someone else. One of those little Mulcahy boys, a sharp little shaver who had overheard his father make a comment about the auctioneer, might have said something in his hearing and then the little fellow would have been the next victim.'

The Reverend Mother bowed her head. That, she thought, would indeed be unbearable. The quick-witted Jamie, or little Frankie, the 'chip off the old block', they, also, could have been in danger. It was consoling to bring those small faces in front of her mental eye and to use them to banish any regrets or scruples. After all, her patron saint, Thomas Aquinas, had condemned useless repining once action had been taken.

The rest, she thought, the rest was up to God and to the law court. She had another half dozen urgent problems to deal with, problems where the welfare of children under her care was dangerously threatened. There was no point in brooding over the past. '*Nullum praeteritum est eligibile*,' she murmured. Then aloud she said briskly, 'Well, Dr Scher, now tell me. How did you find Sister Assumpta, today?'

For my brother Dominic with much love.
And a hope that the book will remind him of our shared
memories of Cork city.

"Viveri bis, vita posse priori frui."

ACKNOWLEDGMENTS

M any thanks to all who have helped to bring this book to publication: my husband who keeps me supplied with strong coffee and wood for my stove; my agent, Peter Buckman, always so helpful and quick to spot a discrepancy; my editor, Anna Telfer, who is the ideal editor, combining appreciation with a clear memory for time sequences and repetitions; copy editor, Holly Domney, who has such a keen eye to spot my many inaccuracies and all at Severn House who work so hard to turn my story into an attractive book.

Lightning Source UK Ltd.
Milton Keynes UK
UKHW011233110419
340873UK00002B/52/P